Ⅱ0666699

Tracy Farr is a novelist and short story writer who used to be a scientist. She grew up in Australia, and has lived in New Zealand for more than twenty years; she calls both countries home. Her debut novel, *The Life and Loves of Lena Gaunt*, was longlisted for Australia's prestigious Miles Franklin Literary Award, and shortlisted for the Western Australian Premier's Book Awards and Barbara Jefferis Award. *The Hope Fault* is her second novel.

tracyfarrauthor.com
@hissingswan

The Hope Fault

Tracy Farr

Aardvark Bureau
London

An Aardvark Bureau Book
An imprint of Gallic Books

First published in 2017 by Fremantle Press
Copyright © Tracy Farr
Tracy Farr has asserted her moral right to be identified as the author of the
work.

First published in Great Britain in 2018 by
Aardvark Bureau,
59 Ebury Street,
London,
SW1W 0NZ

This book is copyright under the Berne Convention
No reproduction without permission
All rights reserved

A CIP record for this book is available from the British Library ISBN
9781910709436

Typeset in Perpetua by Aardvark Bureau

Printed in the UK by CPI (CR0 4YY) 2 4 6 8 10 9 7 5 3 1

For S.

Maps are of two kinds. Some seek to represent the location of *things* in space. That is the first kind – the geography of space. But others represent the location of things in time – or perhaps their *progression through* time. These maps tell stories, which is to say they are the geography of time ... But these days I have begun to feel that stories, too, are basically concerned with spatial relationships. The proximity of bodies. Time is simply what interferes with that, yes?

Dylan Horrocks
Hicksville

RAIN

It was in fairy-stories that I first divined the potency of the words, and the wonder of the things, such as stone, and wood, and iron; tree and grass; house and fire; bread and wine.

J.R.R. Tolkien
'On Fairy-Stories'

Friday

THERE'S A BIG BLACK CLOUD OVER CASSETOWN

Iris flicks the car's headlights on, even though it's not long past midday. There's no rain yet, but you can feel it in the air, smell it coming. When they'd left the city that morning, they'd driven three hours south in midwinter sunshine, under skies of unbroken blue. Then just out of Cassetown they drove in under a thick dark cloud that filled the whole of the sky to the south, and turned the day dusk-dark.

Kurt's in the front passenger seat, next to her. In the rearview mirror, Iris sees Luce in profile, headphones framing her face, eyes closed. She's slumped against a pile of bags and bedding, her hand twitching at her phone as it has been all the way south from the city.

Iris looks back from the mirror to the road, sees the sign for the bridge ahead. She feels the lift in the road take them over the bridge, and she flicks the indicator stick with her hand – flicks it without thinking, starts to turn the wheel, the arc of the turn so familiar, though so long untaken – the flick flick flick to turn right, past the FOR SALE sign overlaid with a diagonal red SOLD sticker, into the driveway of their old house.

The big black cloud holds onto its rain while the three of them pile out of the car, and Iris unlocks the front door of the house. They all stand for a moment in the doorway, then they split apart to wander the house. They claim rooms and beds, open and close cupboards, draw curtains. They breathe in its smell.

The rain holds off as Iris watches Luce and Kurt surge out the side gate and down the path to the bay, like the little kids they were the last time they were all here together. Iris unloads their gear from the car, brings in bags of food they've brought from the city for the weekend, stacks flattened cardboard boxes and packing tape in the hallway. Rain holds off, still. Luce and Kurt reappear, arms loaded with driftwood, pockets tinkling with shells. They bring in wood from the shed at the back, get the stove in the kitchen fired up. Iris makes tea. They all settle in. The kids – her grown-up son, her teenage niece – slink off to their rooms, leave Iris in the kitchen. She stands up, moves to the sink to wash the mugs. Out the window, out the back, above the tin roofs of the shed and the old washhouse, the sky's solid, dark, but still dry.

It's not until two hours later, when Paul and Kristin's car pulls into the driveway, that the first fat drops of rain start to fall. Iris meets them at the door, kisses Kristin on the cheek, inhales the baby's smell, waves to Paul. She bustles Kristin and the baby inside, out of the rain, into the kitchen, to make more tea, to get the baby settled. By the time Paul has hauled their gear inside – the travel cot, the clip-on high chair, the stroller, all the bags and toys and things a baby needs, all of them stacked down the hallway, next to the empty packing boxes – it's a full-on, pelting deluge.

ALL INSIDE THE HOUSE, NOW

They're all inside the house, now, and have been since the rain. They're in rooms that lead off from the central hall that stretches from the front door, down past the pile of baby things and packing boxes, down and down and down past bedroom doors and cupboard doors, open doors, closed doors, past paintings and photographs and drawings and posters hung and pinned and sticky-taped and Blu-Tacked to its walls. The hallway ends at a dogleg to the bathroom, then it crooks past the bend and leads on to the kitchen. You can barely see, in the darkness. If you opened the front door, even if you opened all of the doors of all of the rooms that lead onto that hallway, and even if you opened the curtains and blinds and windows of every single one of those rooms, still the hallway would be dark. There's a single light — just a bare bulb on a cord — halfway down, high up, hanging just below the pressed-tin ceiling. It stays on all day and all night. The hall — the whole place — has the beautiful smell of old house, and the sea: of books and papers; faintly of mice, somewhere within a wall; of musty linen, of mothballs, of old face powder (though none is ever used); of wax crayons and pencil sharpenings; and the salt-metal tang of towels from the beach, flung over doorknobs and chair backs and left to dry.

They're all inside their rooms, now, listening to rain on the roof. It's pissing down, guttering and gushing, sinking into the earth, wetting, muddening, all damp and glorious. Kurt's lying along the sofa in the little room, drawing, his arm curled around — out of habit — to hide the page, though there's no one there to look.

His feet are up on the sofa's arm. A sketchbook rests on his thigh, and one knee is bent to prop the surface to a good angle for drawing. He's pencilled the six-panel page he thought of in the car on the way here. He thinks about getting up, knocking on Luce's door, showing her how he's translated what he imagined into a series of images, a composed page, a piece of story: a scene. But he doesn't get up. He chews his pencil. He listens to the rain. He flicks back through the pages of the sketchbook, past rough ideas, sketches for story lines, glued-in pieces of paper. Some pages are bright and beautiful, inked and fully coloured. Some pages have just a line or two, a shape, a phrase. Some have a wash of watery grey. He flicks forward to a blank page, puts pencil to paper, and starts to draw the rain.

Three doors down and across the hall, his cousin Luce is on the floor, wedged in the gap between her bed and the window, pillows and sheets and quilt all pulled off the bed and tucked around and under her. Her elbows are pulled in tight against her sides. Her knees are up in a V, and the laptop rests on them. She doesn't think about her fingers on the keyboard, the trackpad, doesn't think about how they move, what they do. She's scrolling through stuff she cached before they left home in case the wireless was shit here. And it's shit here. Of course it is. Her phone beeps, and she grabs it from where it lies on the centre of the bed, thumbs the screen alive, reads the text – *Hey Lulu, busy here so not driving down til tmrw, txt me if u forgot anything, and I can bring. Mum x* – and replies – *K* – then blanks the screen and throws the phone back onto the bed. As the phone hits the mattress – a soft thud, a muffled beep – Luce hears a sharp strange sound from a few rooms away. It's like a parrot trapped in a cupboard, but it's probably the baby, so not her problem. She listens for a moment, her head on its side, but all she can hear is the rain.

One door along, and back across the hall, Kristin grabs the pillow and pushes it to her own face to muffle her shriek, her squawk. Paul pushes into her, kisses her, shushes her, 'Shhh, shhh, love,' both of them laughing with keeping quiet, with the unfamiliar bed, with the proximity of the others. Kristin shifts her hips, tensions her body against his. His hand brushes her breast, and her body and mind fill – in a biochemical wave – with their baby, asleep in the room next door, just a thin wall away. She reaches her arm out over her head and places her hand flat against the wall, feels the old wallpaper corrugate against her palm. Then Paul moves faster against her, in her, and her hand raises up until only the fingertips touch the wall, then one finger, then she lifts away completely, and her cry gives up to the high ceiling, to the shush of the rain.

The last time Paul had been in this bed was with Iris. They were still married, then, but already falling apart. Then, he'd driven down from the city, leaving late – leaving Kristin, and the delicious cheating tangle of her sweaty sheets – arriving in Cassetown long after Iris and Kurt had eaten. He remembers Iris reading a bedtime story to Kurt, remembers trying to walk in quietly, but treading on Kurt's Lego, strewn everywhere up and down the hallway. He'd stumbled, sworn, kicked Lego into the darkness. Was it really ten years ago? More? Kristin shifts under him. He moves his leg, and knocks the book from the end of the bed to the floor. Kristin had been sitting on the end of the bed, reading the book – a map on the front cover, reaching around its spine to the book's back – when Paul came to her, after he put the baby down to sleep in the room next door. Their beautiful baby, their nameless girl, lulled to sleep in the rain.

In the middle of the room next door, a thin wall away from her parents, the baby sleeps in her cot, arms L'd either side of her head in surrender. She is fat, fed, loved; she wants for nothing but a name (poor lamb). A few steps away from the baby, Iris has just stepped in, *in loco parentis*, to check her: sleeping on her back, window closed, heater on low, not too many bedclothes. Iris has her arms up, too, in the same position of surrender. She leans in against the thin wall, her palms and forearms pressed into it, her forehead pressed against it.

She hears the thud of a book hitting the floor, hears murmurs of love through the wall; she hears the old-man snore of the baby behind her, and she hears the heavy fall of the rain.

Yes, they're all inside the house, now, while outside the rain still falls. Gutters run with it, downpipes rush.

Iris pushes away from the wall and moves back to the cot, puts her hand lightly on the baby's full belly, feels its rise and fall. The baby snuffles, its breath curdy, sweet, animal.

Iris leaves the room, closes the door gently behind her. Her phone vibrates in her pocket. She fishes it out, unhooks her glasses from the neck of her shirt, swipes, peers: Marti.

Hey Rice, I can't get away til tmrw, txt me if prob. Hope Lulu behaving. Mart x

Iris taps back.

All good, don't worry. Lulu no trouble, as always. See you when we see you. Party starts at 6!! x

She pockets the phone, and stands, quiet, in the middle of the dark hallway. It's been eight years – nine years? – since she's been here, since they let out this house, *as is, where is,* furniture, photos and all, for what they thought would be a year at most before they sold it. Their things are still here; have been, all this time. On the wall opposite her is the old glamour portrait of Rosa, signed FRANK GOLDEN, PHOTOGRAPHER; next to it, the framed dustcover of Rosa's book (the cover from Iris's childhood copy of her mother's book, with IRIS GOLDEN written six-year-old-carefully in black crayon, copying the shapes and serifs of her mother's name, ROSA FORTUNE, in authorial gold print on the front cover): both so faded, both so familiar.

She reaches her hand out, touches a finger to her mother's face, preserved under glass in the photograph. All the people are inside the house, now, all together, the people she loves.

Iris steps down the hallway, arms out either side of her, feeling her way as if by Braille. Her fingertips trace doors (bedroom doors, cupboard doors, open doors and closed doors), doors into rooms (the baby's room, that used to be Kurt's; Paul and Kristin's room, that used to be hers and Paul's; Luce's room, that's always been Luce's; the little living room that Kurt's in now; the middling room, where she will sleep, that she will share with Marti). Her fingers skip over their paintings and photos, their posters and drawings, past the dogleg at the bathroom, and on into the kitchen. Sitting at the table in the rainy-day-afternoon-dark, she feels their old house hum, with the people all inside it, and outside, only rain.

WHEN DOROTHY GOES TO OZ

Kurt slams down onto the sofa next to Luce, his black notebook clutched to his chest.

'This is what I've been working on,' he says. 'It's not finished, not even close. Just ideas, really, so far.'

He places the book – carefully, with ceremony – onto the table in front of them, opens the cover, reveals the first page. He leans in over it, his back hunched, and Luce leans in with him, mirrors his pose, the shape of him.

She's used to seeing film storyboards, from her mum; she's grown up with them, they're as normal to her as newspapers, or novels. This is loose, though, somewhere in between a comic, a graphic novel, a storyboard. Each frame is drawn in pencil, then inked over, right on the page, with black – no colour, just the black ink over carbon-slate-grey of the underlying pencil. He hasn't erased the pencil anywhere, so the bones of each frame – its starts and stops, its dead ends and doodles – are there to see, shadows under the black ink.

'It's one of the stories Mum used to read me when I was a kid,' he says, 'from Rosa's book. The book of faery-with-an-e tales.'

He lets her leaf through at her own pace. She's eager to get the story – the sense of it – but stops to linger on this page, and that, taking it all in: not just the words and the pictures, but the shape and flow of it all together.

'I was trying to sort of reinvent it, you know, for –' He nods in the general direction of the bedrooms, the rest of the house.

'The baby?'

'Yeah. They're great stories, you know? And they're in the book. Rosa's book. But I wanted to retell them, to pass them on. Like a tradition. Pass them down through the family.'

'But the baby's not related to Rosa.'

'Yeah, I know. I keep forgetting, but I know. Rosa's *my* grandmother, not the baby's. But the baby's my half-sister, so the connection's there, right? As if Rosa's her half-grandmother, or something.'

'Yeah, not really, but whatever.'

He shoulder-butts her, gently. She leans into him.

'No, no, I get it. Kind of like Rosa is to me, kind of a step-grandmother or something. It's a good idea. This is really good. Like, amazingly good.'

He nods, as if he knows this already.

'So – it's going to be a comic?'

He shakes his head, pushes his finger against the bridge of his glasses.

'Yeah, that's the trouble. Probably comic – graphic faery tale, I suppose – but I dunno. I actually thought film, when I started, like an animated short, playing around with how colour is used. Like, for this one, I want to start in black and white, like this,' he flicks through pages, points at frames, 'then introduce colour here,' he flicks pages again, stops, points at the page, jabbing it with his finger, 'when the colour comes into the narrative: boom!'

On this page, after pages of black ink on white paper, there's a small patch of blue at the edge of one frame, then the colour builds in each of the six frames that follow. Then, on the facing page, the single frame – the final frame of the story – is flooded with blue, a range of shades, filling the frame, filling the page, picking out elements of the intricate image, focusing the eye, calming and exciting at once.

'Oh, wow,' Luce says. 'It's like letting light in after being in the dark.'

'Yeah, that's what I want, that difference, that transformation. A different world, with colour.'

The colour on the page feels disruptive after the clear, clean monotone of black on white. She turns the page and the colour disappears, then pages later it reappears, but green this time, deep green, grass green, sea green all in the final frame. It's an accent, an emphasis, used for effect, with thought.

Kurt leans in and turns the pages.

'I'm not sure about this one though.'

The book is open at a page of full knock-your-socks-off colour. Luce closes her eyes, slowly opens them. Her eyelashes blur the image, then it comes into focus as she opens her eyes wider, until she's staring, eyes focused on the image on the page. It looks unfinished, still in draft. But that's almost its strength. The colour Kurt's used is brighter than watercolour, but with the underlying pencil, the ink outlines, somehow rendering it subtle.

'Oh, it's the swan story! I love that one! It's creepy.'

'Yeah, the colour might be a bit much, though. I think I prefer the single-hue washes, just the blue or green or whatever accents.'

'It's like when Dorothy goes to Oz. Like going to sleep in black and white, and waking up to full colour. Nice; you've done the bit with the swans swimming off. That's beautiful. Oh, and look at the little guy! The mannikin. Nice. I always loved that bit.' Kurt's bag is on the floor by their feet. He reaches into it and pulls out a book, opens it at a page marked with a flag of coloured paper.

'Yeah, it's not quite the last bit of the story, but I like it. Here: "The black swan and his shining mate swam to the centre of the river, their necks entwined together. The good wise woman leaned in likewise to her little mannikin" – blah blah blah – "four of them, two by two, paired now for life." I always liked that bit too. It kind of works.'

Luce takes the book from him, closes it, looks at the cover. She lifts it, smells it, smiles. She traces the indentations of the embossed words, all but traces of the gold worn from them.

'I haven't seen this for years. We haven't got it. At home. Iris always read me yours. This one.'

'You can borrow it. If you want. I'm trying not to look back at it while I work. I want to leave myself room to move away from the stories, to really retell them my own way. They're really vivid in my head.' He rubs his hand over his hair, musses it behind his head on the right, behind his ear, jabs his finger at his glasses.

Luce doesn't answer him. She's settled into the corner of the sofa, her legs pulled up by her side. She has turned to the first page of the first story in the book.

ALL MY GIRLS, IN THE KITCHEN!

Iris, passing the doorway to the big room, sees Kurt and Luce there together. She stops, leans against the door frame, pretends to sort through the collected tat on the sideboard in the hallway – old keys, bits of paper and notepads, feathers and stones, unmatched hose connector pieces – but really, she's listening, watching. She watches the two of them sitting there, their heads together over an open book, the shapes of their heads – the shape they form together – so familiar. Their hunches match each other, their rounded shoulders containing self; cousins, but they could be siblings. She sees only the crowns of their heads, sees only similarity. The book – landscape, black cover – is open on the low table in front of them. Kurt's finger points to the page, jabs it three times, then flicks up in the air, fingers pinched in to thumb, then pause – beat – then his hand sweeps to the side, palm down, fingers spread in a gesture of *no way!*, then he jabs his finger twice at the next page. He opens both hands outwards, palms up, arms moving outwards, shoulders lifting in a gesture of showmanship. Luce peers in at the page, then looks up at him, smiling, nodding. She says something. Iris can't quite hear her, just sees the shape her mouth makes.

Kurt sits back on the sofa, pulls his legs up, crosses them. He's still talking, but quietly, so Iris can't even hear the murmur she heard before. Luce picks up the book, is leafing through it. She looks up at him, asks a question, makes a comment, nods at what he says. Kurt gets another book from his bag, opens it, points to something, and they lean in even closer, heads together over the page. Luce takes the book from him, runs her fingers over the cover. She lifts the book to her face. Iris watches Kurt watch Luce. Luce smiles, says something. Kurt smiles at her. Luce settles in to read the book. When she lifts it, to read it, Iris sees that it is her mother's book, *Miss Fortune's Faery Tales*.

Iris smiles, but she knows to keep her pleasure to herself, at least as far as Luce is concerned. They used to be so close, the two of them. Luce used to call Iris *my fairy godmother*. Luce, the daughter of her best friend; Luce's mum, Marti, her twin-sister-in-law. Her ex-twin-sister-in-law. But for a year, maybe more, Iris hasn't been able to get close to Luce, and she's pretty sure Marti can't, either. *I was like this*, she reminds herself. She knows she was a difficult teenager, closed off. Poor Rosa.

But the kids are still close. They've virtually grown up together, even though Kurt is six years older than Luce. They were in and out of each other's houses all the time; then when their parents split up within three months of each other, that brought them even closer. And Luce will still let Kurt close. He can lean into her, without her flinching away.

Iris moves, now, down the hallway to the kitchen. She sits at the kitchen table, smooths the list in front of her, her attempt to bring some order to the task ahead this weekend. Now that the house has been sold – sooner than they expected – they're here to sort and pack up their belongings, their long-stored junk and treasures. There's nothing like making a list to postpone action, and Iris's list is random, loose, pointless, little nervous thoughts written down in shorthand, out of list-making habit:

Start in sleep-out – what to keep?
Furniture – need anything?? Kurt?
Rosa's stuff ...
CHINA = kitchen = KEEP!!
Photos etc (scanning – Luce? Kurt? $$)
Plants – cuttings? Dig up => transplant? (Rain!!)
Blanket – unpick? Restart? Finish!!

She starts doodling at the bottom of the page, under the list. She draws an egg; or perhaps it's a stone. She draws a curve around the egg-stone's equator, another below to twin it, then lines that radiate out and down, then another curve, until the egg-stone wears a stiff, sticking-out skirt, a ballerina's tutu – a doodle from her childhood, one she hasn't drawn for years. Down from the egg-stone skirt she draws thin legs, one straight, one bent up to rest foot on knee, each leg ending in a ballet slipper, with ribbons crisscrossing up the spindle-thin legs. Thin arms attach at the top third of the egg-stone, and loop up to arch above it, framing it in the fifth position, *en haut*.

Luce walks into the kitchen. Iris puts her arm over the stone ballerina, puts her head up, smiles at Luce. Luce ignores her, opens the fridge, stands staring into it. She closes it again, walks to the pantry, opens it, closes it, opens it again, then goes back to the fridge.

'Hungry?'

'No.'

'There's plenty of fruit. Crackers? Cheese? We'll do dinner soon.'

'It's fine.'

Luce pours water into a glass, leans against the sink drinking it. In between mouthfuls, she bites the pad of her left thumb.

'What've you been looking at? With Kurt?'

'Nothing. You know. Stuff.' Luce puts the glass down on the sink. 'Mum's not coming. She texted.'

'She texted me, too, maybe an hour ago. Said she'd be here tomorrow.'

'Yeah. Same.'

'She's so busy, poor old Mart. Do you need anything? That Marti was going to bring down for you?'

'Nah. I'm okay.' She bites her thumb. 'Just –'

The baby cries. They hear it start with a whinge and a whimper, rising quickly to a full-on wail.

'Poor love, waking up in a strange room.' As Iris starts to get up, they hear a door open, hear Kristin's voice, *oh bubba, Mama's coming, it's alright bubba*. They hear the baby's cry gurgle to a stop, hear Kristin's *shhh, shhh, Mama's here*, hear her walking up the hallway towards them. She appears in the doorway holding the sleep-creased baby on her hip, both of them with bed hair, neither of them caring. Kristin is wearing yoga pants and a t-shirt. Her feet are bare.

'She's had a good sleep,' Iris says.

'Not *too* good though, eh bubba? Hopefully she'll still sleep tonight.'

Kristin goes to put the kettle on, and Iris stops her, takes the kettle, fills it, flicks it on.

Paul appears behind Kristin, slips his arm around her waist, and kisses the top of the baby's head. The baby reaches her hand out and presses his nose, as if to push him away. Paul's days of bed hair are, like his hair, a thing of the past, but he's grinning a sated grin.

'Look at you, all my girls, in the kitchen! My har-eem. I'm a lucky man.'

'Euwgh!' Luce covers her ears with her hands.

Kristin belts Paul on the bum with her free hand. 'You're so lucky you can cook us dinner, then.'

'With pleasure. What is there?'

Paul starts poking around in the boxes of food they've brought, and the fridge, and Kristin starts bossing him around, telling him what he'll do, in that way she does, that Iris has become used to. It's been ten years since Iris and Paul's marriage fell apart, a year longer than that since Paul fell in love with Kristin. The messy years were over quickly, at the beginning, and – truth be told – they weren't even very messy. They all adjusted. They all got on with it. And they're all just family now. All together, all just family.

And here they are, to get this job done now, all of them in the house, all ready to clean it up, to pack it up, to split it up and sort it out, and to say goodbye to this place.

TIME TO MOVE ON

While Paul is cooking dinner, Iris makes a start on the sorting and packing. She takes the key she's always kept — never handing it over to tenants or agents — and goes out the back door, around to the side door that leads to the old sleep-out. She unlocks the door, the key stiff in the lock, and opens it onto a room stacked high with boxes and furniture, much of it belonging to her mother, Rosa.

It was supposed to be a short-term solution, moving Rosa's things here ten years ago, after she'd sold her house and moved into the retirement village. They'd always planned to spend time sorting through it, working out what to keep, what to get rid of. Until then, they had heaps of storage room in the Cassetown house, their occasional holiday home, where they always planned to move for good (one day; not yet, but one day). Iris thought she could sort through Rosa's things a box at a time at weekends and school holidays, each time they came down to the house; maybe it'd take six months, maybe a year, but she'd get through it. She would check things with Rosa as she went; they could make decisions together.

But a month after she moved into the retirement village, Rosa stopped speaking, just like that: one day she was right as rain, the next, she just stopped. They didn't think it was dementia — though the tests they'd done only went so far (*the cost—benefit ratio of invasive procedures on a ninety-year-old contraindicates further testing*, they'd told Iris). Rosa seemed to know what was happening, to an extent: she would open her mouth when food was brought close to it, she would chew, she would swallow; she learned to sip liquids from the soft silicon spout of a baby's cup. It was unclear, at first, whether she knew who they all were. She had no voice — she whose voice had always been so strong — and she pushed the pencil away when they tried to encourage her to write instead of speak. They were never sure how much she knew or understood. But at least she was cared for, kept well, bathed and dressed and fed.

They'd visited Rosa that morning, early, before they headed south from the city, after she and Kurt had picked Luce up from her grandparents, Jacko and Alba. As Iris walked up the ramp to the High Care Facility of the Dorothy Hill Retirement Village, past the sad winter remnants of roses and lavender and agapanthus, she'd felt the helplessness, born of guilt, that always overcame her when she visited. Rosa – her own mother – no longer knew Iris (or anyone, as far as they could tell). Iris watched her open her mouth, as if to speak, but no words came. No sounds. Poor Rosa, like a tiny, soundless, ninety-nine-year-old bird.

The month that Rosa lost her voice – that unsettled December, ten years ago – was when Iris's family fell apart. Iris came down to Cassetown with Kurt after that, but she had other things on her mind, and never got around to sorting her mother's stuff. Then, after the split, when she and Paul first decided to let the house, they let it to some friends who were moving down south – fully furnished, leaving their paintings on the walls, their cups and saucers in the kitchen, the food in the pantry. That arrangement carried on for years, as it turned out; then, when those friends bought their own place, they found another local family to take the house over on the same terms. It's been odd – they know that – to have people in their house with their things. But they've been happy to leave the house intact, somehow a reminder of them as a family. And neither Paul nor Iris, until now, has needed the money, so the house has sat here, increasing in value, bringing them a steady rental income. It's a decent bit of land, an acre, the old farmhouse on the home paddock, and when Iris and Paul had bought the house (a canny purchase in the 1980s, when land here was still cheap) their nearest neighbours had been the horse stud across the road, the old school house on the other side of the bridge, then nothing much until town. And town wasn't much, then. The town built up around their house, slowly through the eighties and nineties as the wineries grew in popularity, and more tourists came. The last ten years have seen the region grow like mad, the development of the New Town as a commuter hub for fly-in-fly-out workers in the mines up north. These days their house is on an acre of prime building land in the midst of suburbs. They're sitting on a goldmine.

And now Kristin and Paul, with the focused energy of new parents nesting, are building their dream house in the hills above the city, and they need the capital. So Iris and Paul put their goldmine house on the market. It sold quickly. They don't owe anything on the house. They've made a mint. They're going to split it: half for Kristin and Paul, half for Iris, after they take out a chunk to invest for Kurt. The sale will settle at the end of the month – quicker than they'd planned, but that suits them all. Now that it's sold, they want to be rid of it. Move on. That's what people have said to her: *well, it's about time that you all moved on*. She finds herself repeating it, like a mantra – move on, move on, move on – a kind of beat you could march to, or breathe in time to.

Paul has left the bulk of the planning to Iris – *It's your thing*, he'd told her, *come on, it's what you do best*. She's booked the moving van and a rubbish skip to arrive on Tuesday morning – not great timing, but the best she could manage, with the long weekend – and she'll stay to clean up, after that. She doesn't mind. *It's your thing*. She's brought paper and packing tape, and as many boxes as she could fit in the boot of her car; Marti will bring a carload more when she drives down on Saturday.

Not knowing quite where to start, she's decided on the sleep-out, where everything is, at least, already in boxes. Of the dozens of cartons in the sleep-out, Iris targets the one closest to her, stacked at belly height, ignoring the label, just needing to make a start, any start. She has brought scissors with her; she opens them full, grasps

30

them like a knife – carefully, her hand over the blade – and slits the tape along the seam of the box lid, then across each opposite edge, in an H. She slips her hand under the flaps, opens them up and out, bends them back. There's a piece of cardboard cut to fit the top of the box, lidding the contents. There's an envelope (recycled – a label stuck over the old address, and IRIS written across it). She lifts the envelope out and opens it. It's handwritten, her mother's writing. She unclips her glasses from the neck of her shirt, puts them on, and the letters come into focus.

Books – Box 3 of 9
Photography
Photographic method
Some of Frank's books – any of value?

Iris breathes out. It's just a list – not a letter, or even a note; there's no word of kindness or love there – but it links to lives lived, lost, and past; to old memories. She drops the sheet of paper back into the top of the box, folds the box's flaps over it, weaves them in, over and under each other, to close the box.

She sits on the windowsill. There are dozens of boxes, maybe a hundred: not just Rosa's things, but Paul's, and Kurt's, and her own. How did she ever think she'd get the job done this weekend? She'd need fairytale helpers, like the birds that help Cinderella sort the lentils from the ashes.

Her phone buzzes in her pocket. She lifts it out, reads the message on the screen.

Come on Eye-Rice.
Tutti a tavola!
P x

She smiles, shakes her head, types *K*, hits send, and pockets the phone as it swooshes. She doesn't bother locking the door behind her.

Iris joins all of them in the kitchen, all at the table together, at the same moment as her single letter of reply beeps Paul's pocketed phone, and is ignored.

TUTTI A TAVOLA

'Rice! Good of you to join us. Am I the only one drinking?'

'Oh, Paul —'

'Wine? You know you are.'

'Go on then, I'll have a glass.'

'Good lad. Say when.'

'Yep, that's good.'

'Cheers, son.'

'Cheers, Dad.'

'Now, food.'

'No more!'

'I'm stuffed.'

'Well, pass it around, I don't want any leftovers. Lulu? Come on. You're a growing girl —'

'Oh, Paul.'

'— *mangia! Mangiamo!*'

'I said no.'

'No, thank you?'

'No. Thank. You.'

'Well, I'll have some more.'

'Excellent.'

'Whoa whoa whoa! Plenty.'

'Darl, you always cook too much pasta.'

'Oh, does he, still? He always used to.'

'My dears, it's hard to judge quantities for this crowd. I'm used to cooking for two.'

'Oh, look at her reaching her little hands out to you.'

'Though I'll be cooking for three soon enough. Once she's off the tit —'

'Euwgh.'

'Oh, Luce.'

'Breast is best, Lucinda-sky. *It's on-ly natch-ral —*'

'Now you've done it. Once he starts singing —'

'*It's only the beginning —*'

'Oh for godsake.'

'It's going to be a very long weekend.'

'I'll drink to that.'

'That rain is just getting heavier and heavier.'

'At least the kitchen's warm.'

'But the big room's freezing! I was wearing two beanies in there, before.'

'I had socks on my hands.'

'Is there enough wood for the stove?'

'It's supposed to last all weekend. The rain.'

'I suppose the farmers need it.'

'If there's too much, though? What about flooding?'

'Then *the sheep will go marching two by two, hurrah, hurrah —*'

'Was that thunder?'

'Ah, no, sorry. That was me —'

'Euwgh!'

'Paul!'

'Jesus, Dad!'

When they've finished the meal, Paul shoos them out of the kitchen, and starts to clean up, wash dishes, singing as he goes. Luce and Kurt huddle together in the hallway, then disappear to their rooms. Iris, and Kristin with the baby, move through to the big room, settle onto sofas but, even once they've rugged up with beanies and scarves and socks and Ugg boots, it's cold — too cold to stay — so they move back into the kitchen, the only room other than the baby's room that's warm.

Iris makes tea, and eats shortbread from a tin. Kristin eats almonds and goji berries from a plastic tub. The baby rests on Kristin, snugged into her, cocooned in the baby sling that always hangs over Kristin's shoulders, whether it contains the baby or not. Paul squats to feed wood into the stove in the corner of the room. He worries the wood and glowing coals with the poker, adjusts the flue, then straightens and stands behind Kristin with his hands on her shoulders. Iris gestures to the teapot.

'Mmm, nah. Trying to decide between more wine, or straight to bed.' He leans in, puts his arms around Kristin, kisses her neck. Kristin smile-grimaces at him, nudges his head aside with her head.

'You're hopeless. I'm going to put her down. I may be some time. Night, Iris.' She kisses Paul as she stands up.

'Night.'

Paul pours red wine into his glass, sits down across the table from Iris. He holds the bottle up at her, questions with his mouth and eyes. She shakes her head, lifts her mug of tea.

'Cheers.'

He clinks her mug with his glass, lifts the bottle to the light.

'All the more for me then. Cheers.'

He puts the bottle down on the table in front of him, settles back in his chair, and lifts the glass to his lips.

It's the first time Iris has spent alone with Paul since his baby's birth. They settle easily — of course they do — into talk: about the baby (How tired they are, Paul and Kristin! And how beautiful she is, the baby. They find different words to say these two things, over and over, recombining them in ways that are not new, coming back to the simplest forms, so familiar to new parents: so tired; so beautiful); about Kurt (How proud they are of him! How well he's doing! How beautiful he is, their baby boy. Twenty-one!); about Luce (How hard they are, those teenage years! How well she's doing, all things considered). It's safe, this talk of kids — the shared children of their mob, their extended family, their woolly connections.

And as they talk, they lift their voices, incrementally, to make themselves heard over rain that gets steadily heavier, hammering harder and ever harder on the old tin roof.

UNSTITCH THE STARS

When Paul has finished the bottle, and gone to bed — brushing the top of her head with a kiss as he goes — Iris brings a cloth bag from her room and spreads its contents on the kitchen table. There is a rectangle of soft wool, the size of a baby's cot, cut from an old blanket, washed clean and white, and smelling of eucalyptus. There is a metal tin with a hinged lid and, in the tin, loops and small skeins of embroidery yarn, in all the colours imaginable. In the tin with the yarn are needles aligned in parallel on a scrap of stiff wool felt, and a pair of silver scissors, their eye ring sculpted in the shape of a swan. There are pins, a needle-threader, a silver thimble.

Iris spreads the blanket on the table, runs her hand across the lifted terrain to flatten it. There is only a single patch of stitching in one corner, small flowers — or perhaps she meant them to be stars; it's hard to tell, or remember, now. Iris has started then unpicked the stitching twice already, not happy with it. She's been unable to decide what to stitch onto this blanket, her gift for the baby.

She'd been planning to stitch the baby's name, or at least its initial letter, but she's almost given up on that idea. Poor little baby, still without a name. They're all so used to it that it's stopped being funny, or frustrating, or even remarkable. She's just *the baby*. Marti was funny about it last week — typically blunt — when she and Iris met for coffee.

'I'm gonna start calling her Rumpelstiltskin if they don't name her soon.'

Iris traces a large letter R — all serifs and curlicues — with her finger in the centre of the blanket. She shakes her head, wipes her hand over the wool surface, erasing the invisible trace.

Start again.

Iris picks up the blanket, and her silver swan scissors, and carefully unstitches the stars. When she's done, the blanket is bare again: a blank, white page, ready to fill.

SHIPSHAPE AND WATERTIGHT

Before she goes to bed, Iris walks a circuit in the dark, locking doors, checking windows, tugging curtains firmly closed, checking the rooms of the cold, old house. It seems impossible that the roof could keep such heavy rain from coming in on them all. She imagines rain seeping or leaking in, through cracks, through gaps, tracing the spaces between windows and walls, eaves and timber; she imagines weatherboards that are no longer weatherproof. She imagines the integrity of the house compromised, the roof collapsing, great sheets of iron crashing in, and down, all of it failing and falling under the weight of so much water.

But as she moves through the rooms, she finds none of this. No seeping, no damp. There are no leaks. The water is all outside the house. Inside the house, everything remains dry. Everything holds.

Everything's watertight.

All is shipshape.

She stands in the dark of the big, cold room, her hand pressed against the heavy glass of the door that runs the length of one long wall. Rain sheets against the door, renders the glass as dark liquid, though she feels it solid under her hand. She takes her hand away from the glass and touches it to her face, feels it cold but dry against her skin. She pulls the curtains together, overlaps the fabric to close them firmly against the night and the cold and the rain.

The rain gets heavier, and heavier still, but they're all safe inside the shipshape, watertight house, now, drummed to sleep by the noise of rain on the roof, battering against their dreams.

Saturday

DREAMING IN LIGHT AND DARK

Luce wakes while it's still dark, to a sound she can't understand. It's the voice of a strange bird, or an angry cat, but not quite either of these. She lies on her back, staring towards the sound of rain hammering on the roof. She hears doors open and close, footsteps in the hallway, soft voices. The bird-cat sound gets louder, and comes into focus: it's the baby, crying. Voices murmur through the walls. The baby's cry goes away. Luce rolls onto her side and pulls the quilt up over her head, tucking in tight with the sound of herself.

Kurt sleeps in his clothes, and dreams of a page in a notebook, ink-washed deep black, split in the centre by a wedge of page-white light, that wedge of light with a figure in shadow at its centre, the figure itself casting a shadow upon another figure, something he can't quite see, or touch, or draw. He floats above the page, pencil in his hand. He dreams in light and dark.

Iris wakes early, and pulls on a jumper and a woolly hat while she's still in bed. She steps out of bed and straight into Ugg boots. She walks through the dark house to the kitchen. She crouches by the stove, opens its door, pokes the ashes and embers, blows to raise a lick of flame, catches it with paper and kindling. She fills the kettle with water, switches it on. She stands at the sink, looks out the window at rain waterfalling from gutters. She checks the fire, feeds it with wood, adjusts the flue, latches the door closed. She makes a pot of tea, and takes it back to bed.

When Kurt wakes, it's not quite light outside; it's the dark light of not-yet-day, clouded with rain. He smells coffee, and the dark acid ash of burnt toast. He picks up his glasses from the table next to the bed, puts them on, pushes his finger against the bridge of them, sliding them up his nose. He can hear voices from the kitchen: Paul, Kristin. He sits on the side of the bed, steps into shoes, leaves the laces loose. He runs his hand through his hair, pushes the bridge of his glasses again, puts his hands in his pockets as he stands.

Luce is the last to wake and wander to the kitchen. They're all sitting there, around the table, nursing mugs, putting off the moment when they'll leave the warmth of the fire. Luce stands with her legs backing onto the stove, feels the heat work through the fabric of her pyjama pants, feels it hot on the backs of her knees. She stays there until it shifts from good-hot to too-hot, then she pours herself tea from the pot, puts toast in the toaster. She pulls a chair up to the table, sits between Kurt and Kristin. The baby is on Kristin, in the fabric sling. Luce lifts the toast to her mouth, takes a bite. The baby watches her, blows a wet bubble from its slobbery mouth. It's sort of disgusting. It lifts its hand to its face, spreads the spit, then reaches its hand towards Luce, grabs at her toast. Luce shivers, and leans away.

THE CAT AND THE SNAKE

Iris is washing the breakfast dishes when the cat kills the snake. First she hears a scrape, a sound from outside, like a voice, but not a voice, more like paper rasping. The window in front of her, over the sink, looks out over the back verandah that stretches right along the back of the house, sheltering it from the rain. Iris sees a dark shape move, outside, on the cement paving. She sees the moving shape again, but her brain has trouble making sense of it: it seems to be a cat, a thin grey kitten, leaping across the frame of the window like an Olympic gymnast with a ribbon. As she watches, her brain interpolates, interprets: the cat is the gymnast, and its ribbon is a snake.

The cat rears up, makes itself big. Iris sees it from the side, in profile. Then it's down out of sight again. She moves her face closer to the window, angles her head to see. The cat hunches over the slim ribbon of snake, the cat's back a curve, its hackles up. As she watches, the cat swipes its paws and scoops, and the snake curves through the air, patterning a C (for cat), then an S for itself – describing itself – falling a metre distant from the cat, which turns its back determinedly, lifts its paw, licks it, then smoothes its snout, its eye. It passes its paw over its ear, as if to brush back a lock of hair shifted out of place. *Debonair* is the word she thinks of. The cat glances snakewards. The snake lies still. Iris opens the back door, watching for movement, but the snake remains still, misshapen, a comma written on the red cement. The cat looks up at her, trills, then keeps grooming.

Iris takes the shovel that hangs on the rack on the wall (next to broom, hedge clippers, outside torch, tomahawk, pruning saw), shuffles closer to the snake, raises the shovel – holding it vertical, both hands clenched together, like a medieval knight with a sword – and brings it down to halve the snake. The pieces separate. She shivers, involuntarily; the pieces of snake remain still. Iris pushes the pieces of snake with the blade of the shovel. The cat lies on the cement, head contorting to lick its shoulders, under cover of the verandah, out of reach of the rain.

From where she stands, in the doorway to the old washhouse – not really inside or outside – Luce watches the cat with the snake. She sides with the snake – the beautiful slidey slip of it, the no-ears glide of it, the slink of it. Poor snake, thrown airwards by claws, the yowl of cat, its hunting ways, its cruel teasing fling of the done-nothing snake (just slithering along minding its own business). Cat flings snake again and snake flies, shimmers in the rain-grey light. Cat turns away and licks its arse, then pounces again. Then cat freezes like a statue, and snake freezes too, no wriggle, no shimmy left in snake. Cat sits back on licked arse and starts to lick face, lick paw, smooth paw over face, smirking at snake. Then door creaks and bangs its shut noise, and cat jumps a moment, then keeps licking. Snake doesn't jump. Snake's lost its jump, not that it ever had any. And Iris is standing there, and she has a shovel in her hand, and no no NO she lifts it and drops it onto snake, delivers the final, mortal blow.

Luce feels the sick rising in her, up her snakey gizzards, up her snake-thin throat pipe innards, tastes it in the back of her mouth, like acid Vegemite. She imagines it viscous, dark grey-green streaked bile-yellow.

Iris stands over the snake, the murder weapon (a.k.a. gardening implement) still in her hands. The cat is weaving between her legs, rubbing its oily scent head smell onto Iris, who probably can't even tell the cat is marking her. She probably mistakes it for love. Luce watches Iris poke the shovel at the snake. The cat lies on the cement now, contorting, licking its arse again. Iris turns, walks away, back inside (creak, bang, shut). Luce waits, then walks, past the cat lying on the cement (blood-red cement for a killer cat), to where the

46

snake lies. Cat lifts its head as she passes, blinks its eyes at her, that long smirking blink that cats do.

'Murderer.'

The cat closes its eyes at her.

Luce stands now where Iris had stood, and she looks down – as Iris had – on the snake. Snake no longer forms a snaking curve. Snake is uncurled, in two pieces, blunted, like disgusting sausages, connected by the thinnest cord of twisted skin. The snake is unmade. The snake-unmaking break is clean, clear, precise. There's no ooze, no snakeblood. She doesn't know what colour snakeblood is, or should be. The snake's skin is the colour of old metal, or beautiful hair. She pushes it with her finger, rolls the tail-end sausage over, exposes a paler belly, golden, sand-coloured. She runs her finger up its length, feels the texture of its scales, like cold, carved lumps.

Creak, bang, and shadows above her. It will be Paul, and Iris. She turns, looks over her shoulder. No: it's Kristin and Kurt with Iris. Kristin has the baby tied across her belly, in that fabric thing, the baby holster. Luce can just hear the baby snuffling. It snores like a drunk old man, the baby, makes a noise bigger than the size of it. Kristin is patting its back, sort of patting-rubbing, as if she has a sore (snoring) belly. Luce reaches out again to the snake parts, runs her finger down the snake's broken belly, and shivers.

'Luce! Don't –'

Iris stops herself. Don't what? The snake's in halves, it's dead, what's the harm? (Mites, or lice, she thinks; or is that birds?)

Luce sighs, strokes the piece of snake again, rocks back on her haunches, stands up, slopes over to lean against the wall of the shed.

'You killed it.'

'The cat had it. I thought –'

'Stupid fucking cat.'

'Lulu –'

'Don't call me that. You shouldn'a killed it.'

'It was dead already, or half dead. The cat –'

'Fuck the cat.'

Kurt nudges the snake's head with the toe of his shoe. 'She's right, Luce. Bite marks. Puncture wounds. The cat killed it. The shovel put it out of its misery.'

'Fucking cat should be locked up. They should be banned.'

The cat lifts its head from the cement, eyes Luce, blinks its hypnotic blink at her.

'Fuck off!'

Luce pushes past them all, in through the kitchen door. Creak, bang. The baby cries out, sharp and short.

'It's probably protected. Endangered. If anyone even cares.' Luce's voice fades away to her room, slams shut behind her door.

The baby cries out again, then snuffles to settle.

'We should bury it,' Kristin says, patting the baby's back.

'Nah. I've got it.' Kurt picks the shovel up from where Iris left it resting against the back wall of the kitchen. He scrapes the shovel under the pieces of snake, screeching metal on cement. The baby cries a whiny, increasing cry as Kurt flings the pieces into the long grass by the fence.

Kurt leans the shovel against the wall. The cat lies on the cement, still licking itself, awkwardly reaching under its own neck, and around to its shoulders. Kurt crouches beside the cat.

'Y'okay, puss?' He reaches out to touch it, but the cat lashes at him. It rears back, hisses, then takes off towards the long grass by the fence, near where the snake pieces landed. The wet grass shimmies as the cat moves through it, then it stops; all is still. The cat has disappeared, into the garden, into the rain.

Kurt pulls back his sleeve. There is one long, deep scratch, a line of blood looped around his wrist.

Behind him, Iris picks up the shovel, hangs it on the row of hooks in the alcove between the back wall of the kitchen and the washhouse.

The baby wakes up properly now, ramps up from a whinge to a wail. Kristin does laps from the washhouse door to the back door to the shed and back to the washhouse, then repeat. She pats the baby, rubs it, murmurs to it, and eventually the crying hiccups to a choked-off sob, then back to snoring snuffles. Still, Kristin walks, does her laps and pats and rubs and murmurs, as if she's forgotten how to stop.

'I'm going to make tea.' Iris is watching Kristin circle with the baby. 'Kristin?'

'Mnh?'

'Tea?'

Kristin stops by the washhouse door. She shakes her head – breaks the baby-taming spell – and smiles at Iris.

'Tea, yeah, tea's good. Peppermint.'

'I'll make it,' Kurt says.

'Ordinary for me, love. Thanks. And Kurt?'

'Yeah?'

'See if Luce is okay, will you?'

'Yeah.'

He goes inside, fills the kettle, flicks its switch.

'Luce?' He tries it quietly to start with, then louder as he walks down the hallway, 'Luce?'

He pokes his head into the big room, but she's not there. Her bedroom door is closed. He can hear music playing, but quietly.

'Luce. Y'okay? Luce?' He knocks gently on the door, then louder when there's no response. 'Luce?'

He knocks, tries the door handle, opens the door a crack.

'Lulu?'

She is sitting on the bed, legs crossed in front of her, laptop open on her knees, earbuds plugged into the laptop, but not in her ears. They rest on her thighs, pumping tinny music – a tiny, rhythmic thumping – into the room.

'Lu? You alright?'

There are tears on her cheek. She doesn't wipe them away. A tear drops, as he watches, from the very tip of her chin. It falls onto her leg.

'Yeah.' She sniffs.

'You want tea?'

'No, I don't want fucking tea.'

'Okay, okay.' He starts to close the door, but doesn't. 'The cat —'

Luce turns to him, glares. 'What.'

It's not a question, the way she says it.

'Doesn't matter. Just — it ran away. The cat. It was weird —'

'Fuck the fucking cat! The snake belongs here, the cat doesn't. The snake should win, not the fucking cat. Or the fucking shovel!'

'Yeah, but —'

'Close the door when you go.' She lifts the whining earbuds, sticks one in each ear. The tinny music goes away.

As he closes the door to Luce's room he hears the creak, bang of the kitchen door, hears cups, hears voices. He heads back to the kitchen. Kristin is sitting at the table with the baby. Iris is making the tea.

'Luce alright?'

'She'll live.'

Iris sighs, puts mugs of tea on the table, sits down opposite Kurt. 'So, have you thought any more about doing something for your twenty-first?'

He shakes his head, pokes his glasses. 'Ah, it's just not important, Mum.' He's ready to start the argument again. 'It doesn't mean anything. Twenty-one; it's outdated. I've been legal to drink for years. To vote, to drive. There's nothing that kicks in at twenty-one any more.'

'I gave you a key to the door when you were twelve.'

'You did.'

'Even in my day it was a bit meaningless.'

'Well, then.'

'But I still think we should mark it. We don't have to have a party.'

'Good.'

'But I want to celebrate it. Your dad does, too. Doesn't he, Kristin?'

'Yeah, yeah, sure.' Kristin nods, stays neutral.

'So we agree.'

Kurt shakes his head, rolls his eyes. Iris ploughs on.

'Look, I know you don't want a celebration, but is it okay if we roll your twenty-first in with Rosa's one hundredth? Just family. Just – I dunno. Just. A quiet little thing. For us. Before you go back to uni.'

'Yeah. Sure.'

'Thanks, love. Really. Thanks. You know we miss you, now you're away.'

'It's eleven elevens.'

'What?'

'A hundred and twenty-one. Me plus Rosa. Our ages. Eleven elevens. Eleven squared.'

'So it is. And a palindrome, one-two-one. Symmetrical.' Iris lifts her mug of tea, raises it towards Kurt. 'I'll drink to that.'

Kurt clinks his mug against hers. They lean back into their chairs, distance bridged by their shared, nerdy love of numbers and patterns and order.

Kristin sits across from him. The baby is sleeping on her, its hand the only part of it visible, reaching up to rest palm-down, fingers splayed, flat on the bare skin above the neckline of Kristin's t-shirt. Maybe it feels her heartbeat, or her breathing, with its pink starfish hand, its little fat fingers.

Kurt raises his own hand to the same position on his chest. It rises and falls with his breath, but he can't – he doesn't think – feel his heart beat. At the edge of his sleeve, he can see that the line of blood where the cat scratched him has smeared, blotted, hardened in places to little lumps of dark red enamel. It has blotted through the fabric of his shirt, making unreadable patterns, like a badly applied stamp.

'That's nasty,' Kristin says. 'Cats can have that disease. Cat scratch fever. Dirt bacteria, or something. From digging when they crap. You should clean it with disinfectant. Maybe you need antibiotics.'

'It's fine. Hey, should we do anything about the cat? Look for it, or something? Make sure it's alright?'

'I think it's feral.'

'You should definitely clean that scratch.'

'I might look for it. The cat.'

'Just don't bring it home.'

'I won't! I won't. I just —'

'There's a first-aid kit in our car. I'll get it when the rain stops.'

'— if it's out there, with a snake bite —'

'It's not your problem, love.'

'I know. I just — yeah, I know.'

His index finger traces the bracelet of blood at his wrist, the skin tightening around it. He imagines himself tiny, under his own skin's surface; he closes his eyes and sees cartoon cells, mobilising, flaming, flaring, healing.

STITCH THE SNAKE

Will they ever find out what happened to the cat? Whether it survived or whether – snakebitten, or simply neglected, unfed – it died, the winner becoming the loser: a circularity of killing? In Iris's mind the real snake becomes a mythic serpent, tail tucked under tongue, forming a circle without end, looping infinitely. There's no top, no bottom; no beginning, no end.

That's how Iris stitches it, in bronze thread for the snake's body. She stitches the snake, makes it whole, in a continuous line that describes the edges of the blanket. The straight line curves and snakes (yes: *snakes*) to loop in on itself, to connect, to make a frame. She stitches in parallel to this the looping line, the train-track double, a mirror, a twin, then she spaces the stitches wider apart at the end – in the centre of what will be the foot of the blanket – and makes the bulge a head. Then she makes the head (the unseen, unstitched mouth) consume the tail, where those train-tracks V together to a point. The bite forms the loop, the circularity, the continuity. It makes the whole. It's an illusion, of course. There's no snake; no head, no tail, nothing but stitches, tiny lines pointing in and out of the wool of the blanket, roughly representing the snake, cartooning it, lacking realism. Iris moves her head close to the blanket, to the stitching, until the stitches blur. She moves her face closer still, puts her head on her hand, looks across the pale surface of the blanket, into nothing, into everything. The snake-shape frames the page, the canvas of the blanket, ready to be filled.

REMIND ME WHOSE BRIGHT IDEA THIS WAS

Everyone's busy and fussy and loud, as if they're retaking the house with their noise; one long, last hurrah before they leave. They're not just packing up, this weekend, packing boxes, packing the house; they're getting ready for a party.

Paul dubbed it a housecooling party, put the word out to friends, to everyone at work.

'If you're down south for the weekend, just drop in. Open house. Bring a bottle or three. Bring anyone.'

People accepted the invitation, said they'd bring the kids, a friend, the whole family. And more and more people have said they'll come. Over the last few weeks, Iris and Paul have both bumped into colleagues and ex-colleagues, neighbours, old friends, all of them heading down south, all of them keen to converge on the house. It's as if the whole city's moved south for the holidays.

They'd planned – in the usual way of this place, even at midwinter, expecting the weather to be fine – for the party, big or small, to drift outside, for food on the barbecue, dancing on the deck, smokers on the lawn. But the rain will keep them inside, tonight. So they will fill the house with people, with sound, with all of them. They'll fill it with kids underfoot, with beer, with wine, with food, with music. This is how it used to be, this house of theirs. And they're here, now, to make it that way again, then to unmake it; to give the house a good send-off, before they move themselves on.

And so: glasses remain unpacked, and bowls and plates stay out, for food. The fridge is not emptied, but filled, in anticipation.

'Why don't I go and buy plastic cups instead?'

'Oh, Paul. No.'

'No! Such a waste, when there's everything we need here. It's fine. We'll pack the kitchen tomorrow. Or Monday.'

'The movers aren't coming til Tuesday. There's plenty of time.'

'Honestly, who has a party when they're trying to move out of a house?'

'It's the perfect time. Everything's disrupted anyway. Why not celebrate?'

'Remind me whose bright idea this was.'

Paul puts his hands in the air, palms forward, surrendering. 'Mea culpa, baby. But you'll love it.'

'I won't love it. But I'll cope with it.'

Paul scoops his arms around Iris, waltzes her around the kitchen table.

'But Iris, there'll be dancing! Tonight we'll dance the night away. For tomorrow, we pack.'

AT THE BAY

Kurt stands outside, under cover of the back verandah, out of the rain. Through the window he watches his parents dancing together in the kitchen, his mother laughing. He wishes he smoked, for something to do with his hands. He picks up his pencil, balances it between his index finger and middle finger, touches it to his lips. There, round his wrist, there's the track of the cat's scratch, already fading.

The rain has eased – it's no longer overflowing the gutters – but it's still steady. He has made tea, brought it outside to get some peace, some space, before they all start packing. He's lost count of the cups of tea that have already been made in the house this morning. After living through twenty years of his mother's endless cups of tea, he's managed to forget it in the six months since he moved out. It annoys him – her endless tea, and his forgetting – though he doesn't know why.

He opens the sketchbook on his knees, puts the pencil to the page and lets it move; just doodling, nothing forced, nothing in mind. He finds himself making vertical lines, darkening the page with rain. A shape, not quite discernible, almost emerges. He keeps the pencil moving, but the shape remains hidden, behind the lines of rain on the page.

The rain has eased to mist, now. He closes the sketchbook, puts it in the big pocket of his jacket, zips the jacket to the neck, flips the hood over his head, and goes through the gate at the side of the house, to follow the path by the river to the bay.

The river's running faster, fuller, deeper than he ever remembers it running. The riverbank path is fine grey sand, becoming more and more rocky the closer it gets to the beach, where the river widens and flows into the bay. In summer you can't walk with bare feet down the rocky beach without burning your soles. But today at the bay it's cold, the wind coming in off the ocean, whipping salt at him, so he can smell it, taste it. The hood of his jacket flips backwards, exposes his face, his hair. He flicks the hood back up, hunches his shoulders to keep it in place, tucks his hands back in his pockets.

No one should be swimming today – you wouldn't expect it – and it's not the hour or weather for fishing, so he thought he'd have the bay to himself. But there's a mob of kids with a couple of dogs, local kids with nothing better to do. He feels conspicuous, in his towny black, like a black swan wandering strange, out of place, on the beach. His boots crunch and scratch the pebbles underfoot, and one of the kids turns, then they all turn, to watch him for a long moment; then they turn away, back to their business. He walks to the big flat rock close to the river, where the beach starts to angle down to the water. It's a gently sloping surface the size of a large bed, crisscrossed with patterns, crevices, cracks, slick with wet from the rain. He lowers himself to sit on the rock, hunches in over his bent knees, feels the long-ago-familiar face of the rock under him, pressing into him. He puts his hands by his sides, presses the palms flat onto the rock. Fingertips flex, and his right hand finds the curve at the edge of the big flat stone, fits it, grabs it like a handle, holds on tight. He feels the wetness start to seep into his jeans, feels wet turn to cold at the points where flesh touches denim.

The kids are busy at the river mouth. They're all drenched, soaking wet. They're wearing shiny basketball shirts and hoodies; clothes that aren't right for the weather, thin, quickly soaked through. There's one black dog right in there with them, a mad barker, lolling and lolloping. Another dog, black and white, more serious, is hanging back, watching, crouched up the beach on its haunches, front paws out, ears up, attentive, as if it's watching skittish sheep. The dog glances up at Kurt, then back, up, then back at the kids, its flock;

57

seven of them? Eight? *Count the legs and divide by two*. His dad always made the same joke when they drove down here, when he – Kurt – was a kid, when they passed sheep in a paddock.

'How many sheep are there? In the paddock, Dad. How many?'

'Count the legs and divide by four.'

It was their call and response; one of their silly rituals.

The kids are running in and out of the water – the darkened, murky water, where the river meets the ocean – in and out, up and down, over and across, up the beach to forage for wood, carrying big branches and whole bushes back to the water. One of them has a tyre, splaying black fibre, and he drags it, backwards, bent in two with its weight and density. They've got some rope; they're tying bits of wood together to make a terrible bastard of a raft. They're standing on the tyre, pushing each other off. All that stuff kids do. All that stuff he's watched kids do. All that stuff. He presses his palms onto the rock, his fingertips seeking clefts, lines, something to hold onto. It feels good to have something solid to grip. He spends too much time seeking metaphoric purchase, holding it together, not letting the cracks show. Not letting people know there are cracks.

The kids have gathered around now, looking at something; he can't tell what. They've lined up, curved in an arc, all facing the water. They're mostly the same height, the same whip-thin, stick-thin – he can see that now, with them all together – except one bigger kid who's tall, stocky, built like a fridge. And there's one small kid, a head shorter than the others, maybe someone's little brother, or just a runty short-arse. The kids are standing, contemplating, their heads all bent. The noisy black dog is snuffling the backs of their knees, trying to break past the line, trying to see what they're all looking at. The runty kid kicks his leg backwards at the dog, and the kid next to him pushes the runty kid in the back. Not hard though. Just a don't-do-that shove. The watchful dog still watches.

One of the kids is talking. One of the middle-sized ones. Then one of them bends over. Two of them have sticks, and they poke them out towards the water.

A car pulls into the carpark then, a shiny metallic green ute. It pulls up and parks at an angle, *dee-da-doo-doo* tooting the horn. A black wool beanie leans out of the car window — *Carn youse!* — and the kids pelt up the rocky slope of the beach, and up the wooden steps to the carpark. Kurt watches four kids and the noisy dog pile in the tray of the ute as it reverses out, then takes off. Two other boys follow the car, running at first, as if they might catch it, then walking as it speeds off, unreachable.

One of the kids stays where he is by the water, watching the others go, then glancing up at Kurt, then turning back to the water, to what Kurt can now see is a dark shape — something — floating just below the surface. The watchful dog crawls on its belly, closer to the water, closer to the boy. The boy pats its head, and the dog raises its nose, nuzzles then licks the patting hand. Both of them, the kid and the dog, look out to the thing in the water. The kid has a stick, he uses it to poke, to reach out.

Then the dog barks — at a sound Kurt can't hear? At nothing? — and takes off, sprinting up the beach, close enough to Kurt to spray pebbles up with its long lurching legs. Kurt turns to watch the dog disappear into the scrub fringing the top of the beach.

When he looks back, the kid's not there. There's just the dark shape in the water.

Kurt jumps off the platform rock onto the pebbles and sand, and starts walking. His feet are almost deciding to run, to panic. Just as he gets to the steps at the far edge of the beach, the dog pelts down through the scrub and appears ahead of him, bursting out onto the gravel of the carpark, and — somehow — the kid is there, to meet the dog. The kid looks at Kurt, lifts his chin slowly, holds it a moment — in a challenge — then lowers it, then he turns away, and he and the dog head off up a track, disappearing into the scrub.

Kurt turns at the top of the steps, looks back down to the empty beach. The long stick the kid was using rests on the rocky bank, parallel with the river's flow, pointing the tea-brown dark of the river towards where it empties into the grey-green sea.

IN THE WASHHOUSE

When the rain falls like this, misty in between showers of proper dumping rain, everything is soft, feels and looks soft, smells soft. Even colours soften. Intentions soften, too. Luce sits under cover, just inside the door of the old washhouse, and listens to the rain, watches it fall and pool and wet, just a metre from her feet, while she's dry and warm. She sits in an old plastic garden chair, with her legs drawn up in front of her, feet on the chair, chin resting on her knees. From the shaded dark of the washhouse, she looks out into the daylight (the soft light, the soft light rain). She holds in her hand one of the stones she picked up and pocketed at the bay yesterday, when she and Kurt ran down there before the rain started. Before all this rain. She thinks about the cat (that murdering cat), and how — even though it deserves punishment — she couldn't bring herself to do it, to throw this solid stone at that soft, grey head. Her finger remembers the feel of the snake's skin, its sleek, dry cool; its stillness. But she doesn't think she could punish the cat for what it did. If she ever even sees it again.

Her hand is heavy with the stone. It's smooth, a dark brown that's almost purple — like the colour of dried blood — with freckles of caramel in it. It fits in the cup her hand makes when the fingers curve up, and the thumb curves around. She lifts her hand with the stone to her face, holds it against her cheek, presses it there, until its smooth cold makes her shiver.

The side gate creaks. She watches Kurt move through it, close it, walk across the yard towards the back verandah. He is hunched deep into his jacket, head down, hood flipped up, so she can't see his face, just his hair hanging down at the front, like a scarf, or a dark decoration. He opens the back door to the kitchen. For the moment that the door is open, Luce hears a voice, then another, then laughter, then – creak, bang – Kurt disappears into it, and takes the sounds with him.

She stands up, puts the stone in the pocket of her jeans. It makes a bulge, low in the front. She cups her hand around the fabric over the stone, presses it against her. Her phone buzzes in her hoody. She reaches into the pocket of her jeans, removes the stone, squeezes it in her hand. She swaps the stone for the phone, pushes the button, swipes, hunches her head over the screen.

'Love, you're wet!'

    'There's soup on the stove if you want it.'

    'Let me hang your jacket up –'

    'It's fine. I'm fine.'

    'And bread. Here –'

    'Yeah, okay. Thanks.'

Kurt sits at the table, lets Iris put soup and bread in front of him, lets her rest her hand on his shoulder, just for a moment, without shrugging her off. The noise of the kitchen wraps around him, warm but somehow annoying, like a wool jumper with a scratchy label. He's aware of the notebook in the pocket of his jacket; the weight of it. He closes his eyes against the chatter in the kitchen. He can see the panels he drew at the bay. The boy, the dog, the dark shape in the water; the rain, the disappearing, the panic; the lifted chin, the eyes turning away, the dog's turning tail.

Luce creaks through the door, lets it bang behind her. Kurt is sitting, eating; they all are, around the table. Iris half gets up, asks her all the food questions. No, she doesn't want soup. Yes, she's sure she doesn't want soup. Yes, she's fine. No, she's not hungry. Yes, she had a big breakfast. Yes (again), she's fine. She stands just inside the back door, her hands in the pocket of her hoody, one clutched around the stone, one around the phone. In the old lounge chair on the other side of the table, Kristin sits nested in cushions on a crocheted rug, the baby on her (of course, as always). Kristin lifts the baby, flips her in her arms like handballing a footy, or rolling a ball of dough. She presses the baby against her skin. The baby bumps at her, like a blind puppy. Luce shudders, rolls her eyes. The whole room smells of baby. She goes to the stove and stands with her hands out towards it, an excuse to turn her back on Kristin and the baby, on all of them.

'Hi, darl. Where are you? Have you left yet?'

Iris talks too loudly into the phone. It statics in the gaps, the response audible but unintelligible, so there's only one side of the conversation.

'Yeah, I know, we pretty much drove into it. It was amazing! It poured all night. It's eased a bit now, but not for long –'

'Is that Mart? Tell her Evie's coming tonight. She emailed me.'

'Paul says Evie's coming tonight. I know! Did you –'

Luce gets a bowl from the cupboard, lifts the lid off the soup on the stove, clatters it.

'Tell her Evie's bringing the new man.'

'Did you hear that? He said she's bringing the man-child.'

Luce slops soup into the bowl, clashes the lid back on the pot. She rummages in the cutlery drawer until she finds a spoon she likes. She takes her time. She tings the spoon against the rim of the bowl as she takes each mouthful of soup.

'Alright, well don't leave too late. The roads'll be slippery.'

'Take it slow, sis!'

'Did you hear that? Okay. Drive carefully. See you soon.' Iris moves the phone from the side of her face, holds it in front of her at arm's length, peers at it, does a thing with her mouth, taps the screen, pushes the button, puts the phone on the table.

'That was Marti.'

Luce looks up, catches Kurt's eye. She puts her tongue in behind her bottom lip, puffs it out fat and dumb, widens her eyes, wobbles her head. Kurt cracks a smile. Luce smiles back, but she keeps her head facing down to her soup, so no one else can see.

STITCH THE DIAMONDS

Stitch a hand of cards to mark the baby's Diamond clan. Stitch the first two cards for Jacko and Alba (he's Jack o' Diamonds, she's the Queen). Stitch Auntie Marti as a Joker (Joker's wild, for any card); stitch her blonde-haired, blue-eyed, laughing; make her laugh a red-stitched smile. That makes Paul another Joker; make him Marti's twin, her pair. Edge his face with rust-red beard, and stitch it salt-and-pepper grey. Stitch Kristin as another Queen (of hearts, of course), and complete the hand: full house.

ROCK PAPER SCISSORS

They're all around the house, now, all of them. Each of them's busy, focused now on packing: there's newspaper and scissors, packing tape and boxes, bubble wrap and bin bags. They unpack shelves and cupboards, and then – like building a drystone wall, or playing Tetris, judging space and place, rotating each piece to position it perfectly – remake them as careful layers in boxes as they go.

Iris watches Luce, on the other side of the room. Luce has stopped packing books into boxes and sits, reading, one hand on the book in front of her, the other poised above the page, moving between the page and her face, hovering, where it needs to be. Only her hand – this hand – moves. The rest of her – the core of her, and her legs, her shoulders – is still. There's a stillness and measure to Luce, solid as rock, marble-smooth. A beautiful measure, timeless and forever.

Luce sits on the floor, her back against the sofa, her feet on the low table, a book propped against her knees, on her thighs. Iris has given everyone jobs. Iris has given her boxes to fill.

'Just pack everything. We don't have time to sort things. The movers are coming on Tuesday. Make sure you label the boxes.'

The empty, flattened boxes that Iris brought down in the back of her car are piled in the hallway, with rolls of that old-lady-undies-brown tape. Luce has filled one box already, written on the top of it OLD BOOKS, in big letters; then, slightly smaller, PACKED BY; then, biggest of all, LUCY FLINT. She took longer to write the label than she did to pack the box.

She looks up, across the room, at Iris and Kurt at the table, wrapping, packing. They look busy. Kurt stands and tapes a box closed. There's the skritch sound of the tape, high-pitched, like ripping your eardrums apart. She closes her eyes until the noise stops.

She's onto the bottom shelf of the bookcase now, halfway through her second box. The book she has just opened has a cover of thick brown card, dark with time, almost chocolate in colour. It smells of dust, the smell of secondhand bookstores. Iris told her that that smell is the smell of a fungus, that lives on paper. Luce opens the book – the cover opens out into her, hits her in the chest, before she folds it carefully over to her left – and, on the first page is a photograph, and three spaces where photographs must have been, but are no longer. There are mounts to show the corners of the missing photographs, and writing below where they would have sat. She turns the pages, more interested in the gaps than the photographs that remain in place.

Iris is wrapping glasses and china in newspaper, nesting them in boxes. Kurt stacks a taped box to one side, then sits back down, across the table from Iris. He's been helping her pack, but he's been sidetracked, first by the words on the newspaper (he sat, quietly, reading for some time), and then by the actions of wrapping, of cutting: paper, scissors, reminding him of rock.

'It's universal. There's some version of it in most cultures. Different names, of course. Different objects. But it's fundamentally the same. Always three things. Three's just one of those numbers. There's something about primes, but three in particular.'

He talks with his hands. He leans in, animated, to make a point to her, then leans back, flings his head sideways. His hair arcs back, uncovers his face.

'It's circular, never-ending, that's the beauty of it. No one thing wins over every other thing. Any choice you make might win, or it might lose. There's the *potential* to win with each choice, each move, but there's also the potential, each move, to lose.'

He makes a fist with his left hand, pumps it up and down three times, then opens his hand out flat, palm down, thumb tucked in tight at the side.

'Even paper can win. Paper wraps rock.'

He forms a fist with his right hand, folds his left hand around it, brings both hands in under his chin.

Iris forms her first two fingers into a V, and scissors them at Kurt's wrapping hand.

'Chop-chop. Scissors cut paper.'

Kurt's right hand, rock-fist, nudges Iris's scissorhand.

'Rock blunts scissors.'

Iris wraps her other hand around Kurt's.

'And paper wraps rock, again.'

Kurt leaves his hand there, big in Iris's smaller hand but nonetheless enveloped, for a moment, before withdrawing it, placing both hands, one on top of the other, flat on the table in front of him. Iris had leaned forward to reach Kurt's hands; she leans back now, leans back into the chair. She wants to hold him, but instead she gives him space.

She remembers: a long flight home, Kurt sitting between Iris (in the window seat) and Paul (the aisle), Kurt with a Lego alien robot that he took apart and put back together, reconfiguring it, over and over.

'More stable,' he'd said to himself, planting the three limbs on the tray table, jiggling the tray table up and down, back and forth, making a little quake.

Angry eyes peered over the seat in front of him.

'Sorry,' Iris said to the angry eyes, and put her hand on Kurt's hand.

'Don't rock it, sweetie. It's annoying the people in front.'

'Stableman! Rock. And. Ro-o-o-ll!!'

Kurt rocked the plastic figure back and forth, making rumbling noises. Iris could hear the angry-eyes-woman hissing.

'Can Stableman do paper scissors rock?'

'Don't be silly. He hasn't got hands. He's got tools. Impendages.'

'Ap-pendages.'

'Ar-pendages. He's got ar-pendages.'

Kurt formed his left hand into a closed fist, pumped it up and down three times, bobbing the plastic man in unison. On the third bounce, his left fist opened to a two-fingered V, fingers snapping scissorlike at the plastic figure's head.

'Stableman beats scissors!'

He crashed the figurine onto his hand, 'Ah! Argh! Take that, scissorhand!' Then, predictably, 'Ow.'

Iris reached over and took his hand in between her hands, rubbed it, then lifted it to her mouth and kissed it.

'Mu-u-um.'

He'd wriggled his hand away from hers. She let it go, patted it as he rested it on the table. She grabbed Stableman from Kurt, planted a kiss on his head. Kurt rubbed the plastic helmeted head on his t-shirt, erasing her kiss.

She remembers when he was a tiny boy, a teenage boy, and everything in between. He will remain her tiny boy. Even now, when he towers over her. He has towered over her since he was thirteen. She still thinks of him as tiny, and soft. A tiny boy holding onto her hand.

She will always see the little boy in him, not the man. This is what she struggles against. And this is what she struggles never to lose. Never lose that tiny boy, for only she remembers him. He is hers forever, that tiny boy. She cherishes him, and holds tight his hand. She feeds him and comforts him, stills his racing mind with her finger, tracing a circle on his forehead. She stills his fears, his overreaction to what he imagines might happen. His is an active mind; is and ever has been. She formed it. She was there when his imagination formed; she created the environment in which it grew. She is to blame (or thank).

She can still hear him, his boy's voice, him as a child. She kept his answering-machine message on the phone long after anyone ever left a message, long after it was needed. His not-yet-broken voice, that she could phone, and speak to.

Twenty-one years has gone in a flash. Imagine another twenty-one, and another. She has lived for nearly three twenty-ones. She remembers life before Kurt. He cannot imagine life without her. They have co-existed for all of his life. There can be no memory where experience has not lived. Only inference. Imagination.

The rain starts up again, hard on the roof, percussing the heart of the house. Each of them looks up at the noise, makes an O with their mouth at the ceiling.

THE THING WITH FEATHERS

'I found this in the bedroom, on the bookshelf, when we got here. It's so slim, it was between some other books, you know, kind of hidden? I've been reading it. It's all about maps and land and love, somehow. He's a poet from the sixties, seventies. I looked him up this morning, on my phone. He was maybe a little famous, back then, but a little mysterious. He published as Zigi, this one name only, and everyone thought he was ripping off Bowie. Or maybe he *was* Bowie. But it turned out he was this German-Israeli guy, and Zigi was just a nickname he went by, short for Zigmund.'

Iris and Kristin are sitting at the table in the kitchen. Paul and Kurt have gone to get beer and wine for the party; Luce is in her room. Iris pours more tea from the pot, takes another piece of shortbread from the tin. Kristin drinks from an enormous glass of water, and eats carrot sticks that she has cut and assembled on a plate in front of her. The baby sleeps on Kristin, in the green fabric sling looped across her front. All Iris can see of the baby is a thin crescent of head, silky hair dark against the soft, padded curve of the sling. Kristin rests her hand on the book on the table in front of her as she speaks. She is intense, staring; but Kristin is often intense, staring, and Iris barely notices it any more, in the same way that she barely notices the overlay of Kristin's faint accent, her oddly placed words, as she speaks.

'The poems are good. They're beautiful, simple. He was – it turns out – a scientist. A geologist. The centre of his book of poems is a haiku cycle based around this idea of fault. But it turns out to be a literal fault, a geological one, that he worked on as a young student, as a geologist. So, like this: "The most common shape / of the fault trace is an arc / concave to the north." This is one of the haiku, but it's about the geological fault, you know, that he actually worked on. He made a map of it. He "mapped it".' Kristin wiggles her fingers in the air. 'This is what you call it? When these poems were first published, when this book came out, the fact that he was a scientist, that wasn't known. That only happened quite recently. I think maybe he's been rediscovered, you know? According to the internet, anyway. I just really like the poems, though, the science–art thing. And the German–English thing is interesting.'

'Did he write them in German?'

'I dunno. I think in English. But maybe that's why I like them, because they're not written in his first language. There's a click, you know, a something, a missingness in the language. It's maybe something about the distance between the German and the English, the distance between science and poetry. Lots of distance, of displacement. And yet so many connections. It somehow works. There's something about displacement that makes good poetry, I think.'

Kristin picks up the book, hands it to Iris. It is slim, so slim, in the way that only poetry books are. Slimmer than a notebook. Underneath the book's title – *The Hope Fault* – the cover shows a map, in black and white, overprinted in pale orange. Lines and marks. She turns the book over. At bottom right is a tiny, blurry photograph, black and white, of a young man with dark hair, thick 1960s glasses of a type that is fashionable again now. His finger is raised to his mouth in a pose that's coquettish. Iris peers in at the small, grainy photograph, trying to see the detail, but the image becomes more unclear, resolves into dots, so she can hardly make sense of it.

She flicks through the book, closes it, turns it over so the front cover faces upwards, holds it towards Kristin, who waves it away.

'Oh, I'm done with it. You should read it. You'll like it.' Kristin leans in close to her, puts her finger on the cover of the book. 'So. Our thinking is so fucked – you know, we've become so desperate – that last night we were even talking about this.' She points, jabs her finger again at the book, at its title. 'For a name. For the baby. Hope.'

'Mmm. Hope's nice. A nice name.'

'Oh Iris, come on. Hope. Hope *Diamond*.'

'Oh.' Iris splutters, nearly spits out her tea. 'Oh, no.'

'I know. Can you imagine? It's like a porn name. Or a Bond girl. But we didn't even notice until we'd almost decided, you know, almost talked ourselves into it.'

'Oh, I would've told you. Or someone would've. It's too bad, Hope's a nice name. Old-fashioned, in that good way. Like Faith. Or Charity.'

'Yeah. Well, the thing is, it made us decide to decide.'

'What do you mean?'

'Well, we thought while we're here – all of us, here in the house – we should do it. Name her. What better time, you know?'

'But you haven't decided on the name?'

'We haven't. Not quite.' She sips her water, rearranges the carrot sticks on her plate. 'But we need to, anyway. You know, they give you only three months, and you must do it. Register. So we will. This weekend. Paul and I talked about it last night, for ages, after Paul came to bed. We want to have a naming party. Sort of a ceremony. On Monday, before we close the house up. What do you think? Is that okay?'

'God, of course!'

'Just simple, just all of us, family, you know? Maybe outside, if the rain ever stops.'

'I'll make a cake. *Pat it and prick it and mark it with B.*'

'Bee?'

'It's a nursery rhyme. On top of the cake. B for Baby.'

'Ah, Baby. Not for much longer.' Kristin's hand drifts to the baby's head, rests there lightly. She dips forward and kisses the baby's forehead, almost as if she doesn't realise she's doing it.

They've all called Kristin and Paul's baby *Baby* for so many months that Iris has come to think of this as her name. But Baby needs her own name. Names are important, Iris thinks. Long ago, a name was a magical offering. Spinning straw into gold, guessing the names of sprites and goblins and otherworlders, that's a thing of the past, of myth. The world doesn't work that way any more. And yet, a thing — a person — isn't quite itself if it's nameless, or un-named, or wrong-named.

'Oh.' Kristin has her hand inside the sling, checks the whimpering baby. 'You're wet. Come on, little Hope Diamond.'

'I'll do it. Let me.'

Iris moves around the table, reaches her arms out. Kristin lifts the baby out of the sling, hands her to Iris, then hands her the nappy bag that's slung over the back of the chair in the corner of the kitchen. The baby is heavy in her arms, and Iris can feel the damp through the layers of both of their clothes. She holds the baby against her shoulder, talking quietly as they move from the kitchen, down the hall. The baby holds herself out from Iris's shoulder to get a good look at her. As they move through the door from the hall to Iris's bedroom, the baby reaches out her hand and places it, flat, fingers spread like a star on Iris's cheek.

Iris bends down and puts the baby on her bed. She kneels on the floor, unwraps the tiny clothes, unpins the cloth at the baby's belly. She grabs both feet around the ankles with her left hand, lifts her up, pulls the damp cloth out from under her with her right hand. The cloth is thick, folded and wadded, soaked with the sweet hot wee of a breastfed baby, so sweet you could almost drink it. When she puts it down beside her on the floor, the nappy stays shaped in the curve of reaching to cup the baby from front to back, tummy to tail.

When she's changed the baby, and taken her back to Kristin, Iris offers to mind her.

'Everything's done for tonight. I was just going to sort through some boxes, so I can watch her while I do that. You could get some rest. Read a book. Do some Pilates. Whatever.'

'Oh, I've done some already today, before she woke up. It's okay. But maybe while I have a shower? That'd be great.'

'Good. Go. We're good. We might go and sit outside for a bit, watch the rain.'

'Perfect. One moment.' Kristin leaves the room, returns a minute later with a fine merino wrap, and a green woollen beanie topped with a long knitted curl, that she fits to the baby's head while Iris holds her.

'There. Just like Mr Curly.' She leans in, kisses the baby's head. Kristin's hair smells of tea-tree and sweat. 'Ah, and this, too.' She takes the book from the table, slots it in between Iris and the baby, wedging it there. 'Maybe you will read her some poems of Hope.'

The baby's hand reaches towards the book. Iris snugs the wool wrap around them both, book and all, and they head out through the kitchen door to the verandah.

Iris sits under cover of the back verandah, the baby hugged to her front. She feels monumental, holding the baby, feels herself solid and stable, immobile, carved from stone, all out of proportion, a Henry Moore statue, woman with tiny child. The movement – the only movement – is in her and the baby, their breath and blood, their fluids. Even the air around them is still. There's no wind, and the rain has eased, falls gently, straight down.

She holds her free hand in front of her, flexes the fingers, turns the hand palm up, then palm down, spreads the fingers, holds her hand still, hovering just above her knee. There are tiny movements of the fingers, the fingertips twitch as if trying to keep their balance. She cannot see her pulse – nothing as overt as that – just its little tremblings. She thinks of Rosa's hands, how they shake now, how they claw and grab, and fail to connect. Her own hands – when she thinks, like now, to look at them – show her age. She flexes her hand up at the wrist, straightens it. The skin slowly sinks back to shape.

She turns her hand over, so it is facing palm upwards again. Now she can see the movement of her blood, can see – just – the pulse

pulse pulse under the skin in the soft underbelly of her wrist, near where veins branch and cross. She rotates her hand in the light – yes, at the base of the thumb, too, she can see the pulse moving under the surface. Like a swan, paddling madly underwater, gliding serenely above.

Iris wonders, not for the first time, how to describe the relationship the baby has to her. *My son's half-sister. My ex-husband's child. Step-niece.* Almost. The baby has nothing of her – of Iris – in her, even though she is her son's sister. *The half-sibling of my offspring.* It's a common enough relationship, but there's no word to describe it, to define or delimit it. Nor is there a word for what Iris will be, to the baby. The baby, when she grows, might describe Iris as *my brother's mother*, or *my father's first wife*. Perhaps just *an old friend of the family*. Or not even that.

A noise like paper fluttering comes from the baby. Iris has to pull her chin in to her neck, rear back to focus on the baby's face. She is asleep. Iris kisses her head, and the Mr Curly curl – upright, like a feather on the baby's hat – tickles her nose.

'Hope,' she whispers to the sleeping baby, 'you're the thing with feathers.'

She picks up the book of poems with her free hand, opens it, and starts to read, quietly, sounding the poems out; not quite reading them out loud, but whispered on her breath, so she can only just hear their rhythm and feel their weight.

COMPASS POINT

Seam. Fold. Slip. She has searched for him on the internet, on her phone – this Zigi, this poet – and found the geologist, Zigmund Silbermann. She has found his books, his scientific papers and geological bulletins, texts thick with words of rocks and measurements and certainty. She has searched images, and she has found his maps.

They are old-fashioned colours – Commonwealth Pink, teal, yellow, blue – the colours of long-ago classroom maps. The lettering on the maps is close and neat. She pinches her fingers apart to zoom in to see detail large on the screen. She imagines a hand holding a pen, dipped in ink. Or perhaps a pencil, sharpened – as her mother had always done it – with a knife, whittled to a perfect point, kept sharp, precise, controllable. She thinks of her mother, and the work she did, colouring photographs, long ago; the precision it must have taken. Lick the tip, dip to colour, bend yourself in close to the page and gently, lightly, touch the tip to it.

There are marks and hatchings, unreadable areas of colour filling outlined areas, patterns hatched left, hatched right, crosshatched, dotted, herringbone. A streak of solid sky blue reaches almost right across the map, overlaid with words like spells (or, yes, poems): *Vitric lithic and crystal tuffs sandstone / coarse basal conglomerate / marine fossils rare few beds of / fragmental plant remains.* She pans around the space of the map, the face of it. It is unreadable to her. It makes no sense. She can read the individual marks and words and colours and numbers well enough. She can read the colours as colours – as pattern, as shape and form; she can read them aesthetically. But lines that read to her as darts or seams marked on a dress pattern have different meaning on the map. Their sense is not her sense – she can't decipher their code.

Loops and folds of pink and orange course through the map, loop out of its frame, loop back into it. Phrases interrupt the shapes and lines: *steep & broken. Steep & broken. Attitude clear but evidence uncertain. Attitude clear.* Lines are inscribed in little marks, like blanket stitch, or inches marked off on a ruler.

North is not straight up, to the top of the map's page, but lies instead at a lazy angle, as if the earth has tilted to fit map to page. The compass point is simple and beautiful, and reminds her of a Christmas star. The word *True* is written above it.

STITCH A FRAGMENT OF A POEM

Take the book of poems as a guide and stitch hope, stitch fault. Stitch a fragment of a poem, show how the poem maps the land. Stitch the fault as an arc, concave to the north. Make a border, shade it blanket stitch; make an edge, mark a cliff. Give the flatness third dimension, give it height; stitch the ground uneven. Stitch seams. Stitch folds. Stitch darts. Stitch a pointer to true north, but not straight upwards; stitch it lying lazy. Stitch *True* above the compass point.

RUMPELSTILTSKIN, RUMPELSTILTSKIN, RUMPELSTILTSKIN

Luce says, 'There's got to be a ceremony. Like, a party. You can't just start calling her a name, after all this time.'

'Yeah, yeah, that's the plan, Lu. A party. On Monday. Here.'

'A christening, but without the Christ.'

'With fairy godparents?'

'Of course.'

'What about Jacko and Alba?'

'What about them?'

'They'll be pissed off.'

'Nah, they'll be relieved. They've been hassling us about the name ever since she was born.'

'Since before. Ever since we told them I was pregnant.'

'But they'll be pissed off not to be here. Not to be invited. Her only grandparents.'

'If you don't invite them, they might show up anyway. Like magic. Cast a spell. A curse. Like a pricking finger.'

'But you never have evil *grandparents* in a fairy story. *Stepmothers*, yes. Not grandparents. I think we're safe.'

Luce looks at Kristin when Iris says *stepmothers*, but Kristin doesn't seem to mind.

'If you keep saying their names, they'll turn up. Like Rumpelstiltskin, Rumpelstiltskin, Rumpelstiltskin and boom, there, in a puff of smoke.'

'I think that's wrong –'

'Jacko-and-Alba, Jacko-and-Alba, Jacko-and –'

'No! Don't say it!'

'– I think the princess had to guess Rumpelstiltskin's name, and he *disappeared* in a puff of smoke –'

'They'll be fine. Don't worry about Jacko-and-Alba, Jacko-and-Alba –'

'Paul! Don't!'

'We need to bring gifts. Fairy godmothers always bring gifts.'

'She doesn't need presents, Lu. She's got everything she needs.'

'Not *presents*. *Gifts*. Gifts are different from presents. Gifts are sort of – small and magical.'

'Like a magic ring.'

'Beauty. Intelligence. Compassion.'

'A magic story.'

'A magic mirror.'

'Sometimes the name itself is considered a gift.'

'Yeah, but you'll give her the name. I'll give her –'

'It's fine, Lu, honestly –'

'But I want to. I'll make – I'll make a song.'

'Oh, Luce –'

'Oh. Is that not okay?'

'Love, of course it is. It's lovely. That'd be a lovely gift. The best.'

Paul grabs her, hugs her, kisses her golden hair, and she lets him.

'Lucinda-sky. You're the best. You're the crown jewels.'

'With diamonds?'

'With diamonds.'

'Hey, Mum can make a cake –'

'Of course, a Marti Sponge!'

'It wouldn't be a party without a Marti Party Sponge –'

'– and that can be *her* gift to the baby.'

Iris's eyes prickle with love. How Luce has lit up with this task! How impossible she is to predict.

ROUND LIKE A RECORD

Paul was planning to plug his phone through the speakers, but Kurt's vetoed that.

'With all this vinyl? Nah, let's do it old-school, old man.'

Paul surrenders his hands in the air. 'Suits me. Who's DJ? You or me?'

'Aren't you supposed to be on kitchen duty?'

'You think?' Paul holds out his fist.

Kurt matches it. They bounce fists three times; Paul bounces a fourth as Kurt throws a flat hand. Paper wraps rock.

Paul surrenders again. 'The hands have spoken. I'm off to the kitchen. I'll expect music to slice and dice to.'

Kurt pulls one of the milk crates out from the shelf under the stereo, starts flipping through the records. There's nothing more recent than ten years ago, most of it older than that. A mixture of good stuff, and dross.

There are more milk crates, and boxes of CDs, still to sort. He lifts a record sleeve from the milk crate, slides the record from the sleeve to balance between his middle finger (nesting in the hole) and thumb (on the edge). He puts the record sleeve on the shelf, lifts the lid of the turntable and settles the record, places the needle on the lead-in to track one and cranks the volume up loud.

Luce is in her room, fired with purpose, tapping time on the windowsill, thinking about what to put in her song, when she hears the music start, in the other room. She sits back on her bed, leans against the wall, and smiles, starts nodding her head, starts to sing the words.

Iris is in her room, doing one last session of stitching before the party (snipping threads, making marks on fabric), when she hears the music start. She opens the door, and follows the voices. She stands in the doorway, leans, watches. Luce is up on the sofa, her arms windmilling backstroke; then thumbs out, hitchhiking. Her legs are triangling, knees bent, for stability, hips rotating, thrusting to the music. She's singing at the top of her voice. Kurt's on the floor next to the sofa, one arm out in front, the other by his eye – as if to sight an arrow – then he swaps them, pivots at the waist. Luce bounces, stumbles, regains her feet and jumps from the sofa to the floor and Kurt catches her, and they break apart and keep on dancing, watusi-ing and singing all around the room.

'Have you seen the kids? In the big room? God, they're gorgeous!'

Iris finds Paul and Kristin in the kitchen, piling food on plates, glasses on trays. Paul's singing, bouncing to the music as he moves around the room.

Paul's phone, on the table, vibrates. He picks it up, peers at the screen, flicks it, swipes to answer.

'Hey sis, it's party time! Where are you?'

'Tell her I hope she's on her way. It's getting dark already.'

'You hear that? Iris says she hopes you've left. It's dark already. No, we don't need anything, just you. Alright Mart, gotta go, this wine isn't going to drink itself. Drive carefully. See you round like a record, baby.'

Car lights arc across the house and in through the front window, light up the room, light up Kurt and Luce, still dancing. Doors open, slam. Gravel crunches, voices move towards the front door. The first guests have arrived. The party has started.

Saturday night

IN THE MIDDLE OF THE HOUSE

If not for the rain, they'd be spilling out onto the back verandah, and out the big side doors and into the garden, but the people are all inside the house, now, the windows fugged with their breath. This is how it used to be: the house filled with people, with music. It's the right way to send the house off out of their lives. It's not wallowing in the past, or trying to recreate it; it's nodding to it, celebrating it, doffing a hat to it. Raising the roof.

It doesn't take many people to make the house seem full. Most of them are Paul and Kristin's friends, but many of them Iris knows, or at least recognises. Some are neighbours she's never met. She looks around the room at the old people – all of them – and thinks: they're like me; we used to be young. Now, the only young ones in the room are second wives, or grown-up kids.

Across the room from Iris, glasses clink together. From the next room, she hears laughter, and hands clapping, someone strumming a guitar, then tuning it, then strumming again. People turn towards the sound. They move towards it, into the big low-ceilinged room that runs along the side of the house, built out from the original deep verandah, years ago, when they were down here every weekend and all summer; when they'd thought they'd move here one day, and live here forever. A room for kids, they'd thought – for Kurt and his friends, for Luce; or maybe, maybe one day, who knew, Iris was still young enough, Kurt would love a brother or sister – a play room, a music room, where they could make a mess, make a noise, tramp sand in from outside and it wouldn't matter. There's a piano at one end of the room, a guitar stand next to it, and next to that a cane basket full of soundmakers: drumsticks, a tambourine, wooden spoons, chopsticks; maracas made from tin cans filled with rice, decorated with stickers and paint and glued-on glitter; harmonicas and whistles. Someone Iris doesn't know – a man, maybe in his forties, maybe older – has picked up the old guitar and is singing, something bad and bluesy. Is it Creedence? Iris can't tell; they all sound the same to her. She stands up, weaves her way across the room, touching people on the arm, smiling as she moves past them.

Next to the piano, Kurt and Paul stand together, watching the man play, listening to him. Paul leans in to Kurt, says something into his ear, nods his head in the direction of the guitar man as he says it. Kurt's face breaks into a smile – fills with it, lightens with it – before he closes up again, sets it back to neutral. When he smiles, like that, there's a flash of Paul when he was that age, and Iris thinks of the first time she saw him: when she sat on the Oak Lawn at lunchtime, between lectures, eating sandwiches from a brown paper bag. Paul was playing guitar in a band playing so-so Velvets covers. Marti did a Nico, standing smoking at the side, coming in on droning vocals and tambourine on 'All Tomorrow's Parties'. When Iris first heard Paul sing – when he stepped to the microphone, hidden behind those wrap-around Lou-style sunglasses, and sang the first words of 'Sunday Morning' – she fell in love, there and then. Thirty years ago, just about. How young they were, then.

Here and now, Kristin sits on the piano stool next to Paul, the baby held close to her in the sling. Kristin rocks, sways back and forth on the stool, moving slowly, almost imperceptibly, not quite in time to the music.

Look at Kristin with the baby. Iris remembers what that's like, the turned-in-on-yourself feeling of closeness and oneness, of two-ness, of nothing-else-matters. She remembers the focus, the sense – on a good day – of strength (my strong body made this out of food and air and love; I can feed this). Not sleeping; doesn't matter. Have to sleep. Can't sleep. Must sleep. Look at Kristin: how well she looks. She is rested, resilient, remarkable. She is made of Pilates and raw food. She has the vigour of youth, and love.

Paul is next to Kristin, and he leans in to her as he talks, his hand on the baby's head. His big hand protects her, as he once protected

Kurt. Kurt was never tiny in the way that this baby is tiny, though. Kurt was a big bonny baby, the most beautiful, beautiful, all head and limbs; and eyes, her eyes, his eyes looking at her eyes, all recognising.

Kristin has the baby in her shirt, now, the baby's head bobbing at her. Paul's hand is still on the baby's head, so that it seems that Paul is pushing the baby at Kristin. Iris looks away. Her eyes wander to the doorway on the other side of the room, the door that leads through to the hallway and the kitchen. There she is, finally: Marti, framed in the doorway. She watches Marti lift the wineglass to her lips. She imagines the taste of it, the wine, the sweet burn, the escape of it, the sweet of it, the cool of it, of one, then just one more.

MARTI, MARTI, LIFE OF THE PARTY

Iris moves towards the kitchen, but she's lost sight of Marti – big, smoky Marti, the opposite of Iris, loud with that smoker's croak of hers. She'll be out in the rain, on the doorstep, having a smoke, probably on her own; no one Iris knows smokes any more. Just Marti. She doesn't care. She laps it up. When she's in the city, Marti goes to the same café every day, where they all know to bring her long blacks and clean ashtrays in the covered outside courtyard where the chemicals used to be delivered in its former life as a drycleaners.

There she is on the back step, just outside the door, so the smoke drifts inside in little wafts. Iris can smell it across the kitchen, the smell of Marti. She's turned away, talking to someone, but Iris can't see the someone – just Marti, her head thrown back, her big mouth wide in a laugh, wineglass in one hand, ciggie in the other.

Marti has pizazz, big hair; she swaggers when she walks, like a pirate. Iris has never, never, ever seen Marti look or seem uncomfortable in a place or situation. Marti is supremely confident. Marti wears red lipstick, and big colourful wide pants – palazzo pants, perfect for swaggering – and she smokes and drinks too much, and her husky voice oozes *come and fuck me*, but she's a one-man woman, a one-man-at-a-time woman. She's dedicated now to Marco (NewMark), as she once was to Luce's father, OldMark. And to Matt, in between them; DoorMatt, she calls him, because she ended up showing him the door. He couldn't cope with her bigness, her largeness of heart and soul.

'Well, I'm not going to change now. There's the door, Matt.'

Nothing's quiet, with Marti, Marti, life of the party. She swoops, and whoops, a fire-breathing, smoke-belching dragon of a woman. No holds barred, take no prisoners. When you're in her sights, you're a goner: she will smother you with love; she will tell you what she thinks; she will tell you if and when you're being a complete dick. Never fear. You'll know where you stand with Marti.

Marti makes films, and she's loud, like a teacher (like all teachers Iris has known). Marti claps her hands to get attention – even in a gathering of adults, of peers – like a primary school teacher with a class of six-year-olds. There's nothing funnier than Marti, pissed as a parrot, standing on a sofa, clapping her hands over the roar of music, trying to get a party full of people to pay attention.

'Everyone!'

No one ever believes that Marti and Paul are siblings, let alone twins. Marti's like a supercharged version of her brother, all settings dialled up to eleven. Once in a while, though, Paul will crank it up, *pull a Marti*, and it's like watching someone step into a costume for carnival. *Marti Gras.*

Iris watches Marti shift her weight, step aside, as the person she's talking to steps into the frame of the doorway. It's Kurt. Marti puts her arms around him – her beloved nephew – and he leans into her. Everyone does, with Marti. That's her strength: her gathering in. Her warmth. Her big embrace.

And then there's Marti, there in front of her, almost lifting her up with love.

'Rice! Ooh, there you are.'

Marti kisses her, hard, on the cheek – touching, not an air kiss, so Iris can feel the waxy lipstick print she's left there, like a saucy newspaper ad for a strip club.

'Marti, you made it! I thought we'd never see you.'

'Wild horses, love. Said I'd be here. Just needed to get some work out of the way.' Marti waves her hand, waves work aside. 'Marco sends his love. He's flat out, can't get away. So he says. I think he just wanted to avoid the packing and cleaning.'

'Never mind. We'll get by without him. Have you seen Luce? Does she know you're here? She was in the other room –'

'She's fine. I'll find her later. You still not drinking?'

'Not tonight.'

'Excellent, more for me. So: how's it been, carving up the family home?'

'Yeah, okay so far. Strange to be here though. With everyone. After so long.'

'How *is* my brother? And the stick insect? Have they given their poor child a name yet?'

'Actually, I think they're close to deciding. And don't be mean. Kristin's perfectly lovely.'

'I know. But still a stick insect. Bloody vego. She needs a good –'

'She needs a good steak.'

'That's what I was going to say.'

'No you weren't.'

'No I wasn't.'

'Anyway, Paulie's been giving her plenty of, um, steak.'

'Oh no, Rice, no!'

'The walls are thin. The stick insect is loud.'

'God. Oh well, good on them. I'll put my earplugs in tonight. Which reminds me: I'm sleeping where?'

'In the little room with me. I've made up your bed. Come on,' Iris takes her arm, 'you can dump your things.'

They push through, into the crowd, into the light and hum and noise of the party.

WHAT HAPPENS NEXT IS LIKE A PLAY

Even through her closed door, even with her hoody flicked up over her headphones and the drawstring pulled tight for insulation, Luce can still hear the sound of the party, loud and clear. She'd stayed out there for a while – looking through the records, talking with Kurt about music – but, once the house filled with random people she had no clue about (all telling her how much she's grown, and how much like her mother she looks, and blah blah blah), even the music lost its appeal, and she took off to her room.

Since then, there's been a stream of random strangers opening her door. She's stared each of them down, and they've backed out, holding their hands up in front of them, all *sorry love, sorry, just looking for the loo*. She's shifted a chair in front of the door. Not that it stops anyone opening the door if they really want to, but it must give them pause.

She should go out again, get some food. She runs her finger around the empty bowl on her bed, licks chip salt. From outside her room, there's the sound of glass breaking, and a shout, and laughter. She rolls her eyes, though there's no one there to see.

There's no answer when Iris knocks. She opens the door only a crack before it touches something, is gently blocked. She knocks again.

'Luce?'

She pushes the door, sees the edge of the chair that's blocking it, hears the chair squawk as she pushes it and it moves across the wooden floor.

'Luce? Brought you something to eat.'

She pushes the plate in ahead of her, to give Luce a moment, before she opens the door enough to poke her head around into the room. Luce is on her bed, looks up at her. Iris moves into the room, puts the plate (a piece of pizza, a chicken wing, bread, a tiny pile of rice) on the seat of the chair that was blocking the door. Luce closes her laptop, puts it to the other side of the bed.

'Thanks.'

'S'alright. Anything else you want?'

Luce shakes her head. Iris picks the chair up, moves it closer to the bed. Luce reaches out, picks up the pizza.

'Your mum's here.'

Luce nods. Or maybe she's just chewing.

'There's cake. And pavlova. Come out and get some, eh? When you're ready.'

Iris closes the door behind her. She stands for a moment in the hallway, her back pressed to the door, wishing she could do the same: go to her room with her threads and yarns, to stitch and stitch, and shut them all away.

Luce opens the door, just a crack. The noise of voices and the feel of warmth and the smell of wine hit her, and follow her down the hallway. The bathroom door's open, the bathroom empty; she scoots in, flicks the hook over and into the eye on the doorframe to secure it behind her. As she pees, the door handle turns, the door opens a crack, but the hook holds in the eye, keeps it latched.

'Wait!'

She washes her hands, wipes them down the back of her jeans to dry them. When she unhooks and opens the door, there's no one there.

There are people she doesn't know in the kitchen, standing around, filling the room. She can't see any cake. She moves back through the hallway, squeezes between people leaning, talking in the doorway, to move into the big room. The noise of people loudens to a bell-ring sound that clangs in her ears, harsh like a fork in a metal bowl. She flicks her hoody up. She keeps her head down, squeezing through gaps, behind backs, smelling perfume and wine, sweat, more perfume, the sharper chemical tang of aftershave.

She makes it to the edge of the room where the big table is laid with food, and there is the cake, pavlova, fruit, a bowl of cream, chocolates in boxes. She takes a plate, starts to slide a little bit of everything onto it. And then she hears Marti. (She's been experimenting with calling her mum *Marti*, which is her name. *Marti* sounds strange on her tongue, out loud, but good inside her brain.) As if at a command, the crowd parts, and Luce sees her mum – *Marti* – there, across the room, holding court, queen of the party. As always.

What happens next is like a play, as if the movements have been choreographed and practised. Luce watches, feeling like an audience of one. Marti sweeps her arm out, pointing theatrically and, as she sweeps, she knocks her glass, tips it over in front of her. Someone (Swordbearer One) leans over, scrambles to soak up the wine spilling across and off the low side table. Marti laughs, a deep, groggy laugh. She leans backwards in her chair, enjoying the laugh and, as Luce watches, Marti disappears in slow motion as the chair she is sitting on topples backwards. Iris is there, near her, and she stands up, one hand covering her mouth, the other outstretched towards Marti, who is lying on the floor, still laughing. She holds her empty wineglass in her hand, aloft, like a prize won.

It takes three of them – Iris, Kurt and Paul – to help Marti up, as Marti brushes them off, 'I'm fine, fine,' laughing. They stumble her to the bedroom, tumble her onto the bed, pull her shoes off, tuck her under the covers, leave the room dark. Iris brings her a glass of water, puts it on the table by the side of the bed. She places an empty bowl on the floor, tucks a towel over the bedclothes and up under Marti's chin.

'Fine. Fine.'

Iris sits on the edge of the bed, brushes the hair off Marti's forehead. She sits there for the few minutes it takes for Marti to stop muttering and mumbling and slip instead into sleep, signalled by sonorous rumbling deep from her wine-soaked throat.

– – –

The noise of the party fades and builds. Doors open and close, lights are turned on and off, people come and go. No one talks to Luce, but everyone smiles at her. Iris touches her shoulder as she passes. The music cranks up in volume, and people start to dance.

BRIGHT WHITE, SHARP WITH PAIN

Here is Iris, where she finds herself: here, on the bathroom floor.

She remembers going to the bathroom to pee, but getting no further than the doorway before she's hit by the surprise of it, her mouth like an O with it, her eyes wide and breath caught with the sudden rush of it.

First there is pain: sharp and white, like paper; bright white, like light.

Then there is dropping to her knees, getting low to the floor so she can't fall; *so low, you can't get under it*. Then there is falling anyway, and darkness.

Here she wakes. Here she curls into herself, foetal, here on the cool of the bathroom floor. And here is the pain still, in her belly, low, on one side. Pain radiating from a solid point, like a star, like a spike, like a tiny stone. She hears her voice, quiet, a low breath, an *aaaah*, an *ooooh*. Then there is falling again – falling on the inside, for she is already so low, she can't get under it – and again, darkness.

C-CURVE

She wakes again, on the bathroom floor, and the pain is gone, as suddenly as it came, as completely. Here she is, curled at the base of the toilet, a C-curve surrounding the turquoise pedestal. Up close, like this, the crazing in the old porcelain maps like veins, like rivers. There is the sound of the party outside the bathroom door. There is a tender ache in her belly where the pain has left her. There is the slick of sweat on her face, evaporating to leave her cold. She can feel her face pale, pearl-white (is that where the word 'clammy' comes from, she wonders, from oyster, from clam?); she imagines blood all sunk to her core, to her organs; the thick iron spine of it keeping her alive.

She pushes with her hands against the floor, raises herself – slowly – to sit, leaning against the wall, her eyes closed, equilibrating. When she feels herself stable, she half rolls, pushes up onto hands and knees, then – hands on the toilet seat, pushing up, catching the ammonia whiff of pee – she stands, shifting her hands to the basin, resting there. Breathing out through pursed lips – not because of pain, but for fear of it – she looks up to the mirrored wall cabinet over the basin. There is her face, as pale as she imagines it to be. There is the patch at bottom right of the mirror where the silvering has worn, where light falls like dull blank mildew. There are her careful eyes, the skin around them bruised bright from pain. There is her mouth, the lips parted to breathe each breath with a sounded exhalation – breathe in, breathe out; if you can hear it, it is happening.

After she pees, she stands up carefully, testing her balance. She runs the tap, washes her hands, splashes her face with water. The pain is still gone. She watches herself in the mirror, her colour slowly returning.

The doorknob rattles, a voice outside says 'Sorry' as Iris says 'Just a minute.'

She breathes in, breathes out. She tucks her hair behind her ear. She pats her cheeks with her hands three times. She puts a smile on her face in the mirror.

Iris comes out of the bathroom as someone she doesn't know goes in. She opens the door to the room she shares with Marti. In the soft, dim light through the doorway, Marti makes a broad peak in the bed. Iris picks up her bag from next to the bed, checks that her phone, her keys, her wallet are in it. She sits on the bed and pulls on socks, trainers. She shoulders her bag, and shuts the door behind her as she leaves. Through the closed door, Iris can hear Marti snoring and muttering in her sleep.

Iris stands at the door into the big room, the music room. It's only just after midnight; the party is still going strong.

As she walks past the door of the room where the baby sleeps, she hears an adult voice, low, quiet. She opens the door, just a crack, and looks in. Kristin is sitting on the floor, her legs tucked under her but out to the side, like the Little Mermaid in Copenhagen harbour. She leans her head against the side of the cot, where the baby should be sleeping. The baby's feet, in the corners of a merino sleep suit like a pillowcase, spring up and down, lifting up from the pale plain of the cot's mattress, and she burbles at Kristin, who's talking back to her, low-voiced, calm, tired.

'You okay?' Iris whispers into the room.

Kristin turns to her, and Iris sees her smile in the grey shadow light. 'I'm hiding out here so I don't have to talk to pissed people. But even she wants to party. I think she takes after her Auntie Marti.'

'You need anything?'

Kristin shakes her head, 'I'm fine. We're fine. It's nice and quiet in here. Our own little party.'

'Okay.'

Iris closes the door to the bedroom. From the row of hooks near the front door she takes her coat, throws it over her arm. It's only a ten-minute drive to the hospital; she's not worried about driving herself. But she should tell someone. Not Kristin – she will offer to drive her, and bring the baby, and Iris can't bear to drag them out into the rain. Everyone else is pissed – there's no point telling them. But: Luce.

There's a line of light showing under the door to Luce's room. Iris knocks, then puts her ear to the door. She knocks again, louder; she lifts her head away as Luce opens the door, stares out at her, eyebrows raised.

'Lu, I need to tell someone so I'm telling you. I'm fine, but I'm going to the hospital.'

'But. What –'

'I'm fine now, but I had some dodgy tummy bug or something. I'm going to drive myself down to the hospital and just get checked out. I wanted to tell someone, but I don't want to break up the party. Okay love? Just in case it takes ages for me to see a doctor, in case I'm not back in the morning, so someone knows where I am. Right?'

'I guess.'

'But don't tell them tonight, okay? I don't want anyone to worry. We'll just keep it between you and me.' Iris reaches into her bag, pulls out her phone. 'I'll text you when I get there, then I'll turn my phone off.'

Luce's eyes crinkle into worry, her mouth purses. Iris feels a rush of love for her, this girl she loves like a daughter.

'I'm fine, Lulu.' She lifts her hand to Luce's fingers, where Luce holds the door just open, just closed, just on the brink. Iris runs her finger down the bumps of Luce's knuckles, up again, and down. Luce's index finger shoots out straight and loops itself around Iris's finger and they stay like that, linked, holding on. 'Sweetie, I'm fine. You hold the fort, eh.'

Their fingers unlink. Iris waggles her phone at Luce. 'I'll text you, okay?'

''Kay.'

Iris waves her fingers at Luce, then puts her phone and her bag down on the table by the front door as she wriggles into her coat, buttons it, prepares for the dash to the car. She opens the front door, stands looking out at the rain. She turns back to look over her shoulder. Luce is still at the door to her room, leaning into the gap, watching Iris. Iris waves, turns, and steps out into the rain.

Luce watches Iris go. She stands at the door to her room and listens to the party, the mill of people, the rustle of them, the shuffle of them, the hearty laughter and boozy noise. She hears a click, and watches the door to the room that her mother shares with Iris open. Her mother steps out, heads down the corridor – to the bathroom, or to the wine in the kitchen? Whatever. It was disgusting before. When she fell over. *That should be me* is how Luce thinks when her mother behaves like that. *I* should be the one getting pissed. It's not fair.

She hears a phone ring, vibrate. It's close, it's on the table by the front door. Iris's phone. Luce picks it up, swipes.

'Hello?'

'Iris Golden? It's Nancy Smits calling, from Dorothy Hill Retirement Village. Everything's fine, and I'm sorry to call so late, but we've just had a little incident with your mother, and I wanted to let you know.'

'It's not Iris. I'm not Iris.'

'I'm sorry, could you put me on to her?'

'She's not here. She just –' Luce doesn't know whether *not telling* extends beyond the party, so she plays it safe. 'She's just gone out, and she forgot her phone.'

'And I'm speaking with ...?'

'Luce. Lucy Flint. I'm Luce. Her – niece.'

'Of course, Lucy, I remember you. Will Iris be back soon, do you think?'

Luce thinks of waiting in hospitals, of that long boringness. 'I don't think so. I could give her a message?'

'Look, that'd be wonderful dear. Could you just tell Iris that her mother had a fall, but she's absolutely fine, and there's nothing to worry about. We're keeping an eye on her. And could you ask Iris to give me a call? Not tonight – in the morning is fine. Nancy Smits, Ess-Em-Eye-Tee-Ess. She can call me back on this number any time after nine. Okay? And don't you worry, we're looking after Rosa. She's very comfortable. Goodnight, dear.'

She hangs up before Luce can answer.

Luce stands for a while with Iris's phone in her hand. Then she shrugs, puts the phone down on the table where Iris had left it. As Luce starts to walk back to her room, from the kitchen she hears the sound of glass breaking, then a shriek, then her mother – laughing that laugh of hers, unmistakably pissed – then other people join her, all laughing like crazy. Luce stands and listens. Music starts up again, more old-fart music. She goes back to the table, picks up the phone – because someone might see it there and wonder where Iris is, and that'd be almost like *telling*, to leave the phone there as a clue – and tucks it in her pocket, then turns back to her room, to shut out the noise.

STONES, NOT PASSED

Iris feels a kind of tired calmness as she drives. She is washed out, exhausted, but in that state of tiredness that is characterised by a sort of clarity of mind. She can think of one thing, and it is clear to her: drive to the hospital. Her mind doesn't wander to other things, to distractions. It's almost like a state of meditation, of mental stillness.

She's not sure whether it's even worth going to the hospital, but it's better, she tells herself as she drives, to be on the safe side. She can feel the site of the pain, can remember the feeling of it with a bright white intensity. What she feels is no longer pain, but tenderness.

She drives at the speed limit, which always feels too slow, down the strip-mall highway, past lights flickering fast food, carpets, supermarkets, even though they're all closed. She turns off into the carpark of the big new hospital by the ocean. She follows arrows and signs, parks the car. She reaches into her bag, on the passenger seat, for her phone. It's not in the inside pocket; she ferrets through – nothing – then empties everything onto the passenger seat, *fuck, fuck*, but no phone. She must've left it at the house. She sees herself put it down on the table, when she told Luce where she was going; she sees herself gather her bag, fail to pick up the phone. *Shit.* She shakes her head, piles everything back into her bag, climbs out, locks the car.

She follows the signs to EMERGENCY, even though it no longer feels like one. The door whooshes open. She walks into the fluoro-lit space. There's that hospital smell she's never experienced enough to get used to – just enough that it unsettles her. She goes to the desk, hands over her Medicare card.

'Hello love, how can we help?'

'I'm not sure it's an emergency, but –'

She describes the pain she'd felt, the quickness and suddenness of its coming and going. She tells how it was this suddenness that had scared her most.

'I think I passed out. I don't remember. I just found myself on the floor. In the bathroom. But I don't remember how I got there.'

'Did you fall? Hurt yourself? Any bumps.'

'No. I don't think so.'

'You had any drugs or alcohol, love?'

'No. No, nothing, I don't any more. Drink.'

'Are you in any pain now?'

'No. None at all.'

She puts her hand on her belly, low, where she can remember the pain being, radiating from.

'It was here.' She finds herself popping up on her toes, to show the nurse where her hand is. The woman nods, types something. 'But it's fine now.'

'Okay, I've logged that. Can I just check your contact details?'

Iris gives her address in the city, explains that she's here for the weekend, gives the Cassetown address. They have a record in the hospital system from years before — *We transferred over the records from the old hospital* — from long-ago summer visits, from when she and Paul were together. She updates phone numbers, her email address.

'Primary contact and next of kin's listed as Paul Diamond.' The woman rattles off Paul's phone number.

'Yeah —'

She could change it, but to what?

'That's fine. Paul's fine.'

'Right, all up to date. We'll check you out and see what we can see, okay? Take a seat, wait for your name. If you're feeling any pain, let us know right away. Don't want you passing out on the ED floor. And you're in luck. It's a quiet night for a weekend so far, touch wood.'

Iris sits down on the plastic chair, careful not to touch anything. She thinks of disease, of some long-ago-read article about hospital-acquired infections. Nose-cone; nose-something. Nosocomial, that's it. Nosocomial infections. The article had made some outrageous claim, like you're better off having surgery in the hospital carpark than in the operating theatre. She tucks her hands into the pockets of her jacket, like a police detective at the scene of a crime. *Leave no trace.*

There are no men in the waiting area, only women and children. A child in pyjamas sits opposite her, cradling its arm, curled up on the lap of a woman. Iris can't tell whether the child – a preschooler, maybe three or four years old – is a boy or a girl. At the other end of the row of plastic chairs sits an older woman, her head dropped low so Iris can see her thinning hair, white at the crown, and dark blonde dye out from there. A younger woman sits next to her, has the older woman's hand in her hand, is patting it, occasionally rubbing it. Iris catches the eye of the hand-patting young woman. They smile at each other. Iris looks down, and sees that her hands are in her lap now; she's rubbing and patting her own hand. She leans one elbow on her knee, cups her chin in her hand, tucks the other hand in, to stop the mirroring.

Although there aren't many people in the waiting room, there is noise leaking from the other side of the swinging plastic doors, from the treatment rooms that she can't see. It's a low hum with occasional clangs, an undercurrent buzz of voices, the murmuring sound of nurturing, with occasional laughter bubbling through. Iris imagines a night that's not quiet; she imagines shouting, the room full of drunks, and schoolkids, and drunk schoolkids; a night full of drinking injuries.

She stands up when she hears her name, and follows a man with a clipboard, pushing through double doors, around corners, past curtains, to a bed that's like a trolley (a *gurney*, she thinks). The bed-trolley is behind another curtain, patterned with flowers like the others. He gestures. She sits on the bed.

'Won't be long.' He hooks a clipboard onto the end of the bed, pulls the curtain half-closed around her, then disappears back towards the waiting room.

She clutches her bag on her lap; she unshoulders it, then shoulders it again, then puts it on the table next to her. She fiddles. She can hear a clock, ticking like a cartoon clock, louder than it needs to be, underscoring the time that she's waiting. She wishes she had thought to grab the bag with the baby's blanket in it; she could have spent time stitching, while she waited. What would she stitch? A clock. A telephone. Little stars, for the bright white pain.

Noises come from behind other curtains. The voices are low, keep to themselves – except there's no keeping to yourself in here; there's nothing substantial to afford privacy, just curtains and lines on the floor to mark out space. One voice is old and angry, hissing, venomous. Another is sleepy, or uncaring, or pissed or stoned, not really connecting, not really listening.

From behind the curtain closest to her she hears a man's voice, low and muffled; she can't hear the words, can just hear the care in his tone, like he's talking to a sick child, or a dog. Then a woman's voice harsh and hurting, 'Jesus, Andrew! I told you. I don't want a fucking engagement ring. I want a fucking sofa.'

A man pushes aside the curtain next to her. Ducking his head under the blue flowered fabric, his eyes meet Iris's. Iris turns away, puts her hand to her bag, pretends to look for her glasses or her phone; anything. She waits a beat, then looks up to watch the man's hunched back – the big, hurt curve of him, all red and blue flannel checks – move away, out towards the waiting room.

People come and go. They close and fling open the curtains around her; they peer in, check the clipboard, smile at her; they tap the clipboard with a pen, they write on it. One of them looks at the clipboard, then at the screen of an iPad, swipes and taps the screen, frowns. Iris can't be sure if he's looking up her records, or checking Twitter.

Different people come, and she has no idea whether they're nurses or doctors or orderlies, nor does it seem to matter. If they introduce themselves, it's by first name. They all seem to have badges with their first names pinned to their chests. Their names are written with thick markers in purple or green ink – 'fun' colours, no prosaic black – all next to the smiling cartoon sun that is the hospital logo.

Another woman comes to her, checks the clipboard, swipes an iPad.

'Iris.' There's a glimmer of a smile, a tired smile, all she can muster to comply with customer service requirements. 'I'm Julie.' She nods to her name badge, the name spelled out in thick red lettering (blood-red, not a good colour choice for a hospital).

'Acute abdominal pain, lower right, yeah? Came and went suddenly? Came in waves?'

'That's right. I passed out, I think. Not for long.'

'Ever had this before?'

'No. Oh –'

Iris has a recollection: a night, cold white pain, waking up on a toilet floor, sticky with god-knows-what. She'd put it down to drink, as she always did, then.

'Maybe, but not like this. This was – extreme pain. Waves of it. Then – really suddenly – gone. I feel fine now. It's probably nothing.'

'Not necessarily. Could be gall bladder. Possibly gallstones, little solid bits in your gall bladder or bile duct. An ultrasound should confirm that. We'll pop you down to Radiology.'

They start to wheel her as the woman keeps talking, of stones, of calcification, of calculus and concretion, a wash of words that Iris has never before connected to her body, to pain.

She's wheeled (on the *gurney*) into a dark room, next to a blank screen and a bank of plastic-coloured machines, with spiral cords like phones used to have. There's a blue-green smock to put on, and she doesn't know whether to put the opening at the front or the back. She goes with front.

She lies on the bed, and gel – 'It'll be a bit cold, just for a moment' – is squirted on to her belly, but low, and off-centre to the right. The bulbous end – like a showerhead, or a dildo – smears the gel on her, makes her feel queasy. It slips over her skin, sliding, spreading the slippery gel on her. She feels it touch the top of her knickers, imagines it wicking into the fabric, slick, undrying. Sick rises in her throat, then goes away. Hospitals unsettle her. She concentrates on the beat of her pulse, imagining she can hear it in her chest, her throat, one-cat-and-dog, two-cat-and-dog, counting the seconds until the bulbous slithering stops.

'Ah!'

The operator lets a sound out, but she's not giving anything away. Iris looks at the screen, its lines of longitude and latitude mapping her body, the heights and curves and shapes of her, pulsing, bulging, unfathomable. The operator taps a button to zoom in, moves the centre of the field of view, the dark and light shapes change on screen. Iris keeps expecting a baby-shape to emerge, a jellybean foetus, as it did twenty-one years ago when she was pregnant with Kurt. The image then was as unreadable to her as this is, now. Then, they'd printed a single image on shiny paper. The paper had started to darken, the image fade, almost as soon as they'd handed it to Paul. It's — where? — in some long-ago photo album, from when people had photo albums. Kristin and Paul would have got a CD, or been emailed the images. Or maybe the ultrasound operator posted them straight to their Facebook pages.

Iris isn't offered a printout, nor a post to Facebook. The operator wipes some of the gel from her, then hands her a clutch of paper towels.

'There you go. Clean yourself up,' she inclines her head to a rubbish bin in the corner, 'and you can get dressed. Wait in Reception. The Registrar will come and talk to you once she's had a look at the imaging.'

Iris sits up on the gurney, wipes the mess from her belly. A wave of shame washes over her. It feels sordid, as if she has soiled herself, or had sex with someone she shouldn't have. She touches her hand to her belly, feels the tight drying stickiness forming a scum, a skin. Then she does as she's told: in the little curtained cubicle in the corner of the dim-lit radiology suite she dresses, places the hospital gown in the plastic bin labelled USED GOWNS, then she heads back to the waiting room.

The clock above the reception desk shows 2:46. The party will still be going.

THE WEIGHT OF IT

Kurt goes outside, kicking the kitchen door closed behind him on the tail-end hum of the party, the stayers. He stands on the lawn, in the rain. He must concentrate to stand; in fact, he sways on the lawn, looking back at the bright house. A shriek – that'll be Auntie Mart – leaks into the night, out through windows and doors closed against the cold. He doesn't feel cold, though. He has a beer jacket on. He managed to remember to grab his actual jacket, too, and he's flicked his hood up. The rain has eased, but everything's soaking.

He shoves his hands into his pockets and stands (sways) on the lawn, listening to the waves, though he can't see them. The sound of them from this distance is all shush and tumble, light and strong at the same time. It's like cars on a distant freeway. Or like that sound when you hold a shell to your ear, that they tell children is the sound of the ocean, but is the pressure in your own ears, little waves of blood whooshing and rushing through your body.

He opens the gate and walks on the path by the river to the bay. There isn't much moon, so it's dark. He has to watch his feet (because beer; because joint, then whisky, then more beer; because dark), to stay on the path. He wants to put his hands up in front of him, to feel his way to the beach, but there's nothing to feel, nothing to guide him there but the sound of the waves, getting louder as he gets closer.

When he gets to the top of the beach, he realises just how hard the waves are hammering in tonight, booming in – not like the calm of yesterday, when he watched the kids with sticks. Tonight you can't hear yourself think, thoughts drowned by sound so loud it thumps through the ground and up through your body. You can feel it in your chest as well as hear it, like music coming at you when you're standing in front of a massive fuck-off speaker. You feel it when a wave dumps, feel that pause before the crash, the thump, the reverberation. The weight of it frightens him.

When he was little, for a few years he went surfing with his dad, both of them learning, neither of them very good at it. He doesn't remember being scared of the waves, back then, when he was eleven or twelve. Something changed, though, and he stopped wanting to go surfing, or even to go to the beach at all, for years. It's only this last year, since he's left home, that he's started going to the beach again, but only to walk, and only when it's cold, windy. He'll wrap himself into his jacket, button the buttons, turn the collar up, or the hood if it's really bitterly cold and blustery. He'll put his hands in his pockets and his head down, and walk.

Sometimes he'll stop to pick something up, but mostly he ploughs on; the walking, the ploughing on, is the meaning of it, for him. His mother's the one who picks things up – always has been. She's always been the collector. When he was a kid he used to bring her things – seaweed or stones, feathers or ferns – and she'd turn them over in her hand, or turn them out on plastic or paper, examine them, name them for him, explain them; sometimes explain them away. He doesn't bring her things any more. She still collects, though. Always the archivist. She doesn't plough on, when she walks. She stops and starts, stops and starts. It takes her forever to get anywhere.

He walks down the slope of the beach towards the dark solidity of the platform rock, and settles on it – his rock, his place, the feel of it so familiar – lies down, looks up at the sky, his gut acid, his head bedspin-tight. Bedspin; rockspin. He closes his eyes, but the bedspin, rockspin is worse. He rolls on his side – recovery position – but the spew doesn't come. He clutches his jacket in around him, grabs a steadying hold of the edge of the rock, pulls his knees up, foetal, closes his eyes and sinks into blackness to the sound of the waves' rush and roar.

Some time passes. In the star-lack night, dark under a sliver of moon, Kurt wakes – does he? – all sick-mouthed, and sees – is it? – two people at the rocky far end of the bay. The two of them are walking close, as if in an awkward embrace, or holding each other upright. His eyes zoom in on them, broach – as if by magic – the distance between him (Kurt) and them (The Couple). She (The Girl) is slim, pale-faced, dark-haired, beautiful (how can he know that in the dark, from a distance?). He (The Man) is broader, taller; he is older (how can he tell?); he is brutish, hard-faced. They walk close to the water's edge. They turn to face each other, their heads incline – his head bows down to hers – and they come together to kiss.

Kurt remembers to breathe.

Then another wave of dark comes.

Kurt wakes suddenly, sits up, stands up on the platform rock. The rain is heavier again, now; he must take care not to slip, so he moves slowly. He sees The Couple, further from him now, out on the point at the tip of the bay. Kurt lifts one hand to shade his eyes – that's what you do when you look to a distant point – but The Girl and The Man merge together, no gap, no light, no space between them. They stay together for a minute, an hour, an age. Time stands still. Time is only now. Like music. Or comics: the now of the panel you're reading, preceded by the past now of the panel before; followed by the future now, the next now. The now and the now and the now, all present at once, past and future bracketing the present, but all visible at once, all their own now. Here's here in the now, the now of the shape of The Couple, there in the frame that his eyes can see.

Kurt remembers to breathe. The now and the now of it: breathe in now, breathe out now. The Couple dissolves and The Man turns and walks away up the rocks. The Girl is not there – not on the beach, not walking with him. Gone. Just like that.

Another wave of dark comes, wet with rain.

Kurt stumbles towards the point, boots crashing harsh over stones and sand, jacket flailing behind him like a great bird's wings flapping across the beach.

He falls into the water. He's on all fours. A wave breaks, and its foam surges up the beach, shushes up under him. He stands up. He wipes his eyes. He can't see – what is it he needs to see? – and his eyes sting from the salt, and the night. He crashes again to his hands and knees, crawls up the shaley shore, stands again and turns to the sea, watches.

There: something. Is it? A dark star in the water. A pale shape, a slender shape, a dark shape. Moving or not moving? He moves closer. A wave comes, breaks, flows. The dark shape changes, slips sideways, as if turning in the surf.

He falls to his knees in the surging sea, and the dark comes again.

EVERYTHING GOES DARK

Luce wakes, fuzzy, from deep sleep to a buzzing, a beeping, a tiny light shining from the floor by her bed. *Hello*, she says, trying out her voice, clearing her throat, *hello, hello*, before she swipes to answer Iris's phone.

'Hello?'

'Is that Iris Golden?'

It's the person who phoned before. Luce can tell it's the same voice, but she sounds different – formal, or something. Serious.

'No, it's me, Luce. Lucy.'

'Could I speak to Iris, dear? It's important.'

'Just a minute. I'll look.'

She looks at the phone for the time – 3:13. She opens the door to her room without turning the light on. The only light is from the rectangle of the screen of Iris's phone, in her hand. The party is over. The lights are all off. She goes to Iris's room, softly opens the door. There is her mum, big and fat and snoring. Iris's bed is empty. She closes the door, sinks down onto the floor, her back against the wall of the hallway, holds the phone to the side of her head, whispers back.

'She's not here. Iris isn't here.'

The woman on the phone draws in her breath – Luce hears it *swhoooooph* suck in air. This is the sound of deciding what to do. Then there's a sigh. This is the sound of telling the decision.

'Lucy, it's very important that I speak to Iris as soon as possible. Is she – when do you expect her to be back?'

Now is the time for Luce's telling. She lets the words out in a rush.

'She forgot her phone. She went to the hospital. About midnight. She's not back.'

'To the hospital? Here? To see Rosa?' The woman sounds confused, or surprised.

'No — here, Cassetown. She was sick. Iris was. Then she was better, she said. She took herself to the hospital, to get — um — like checked up. In her car, she drove. She told me not to tell, not to spoil the party. But she forgot her phone. I don't know — everyone's asleep. Iris isn't back yet.' Luce can feel herself getting panicky, the words mixing up in her head, coming out in the wrong order. Iris shouldn't have done this to her. It's not fair.

'Look, don't you worry, Lucy. I'm sure Iris is fine. You go back to sleep, dear. But as soon as Iris gets back, you must get her to call me. It's important. Alright?' The woman on the phone has a calming voice, one you sort of just want to obey, whatever she says, like a kind teacher, or the school counsellor.

'Yeah.'

'You pop off back to sleep, okay?'

'Yeah, okay.'

'Goodnight, dear.'

'Night.'

The woman ends the call before Luce does. Luce hears the beeping sound of the disconnection echoing inside the phone. She taps it to end. She sits there — on the floor, in the hall, outside the room where her mother sleeps and snores — until the screen on Iris's phone goes to sleep, and everything goes dark. In the darkness, Luce realises: the woman didn't mention Rosa. She didn't say that Rosa was alright, like she did before.

And Luce knows it from the not saying, and from the sound of her voice: Rosa is dead.

ROSA

One hundred fingerprints I hear
A hundred linger in my ear
Counting backwards I count you in

Kristin Hersh
'Counting Backwards'

100. NOW

No earth move, no jolt, just empty whisper. Quiet in the night, night in the bed, bed lift me up, up and down like a bride's nightie. Woman there, tap tap tapping on the thing, phone, she's tap tap tapping. One two three tap, two two three tap, nine ten eleven tap, counting me in, counting me down, five four three two one ... breathe in, breathe out, count backwards til I I I ... O o oh. Rosa.

99. TWO HOURS AGO

There she is, Smits, in-charge woman, phone in hand. Loose, she says. Loose-y.

Rosa, we've left a message for your daughter, she says. Loose-y goose-y, lefty loose-y.

She says I was on the floor. They picked me up, she says.

I am in my bed now. No, another bed. No, it's my bed, but there is a machine next to it; no, a thing. For diving under water. A tank. A mask.

I breathe in, breathe out, as she tells me to, and sense starts to remake itself: had a fall; took a turn; oxygen is helping; Lucy.

They are going south to Cassetown today. They've just popped in, can't stay too long, got to beat the traffic, Mum, long weekends are hopeless.

Iris has brought the boy with her. Little Kurt (who is not little any more, but I still and always think of him as Little Kurt). He is visiting, staying with her, home for the holidays. He is dressed all in black. His hair is black, too. He looks like a big black crow, or a swan. Iris has brought the girl Lucy, too, the cousin. She is prickly that one, like a rose bush. Like thorns on a lemon tree.

But there is something prickly about the boy today, too, about Not So Little Kurt. He has a big black dog on his back. I used to say that to Iris, you've got a big black dog on your back, when she was in a mood like this. I would say it to the boy today, if I could speak. Instead, my hand just claws towards him. He jerks his hand back out of reach, instinctively. Then Iris moves her hand onto the arm of the chair where I'm sitting. She puts her hand there, near my hand, and so I claw at her. Big black dog, big black swan. There's a big black mood in the room today.

The prickly girl, Lucy, is chewing her thumb. That's a nasty habit. And Iris is folding my clothes. That's habit too; that's typical of Iris, making work where none exists; the clothes were already folded, or they wouldn't have been in the drawers. That's what the nurses do, or the orderlies, or whatever they call them. That's their job.

Everyone here has a job. My job is as it has been for years now: to lie here, or sit here, and be subject to their jobs. Iris's job is to worry, to mother. Poor Iris, no one's ever really looked after her, picked up after her, made her meals, washed her laundry; not since her father. Frank, I mean.

97. TEN DAYS AGO

They have sold the house. Iris has come today to tell me this, and also that her boy will visit her next week, fly home from Wellington. His work (or is it study?) is going well. Something about film. Or perhaps I mean maps. Iris is vague. Or perhaps it's me.

Yes, she tells me, they have sold the Cassetown house, so they must empty it.

In fact, she says, the whole famn-damily's going down to Cassetown. She says, Paul and Kristin are going to bring the baby, and Marti's coming, and Luce, and Paul's organised a bit of a party on the long weekend, to lift the roof off the house, one last bash before we clear out.

Your things are there, she tells me. I'll go through them. She takes my hand, rubs it, rub-a-dub-dub. I'll take good care, she says. Kurt'll help.

Now, she says, a verbal handclap to change subject, birthdays! It's Kurt's twenty-first, your one hundredth. We can't let that go uncelebrated. Kurt doesn't want to do anything, so he says. But I'll talk him round, while we're down in Cassetown, talk him into a family thing, celebrate your birthday and his together. We'll all come in to see you. It'll be good. We'll have a cake. It'll be lovely. All of us together, that's the main thing. She takes my hand again, rubbity-rub, pat pat.

She stands, folds my few clothes in their drawers, straightens the tissue box by the bedside. She tweaks the curtains, stands there for a time looking out at the garden, says something about roses, and birds, and the sky, and the weather.

Honestly, I can't be bothered listening.

She shoulders her bag, kisses my cheek.

I hear her talking with the manager woman in the hallway outside my door.

Box of birds, dear, she's a box of birds.

The manager says that, and she means me. This old bird is a box of birds. The manager says this sort of thing: a box of birds, or one of fluffy ducks. Early birds and rare birds, a little birdie told me. Much of her vocabulary is bird-based. Strange bird, that one. I'm a kiwi, she tells me.

96. TWO YEARS AGO

I don't really know why, Iris says. Why now, I mean.

She is sitting in the chair by the side of my bed. She has fabric in her lap, a silver needle flashes between her fingers. Stitch stitch, snick snick with the scissors, the thrill of red thread, a knot, stitch stitch.

I don't really know. It may not last. I just thought, you know, I've been hitting it a bit hard. It's just easier to give it up completely, for a while, than to cut down.

She is talking about drink. She often sits and talks, these days. She talks to me more now than she ever has before. Now when I cannot answer her (and, of course, perhaps that is why). Lately she has been bringing needle and thread, and she sits and stitches and chatters away. This is a new thing, the stitching. She shows it to me. It's not the little fine stitches of traditional embroidery, but big bold strokes that quickly make a shape, give a sense of colour and movement. Sometimes she stitches words, so the effect of words with simple shapes is of a cartoon, or a comic book. She experiments, she tells me.

The not drinking is a new thing, too. It suits her. Her eyes are brighter; the skin on her face is less marked and mapped by the fine red lines that had begun to define her. Or perhaps I'm imagining it.

It's been a week now (she says), and I'm feeling really good for it. I don't miss it. Not really. I don't have any in the house. No wine in the fridge. That makes it easier. Of course, the real test will be staying sober next time I see Marti. I shouldn't blame her, though. I'm an adult. I make my own decisions.

Oh, I remember wine in the fridge. I remember sobriety, and its opposite. I remember choice, and agency, and making my own decisions.

Those were the days.

I hear the tea trolley rattle in the distance. Or maybe it's the medication trolley. They sound the same.

95. THREE YEARS AGO

There's a radio in my room, but they keep it tuned to easy-listening music, soulless stuff. I never hear the news any more, unless I catch it sideways.

Today, when they clean my room, they hobble me into a wheelchair, and wheel me to the day room. They park me there, line me up with the rest of them, facing early morning breakfast television. Our mouths gape, slack with age; we're as helpless as baby birds. One of the staff points a black box, click, click, and the channel changes, flicking from a cartoon sponge to a cricket match, from a close-up shot of vegetables whirring in a blender to a news desk, a human face with a rictus slash of red lipstick, hair that doesn't move.

They call news like this *breaking*.

There is a city, rocked by earthquake. The spire of a cathedral tumbles. A catastrophe of letters flashes on the screen: CTV, PGC, EQNZ, USAR. I sway in my wheelchair, as if registering the aftershock.

94. FOUR YEARS AGO

The boy, Little Kurt, when he visits is sweet, kind. He visits quite often, now that he has left school. He's a good boy, underneath the black clothes, the hair, the look. He sits patiently, quietly. One day last week, when he visited on his own, he sat and rubbed my feet. He *rubbed my feet*! Imagine. The feel of it. His touch. He drank tea with me, from the small thick cups they always use here, cream with a red stripe around the rim, thick and heavy but too small for a proper cuppa.

The boy Kurt, my should-be-grown-up grandson, might have flown off by now to have his own life, I would have thought, might have left the limbo of adolescence. But he seems to cling to it, or it to him. Iris sits and talks about him. He's only seventeen; it's too young to know what you want to do, she says. I could tell her what I was up to at seventeen, curl her hair, turn her head. But he's a good boy, at least, a kind boy (see: foot-rubbing, as mentioned. It's a rare grandson that would do that for his poor dumb, bedridden crone of a gran).

93. FOUR YEARS AGO

Iris folds and refolds the clothes in my drawers, chattering all the while about god knows what. She closes the top drawer then turns around and leans against the dresser. Look at it, the sharp false wood of its cheap edge, look how it's cutting into her through her jeans.

The Norwegian one, Kristin, has lost another baby (I could do a Lady Bracknell, say something about misfortune, carelessness). A late miscarriage, Iris says. Sometimes when she tells me these things I think she is telling them to herself.

It is hard to read her feelings now for Paul, but I think, I truly think, that he is family to her. He is and always will be the father of her boy. I do not think she aches for him. And I think she truly cares for the Norwegian. Poor Kristin, she says. Poor thing.

92. FIVE YEARS AGO

I sit in my chair, watching the door. (What else is there to do?) I can see reflections on its wood; light, coming softly through the curtained window, through cotton voile modesty drapes. I shift my hands in my lap. There is delicate pearl varnish on the nails, from Kurt's visit last week. He painted my nails with such tenderness. His own nails had chipped black varnish on them. He painted over it with my pearl ivory varnish, after he'd finished painting my nails.

Kurt was wearing black when he visited. Not just on his fingernails: on everything. He wore black pants, and a black t-shirt, and a shirt with buttons over the top of that, and that was black, too. His shoes were black. Leather, with laces; heavy on his feet, the soles worn down at the toe.

I close my eyes, lean my head back against the chair. It is comfortable enough. My hands rest on the arms of the chair. I lift my fingers, play an arpeggio on the arms of the chair, both hands at once, from little finger to thumb, and back again from thumb to little finger. Pinky finger. This little piggy went to market. This little pinky. The nailpolish that Kurt painted over his chipped black nails; I can see it. Pearl islands in a pearlised black sea. His fingernails remind me of the photographs I used to colour, when I worked at the studio with Frank, painting flesh tones onto faces and hands, onto necks held high and proud, onto young décolletage and old crêpey bosoms. Pink flesh tones and rosy cheeks. Rosa cheeks. Cheeky.

91. SIX YEARS AGO

Postcard from Dunsborough

Dear Mum,

File this under 'sentences I never thought I'd write': my ex-husband's wedding was lovely, and his bride was beautiful!!!

The ceremony, dinner, everything, was on a terrace overlooking the beach here (the beach on this postcard). Very low-key, untraditional, but all very charming, elegant. I ended up giving the bridegroom away – sort of a symbolic handing over to Kristin. Kurt was Paulie's best man – oh, Mum, it would've brightened your heart to see him, so beautiful, so serious (there's nothing quite as serious as a 15-yr-old!).

Luce was her usual sullen self – the grumpiest 9-yr-old I know. Marti was a hoot, as always.

One awful, awful thing though, that Marti told me: Kristin was pregnant, but she miscarried the day before the wedding. So sad. Kristin's a sweetheart (also filed under sentences I never thought I'd write).

Back soon, see you then,

Love

Iris

90. EIGHT YEARS AGO

From here, I can see myself reflected in the mirror on the dressing table. Not that I need a dressing table. Or a mirror. My room has all the things a person would need if they hadn't lost their mind. That's what Iris says when she thinks I can't hear: my mother's lost her mind, poor thing.

All I really need in this room is a bed and a chair. The nurses, or whatever they are, bring me food, and feed me, and take the food away, and take me to the toilet, and dress me, and put me in the chair, then take me out of the chair and get me back to bed. And I just sit here, sprawl there, not even bothering to hold myself up in the chair, not even bothering to smile at them for their small gestures of care. Sometimes my mouth moves, as if it's trying to say something. Sometimes my hand scratches on the arm of the chair, or in the air, though I do not bid it do so. Sometimes I claw at Iris, or at Little Kurt. I imagine my touch like paper, or pins.

My eyes wander around the room without fixing on anything, without watching, or even really seeing.

89. TEN YEARS AGO

So, that's it. It's decided. I'll stay here.

They don't know what's wrong with me. I am old, is all. So I'll stay here in this room they've moved me to, in the High Care Facility of Dorothy Hill Retirement Village, sentient but silent. Until I get better, that's what they say, but reading between the lines it'll be forever and ever amen. Though how long can it be? Ninety is a good innings, by anyone's accounting.

Iris talks to the person in charge. There they are, in a huddle by the door. Kurt sits in the chair by the window, hunched over a thing in his hands. The thing: a shape, plastic, noise, his fingers moving and toggling and switching, face getting closer and closer to it, light from it shining up to his face.

Iris says: Kurt, for chrissake, at least turn the sound off!

And his face looks up at her, his eyes frown, then the sounds go away, and he hunches back. The person in charge puts her hand on Iris's shoulder, and her eyes crinkle in professional sympathy. How many times she must have done this. She leaves Iris in the doorway. Iris leans there, watches me. Her eyes flick to her beautiful boy.

I can see all of this from my place in the bed. I want to tell her it's alright. I understand. I'll stay here. Don't worry, my girl. I need looking after now, finally, after so many years of only looking after myself. But not by you. You have your own looking after to do.

I cannot speak, but my gap-ridden brain, the strange mass of cells and synapses in my head, still makes connections, sees the light (or the absence of light) behind the eyes of my dear ones, my girl, her dear boy. Imagine it, my brain, my poor brain, the electricity sparking through it. With all its failures and misfirings, it can still read the shape of humanity. It can read the sad unshaping of my daughter's family.

And that makes me think what a marvel it is that all the life in this room came from me: not from my brain, not my thinking brain; a deeper, lower, animal mind that connects me still to Iris and Kurt; my child, and the child of my child.

Iris cries today, just sits by my bed and cries and cries, tears of shame and sadness and self-pity and rage.

I couldn't tell you before, Mum, not while they were doing the tests, but now that you're stable, I thought I'd better. Tell you. Paul's been screwing the fucking crew. A student. A Norwegian student. Kerstin. Or Kristin. Something. Young and blonde and foreign and gorgeous, like a walking fucking cliché. Oh Mum, I feel so stupid. Ugly and old and stupid. The bastard. The fucking bastard. How dare he.

She whispers that, as if anyone here is likely to object to juicy gossip, spicy language.

Her face is blotched red with rage, indignation. Her hands clutch tight around endless tissues, discarded into the rubbish bin by the bed. You'll be fine, I would tell her if I could. I try to tell her with my eyes. I hold her hand with my hand, hold her as tightly as I can. I let her rage.

Kurt, she whispers, is handling it. We've been honest with him, as far as it goes, but how much can you tell an eleven-year-old? I don't think he realises that this is it. This is it, Mum; I've had it with the bastard.

It was Boxing Day, she hisses. Fucking Boxing fucking Day, that's when he told me. In Cassetown, after we got back down there, after we'd had Christmas lunch with you. At least he spared me Christmas Day. The fucker. Fuck him.

I can smell the sour smell of last night's wine on her breath, seeping from her pores. I hold her hand; that's all I can do.

Thank god it's school holidays. He's moving out of the house. Kurt and I are staying down in Cassetown, I've just come up for the day. Marti came down last week, with Luce. The two of us, licking our wounds, making a nest with the kids, going to the beach, pretending everything's alright, drinking too much. Oh Mum, it's shit. It really is shit.

I'm sorry, Mum, I didn't mean to dump this on you.

87. TEN YEARS AGO

The doctor is showing a sheet of film to Iris. The scan, she calls it. They point, they nod. They look back at me and smile with their mouths. After 'the incident' (the person in charge makes scratch marks in the air when she talks) they moved me to this room from the flat I was in. This little room, this little box, not much to it; there's no kitchenette here, no sofa, just the bare basics. It's like a hospital room; even the bed is a hospital bed, all metal and hydraulics and hospital corners. An attempt has been made to give a homely feel. Curtains. A dressing table with a mirror. A little built-in wardrobe. An utterly appalling, ugly 'painting' (I'll give *them* scratch marks in the air) on the wall.

The doctor is holding the scan up against the window to let the light through it, to show the colours, like the cellophane they used to put on the windows, or coloured films over lights to shine on the walls; remember? My brain looks like a big coloured walnut in a half shell of head. I'd fancy a walnut now; imagine it, with blue cheese and quince paste; imagine the taste! Imagine the crack of the shell! But I'm not allowed walnuts. No one here's allowed nuts. The only nuts are the residents. Risk of choking dear, they yell in my ear, as if I can't hear. There's nothing wrong with my hearing, though, that's not what's gone. My hearing is fine, I want to tell them. I can hear every little thing you say. I can hear you when you mutter under your breath, when you lift me and clean me. I can hear you when you complain about the smell and the dribbling and the eternal mundanity of it, when you're standing outside my room and wheedling, trying to swap jobs, trying to avoid the stinking intimacy of old bodies. I can hear you.

I just can't tell you so.

86. TEN YEARS AGO

Rosa?

Rosa?

Mrs Golden?

Rosa, we've spoken with your daughter. She's on her way. Iris is coming. She'll be here in three hours, if the holiday traffic doesn't slow her down.

Mrs Golden? Rosa?

Rosa, you've had a bit of a turn, but you're going to be fine.

85. TEN YEARS AGO

I listen to the radio when I cannot sleep.

Sometimes I hear stories of love: a book being read, a love letter written, a song played for a fiftieth wedding anniversary. When music plays, on occasion I sing. Sometimes I dance, holding myself, smiling at partners not there, leaning in to accept or prompt a kiss, to touch cheek to cheek. Can I have this dance, for the rest of my life?

Sometimes, though, they're stories of hate, of war and politics and profit, of turning back the boats and no more and stay away. Voices raised or reasoned, bitter underneath, little lizard men with evil on their tongues and in their minds.

Today from the radio I have heard only sorrow, great waves of it, and horror, and shifting.

A great shifting quake under the ocean, walls of water breathing in, then out over the land. The radio numbers the dead, the numbers rising to meaninglessness, incomprehensibility: thousands, then tens of thousands, then hundreds of thousands. Imagine – so many people gone, disappeared, drowned. No. It is unimaginable.

Ah-chay, I heard. Ah-chay Province. Indonesia, Sumatra, Thailand, islands. By mid-morning they are calling it the Boxing Day Tsunami, in capital letters that will define it, box it in: the when of it, the festive timing (like Christmas forever triggering Cyclone Tracy). Boxing Day becomes shorthand for hundreds of thousands dead, a million displaced. Imagine more than that though.

Or imagine fewer: imagine one, just one lost, one dear one. The horror of that, even, is unimaginable. (But I do not have to imagine. I remember.)

Oh, that the earth could do this! That the ground shifts, rifts, rips apart under the ocean, and throws that wall of muddy water. One man on the radio said: an earthquake of this magnitude can cause the earth to vibrate measurably.

This big globe, spinning here, cracking and shattering and shifting beneath us. So strong; so fragile. It's more than I can bear.

And in the face of this, what can I say? What can anyone say? I can find no words.

84. TEN YEARS AGO

Postcard from Cassetown

Dear Mum,

It feels so strange to be sending you a postcard from Cassetown, but here we are here, and there you are up there. Because you won't be coming down here this summer, I thought I'd send you a postcard of the bay. You can think of the sound of the waves (and how bloody annoying you find it!).

It's Christmas Day afternoon. We got back safely, before the traffic got too bad.

Thanks for coming to lunch at Marti's. She's not too miserable, poor love. I guess Luce was missing her dad, but she's coping pretty well with them splitting up.

Kurt won't leave the bloody Game Boy alone. He's as happy as a clam. He says to tell you he's got a great game to show you when we come up on New Year's Day. I'm going to bring you some stones from the bay. Remember, at home, for years you kept those stones lined up on the kitchen windowsill? I'll bring you some, for your new flat.

We'll see you next year! Enjoy the rest of this one.

Love

Iris, Paul and Kurt

83. TEN YEARS AGO

My first week at Dorothy Hill Retirement Village hasn't been bad.

Iris and Paul helped me move in. I couldn't bring much — this little flat is barely bigger than a hotel room. I brought a small sofa, a side table; my little dining table with its leaves removed, so it's just a small circle, four chairs tucked in around it. I brought just one small bookcase, and only as many books as fill it. The rest — furniture, books, and all — has gone down south to the house in Cassetown, where there is space to store it. Iris says that it can stay there as long as it needs to. She says she can sort things. She says she'll check things with me. But I think, now, I have what I need here. I'll leave the rest for her to do with as she will.

Summer almost goes unnoticed here, with the air-conditioned closed-in-ness of it all. In a way, it's a relief, after all those baked hot summers I've spent in my house. I walked out the door yesterday, to explore the garden, and realised that it was the first time I had breathed fresh air, felt sun and breeze, in a week. It's mostly paved and tamed, with awful pink old-lady flowers, and agapanthus, and lavender. There are rose beds, of course (these places always have roses). But I followed my nose and found a stand of eucalypts, right in the middle of the place. A sign said POSSUM SANCTUARY: THIS RESERVE OF BUSHLAND HAS BEEN PRESERVED AS HABITAT FOR POSSUMS. A bench at the edge of the trees was in shade, so I sat there a while, resting, breathing. I bent and picked up leaves, their surfaces scribbled by insects, infestations leaving notes I could not decipher, maps to places I will never now go. I crushed the leaves in my hand, breathed lemon, eucalypt, home.

I am in the Independent Living Apartments. It's all very Capital Letters. The other Residents are pleasant enough, and I can keep to myself, or not, as I wish. There is a High Care Facility here should you ever need it, the person in charge said as she showed Iris and me around the (Upper Case) Facilities that first day, and she put her hand on my arm as she said it, as she has said it to all of us, all the Residents here at the Biding Time Village for Old Buggers.

Oh, it's a sensible move. I know that. It's time, if not long-past time. I'm ninety years old, for godsakes. I'm not getting any younger.

82. FIFTEEN YEARS AGO

Iris and Paul have moved house. Close to school, close to the city, near the university; yes it's a good move, yes it's time, but moving the week that Little Kurt starts school? Moving in the stinking heat of February? Not very clever. Still, it's neither my problem nor my decision.

It's a dark house they're moving into, good in the summer heat with its great thick double-brick walls, limestone foundations sitting up off the ground, a solid old pre-war bungalow. Iris took me there the day she picked up the keys, last week. The house was empty, echoing. It smelled of industrial cleaning products on old carpet. It was a deceased estate sale. Of course, she died in a hospice, the estate agent had told Iris. Well, they would say that.

We're going to live in it for a while before we do anything, Iris said.

It's nice enough, and better than the place they've been in, but a little too far from the beach for me. I'd miss the sea breeze.

That beautiful boy, ready to start school! He could walk from the new house, but Iris says she'll drive him.

He's only six, Mum.

You walked to school when you were his age, I tell her, and she gives me one of those looks.

81. SIXTEEN YEARS AGO

I am minding the boy tonight. Iris and Paul are off to a film, or a dinner, something to do with the university. I have come to their house. It seems easier, saves them bringing his things. Saves me making a bed for him. Saves them feeling one of them has to stay sober to pick him up and drive him home.

He babbles on in the bath, about kindy and cartoons. I tuck him into bed, all clean, smelling of powder and soap and toothpaste. He asks me to read to him. He brings me the book – my book! Nonsense, I say, you don't want to read that old rubbish. But my mum is reading it to me, he says. She reads me all the stories. My best story is the one about the baby, he says, the baby and the colour of blue.

Oh, is that so?

Yes, he says. I love that baby.

Then he says: I'm going to have a baby of my own soon. He is all smiles. It turns out, on further subtle questioning, that Paul's sister is pregnant, so the baby will be a cousin for Kurt, not a sib as I thought he'd meant. Ah well. Paul and Iris are so close to Marti and Mark that it will be like a sibling, this baby, handed from one to the next, not quite sure who it belongs to, but belonging to them all. That's the thing with Paul and Martina, the twin thing, that strange closeness. I think Iris thrives on it. I suppose it makes up for her solitary childhood.

Well, enough about babies, I think we'll have something a bit different tonight, I tell him. There is a book about trains, and another about dogs on a beach, and another about a horse, and I read those, do some voices, and he seems happy enough. I don't know what Iris is thinking, reading him those old stories of mine. They're so – I don't know. I did not write them for children.

142

He'll be at school next year. He'll grow before we know it, grow tall, become a man. Impossible to imagine, when they're little like this, but he will. He can read all he likes when he's a man. I doubt he'll want to read my stories then. *Miss Fortune's Faery Tales* — that preposterous, affected spelling. What was I thinking?

He's sleeping now. All children are lovely when they sleep. Iris and Paul will be back soon, and I can drive home. I have a book with me, but I've turned the radio on to keep me company. I have the volume down low, just murmuring, so I can't really hear detail, just the up and down lilt of voices and music, the pips, then the quiet *ta-daah!* of the fanfare announcing the news on the hour.

80. EIGHTEEN YEARS AGO

Postcard from Vancouver

Dear Mum,

This is the market (*produce market* they call it over here, proh-doose, but it sounds so silly when I say it like that) close to our apartment (no one says *flat*). Such a treat to be able to just put Kurt in the *stroller* (that's *pusher* to you!) and walk there – we walk along the waterfront if it's not raining – or hop on the bus. Kurt loves it all – the walking, the bus, the stroller. He loves the market – looks around taking everything in, claps his hands at the buskers. We do counting, and colours, and names of the different fruit and veggies. Fun times, just doing the shopping!

Paul's so busy at the university. Ridiculous that it's called a *sabbatical*, with the *rest* that implies. I'm keeping busy enough with Kurt, and I've lined up a few little bits of work to keep me from going kiddy-mad – I'll be cataloguing at the museum a few mornings a week. There's a crèche there for K. Will six months be long enough for him to come home with a Canadian accent, do you think?

Hope the house is holding together for you. It's the Goldilocks time of the year to be down in Cassetown – not too hot, not too cold, just right. Are those waves keeping you awake, as always?! We're so pleased to have you staying there while we're away, keeping an eye on everything.

Out of room! Postcards, eh!

Love

K, P & I

xxx

79. EIGHTEEN YEARS AGO

I like being here in Cassetown while Iris and Paul and Kurt are away. I spread myself out in the rooms of the house. I take it over, pretend it is mine.

The rooms are filled with the boy's discarded things — a high chair, a cot, a mattress; bags of baby clothes and nappies; cloth books, rattles, hanging gewgaws, a device with straps for jumping in doorways, a bouncinette, a baby bath. They bring things here from the city, keep them at this house, shut them away in a shed or a sleep-out when they are not yet ready to throw them out. There is room here to store, to stockpile (to keep things for if only, and what if).

At night, in the Cassetown house, I often lie awake. Sometimes when I cannot sleep, I stand on the lawn at the back of the house, where I can hear the waves, though I cannot see them. I hear, not so much the water, but what's in the water: rocks rolling, stone tumbling on stone. I feel the grass between my toes. I smell salt in the air. I look to the dark windows of the house, empty and quiet.

In the daytime I walk to the bay, and photograph the heaviest stones, boulders that rest on the beach, that the water can no longer move. This one is flat, like a bed, or a table, marked out with cracks, its surface seamed with milky quartz. I fill the camera's eye with rock, so I cannot see its edges, cannot tell size, or scale.

I pick up smaller stones and slip them into my pockets (I forget about them until I find them at night, when I slip my clothes off and feel their pellet-hardness), tiny reminders of the earth, the action of water.

I do not swim; even on the warmest days I keep to the land, keep even my feet dry. I think of the long-ago geologist, Casse, who drowned, foundering on the rocks, gave this bay its name. When I focus my camera on the water, I find it difficult to frame.

78. TWENTY-ONE YEARS AGO

Dust me grey and call me granny. The child is born. Iris has had a boy.

They have yet to name him. He is healthy, big and bonny. He looks like his father; but don't all babies? Isn't that nature's bid to stop the father from running away, to bond them to the miniature portraits of self? He has his father's long body, long fingers; he has his mother's dark hair and eyes, that she has from her father. He is beautiful, so very beautiful, as not all babies are.

Iris is looking shattered, poor thing. Broken blood vessels in her skin; even her eyes are red like those of a devil goat.

Paul is ecstatic. The whole noisy Diamond clan has gathered at the hospital (of course). Martina has brought bubbly (of course) and a man I haven't seen before. Jacko is loud. Alba fusses.

Martina tries to give me a glass, but my hands are full, taken up with my camera. I prowl the room, try to capture it all: the sparkling Diamonds, Iris's exhaustion (she waves me away with a tired hand, but I catch her anyway). And the mannikin, the beautiful boy: I focus my camera on him, of course, on that new skin, those precious hands, those long lashes. I touch the shutter release gently. He opens his eyes at the sound of it, and fixes his gaze on me. I lower the camera, and greet him.

Hello, my boy. Hello. I am Rosa.

He lifts his chin at me, closes his eyes again.

Iris says: I wish Dad was here.

She means Frank. Dear old Frank.

77. TWENTY-TWO YEARS AGO

Postcard from Thailand

Dear Mum,

We should be home before you get this postcard, but I'll send it anyway. It's so weird travelling when I'm pregnant – it seems the world is full of pregnant women, and women with babies, and I have never noticed it, until now.

People keep smiling at me, touching me. All very strange. Paul's gone into protective husband mode, which is hilarious.

I hope all our stuff arrives safely. It was sad to leave Norwich after three years there – fun times – but so good to pack up knowing that the next time we see our stuff, it'll be back home.

See you soon,

Love

I + P

xxx

76. TWENTY-FIVE YEARS AGO

Postcard from London

Dear Mum,

A blast from your past – Waterloo Bridge at sunset – you must remember this from when you lived in London before I was born?

A friend of mine from uni – you know, the one I told you about who moved back here? – suggested we meet here, in the middle of the bridge. It's beautiful, all the people walking everywhere (so different from home, where everyone's in cars), people crossing the bridge, all dressed in overcoats with umbrellas and briefcases.

Have you ever seen *Waterloo Bridge*, the film with Vivienne Leigh? Full of missed notes, lost opportunities, sad tokens of love.

It's good to be back in London after travelling around for so many months. We head to Norwich next, in time for Paul to start at the beginning of the new term. My first job's to look for somewhere to live!

Love

Iris and Paul

75. TWENTY-FIVE YEARS AGO

Postcard from Istanbul

Hi Mum,

Travelling is crazy. We've been so out of touch. It was good to talk to you from Athens. It's hard to sort the phones out. Crazy. Thanks for sending the mail, we picked it up from poste restante, no problems.

We've been so cut off from news that we didn't find out that the Berlin Wall had fallen until nearly a month afterwards. And same with that thing in Peking, the Tyanamin (sp.?) Square thing. Awful to think these things can go on, and we don't know anything about them. Especially the Berlin thing – we were on the same continent!

You might not hear from us again until we get back to the UK. You can send any mail on to my friend's address in London – or maybe better straight to the university in Norwich? Make sure you send it in Paul's name, not mine.

Call you when we're settled.

Love

Iris

74. TWENTY-SIX YEARS AGO

I spend the weekend with Paul and Iris at the house that they have bought. They're so pleased with themselves, but it's a funny place in the middle of nowhere. An old farmhouse, I suppose, it's a dark and rickety place, the original house all added to with annexes and sleep-outs and louvred-in verandahs; doors that lead nowhere, windows not to the exterior, but to other rooms. There are overgrown paddocks around it, some bush; it is close to the road, and to an old schoolhouse that is falling down; to a horse stud across the road, all new white fences and big money (the only big money in the vicinity, unless you head closer to the wineries). It's an odd place to buy a house, and I see the Diamond clan at work in this. Paul's family used to holiday near here, every summer, and it's always drawn them, he says.

And at least it's near the sea. We walk there, Paul and Iris and I, out the side gate, across a paddock, follow the river and there we are, at Little Casse Bay. It's full of stones and sound and water, not a sandy beach to draw the crowds, the surfers. The beach curves around and out to a disappearing point. It could feel like a lonely place, if you were that way inclined.

That's Point Geologue. Named for the French ship, Paul says as we walk.

It's interesting, actually, a double dose of geology, he says. There was a guy, a geologist sailing with one of the early French explorers, on a ship called *Géologue,* and he jumped ship hereabouts. Presumed drowned, but they never found a body. There've been stories through the years that he survived – went bush, went native, walked all the way to the city, even though the city wasn't settled when he disappeared. One of those stories that pops up every so often. Or someone writes a book about it, some new theory. This place is named after him.

You mean Point Geologue?

I turn my camera towards them, focus as they walk.

Well, he was a geologist, Paul says, but technically the point was named after the ship. His name was Casse; the bay was named for him, Little Casse Bay. And the town. Cassetown. Not that there's much of a town here now, but there was at one stage. Then people moved – better land, I guess. It's cheap now, but if we hold onto it for a few years … well, it won't be a bad investment.

Paul and I think we might move here eventually, Mum. Not for ages – we want to travel first, you know, work overseas, well, we have to really, once Paul's finished his PhD, and there are so many things we want to do – but Jacko reckons this is a good investment. We might plant a vineyard. Or maybe just sell off the land, keep the house. Somewhere to retire early to.

The sound of the waves in the bay is vast and deep and rolling. The waves move the stones, and the sound of it is smoothly deafening. I imagine stone wearing, surface against surface, millimetre by millimetre, invisible layers, turning to sand.

73. TWENTY-SEVEN YEARS AGO

Postcard from Tioman Island

Dear Mum,

This is pretty much the view from our room. Not a traditional bridal suite — we didn't want that — but we are right on the beach, and it's beautiful.

You were right: everyone from the airport check-in to immigration to the hotel bar has made some sort of variation of a joke about newlyweds, Golden, Diamond, and rings. At least my decision to keep my name is less jokeworthy than if we'd hyphenated.

Have you developed the photos yet? Can't wait to see them. Thanks for being wedding photographer *and* Mother of the Bride! It was a lovely wedding. I only wish Dad could've been there, too.

Love from us,

Mr & Mrs Golden-Diamond (I don't think so!)

72. TWENTY-EIGHT YEARS AGO

Now that Iris has moved in with her chap (Golden and Diamond, under one roof) I will have the house to myself. How strange that will feel. Strange for Iris, too, who has grown up in this house. Frank's house. Our house.

It's all been very quick. Oh, he is pleasant enough, this Paul Diamond. He and his family come as a package (a loud and overwhelming package): the loud twin sister, Martina; the jovial father ('everyone calls me Jacko – Jacko Diamond, geddit?') and the quiet mother, Alba. They are in and out of Paul's house (Paul and Iris's house). And now Iris is part of that Diamond family package. Not my cup of tea, but there you go. As long as she is happy.

71. THIRTY YEARS AGO

A door has closed, a chapter ended. I handed over the keys to the photographic studio on the first of this month and by the following week the old sign was taken down, a new one hoisted up in its place. Fortune Photographics, that once was Golden Photographic Studio, is no more.

I retire with a tidy nest-egg from sale of the business. How nice not to have to worry about money! I could have got the pension ten years ago. But it would've seemed wrong, with Iris still at school. It's only now that the time feels right to make the move. Iris has settled into her job. The museum has given her leave to study part-time; she starts classes soon. Finally she is finding her way, her place.

I had thought, at one time, that Iris might take over the studio. When she worked here with me for so long (was it seven years? More?) after she finished school. But this is better: that she finds her own way, moves on from Fortune, that once was Golden.

What will I do? That's what everyone asks me. I can say in truth that I will do as I please, and please my damned self. What joy there is in a life like that!

70. THIRTY-TWO YEARS AGO

Iris has a job (working for someone other than me)!

She will catalogue collections at the museum, process loans, photograph specimens. They have taken her on, she says, because of the experience she has from here, working in the studio. So it has been for some good.

Of course, I will miss her. I have become used to her presence these past years. I've become used to her help, I'll admit it. But she needs to make her way in the world, not linger here with me all day, at home with me all night.

69. THIRTY-NINE YEARS AGO

It is odd having Iris here each day with me, in the studio.

She's useful, so far. It's just for the summer, she says. Until she's decided what to do.

She is — what? — a little shiftless? No interest in travelling, or anything much other than just filling time. Or perhaps she simply doesn't tell me.

I get her to do the dirty work. Well, why not? She mixes developer, stop and fixer; cleans the tanks; disposes of the waste. She does the heavy work. She's young, strong. And she can learn the business. Who knows, maybe one day she'll take it over. Frank would have liked that. Dear Frank.

68. FORTY YEARS AGO

From a 1974 report in the Geological Bulletin, *sent to Rosa Golden*

MEXICAN QUAKE ONE YEAR ON — COUNTING THE GEOLOGICAL COST

The tragic loss of life in last year's Veracruz earthquake is high, but the real number affected may never be accurately known. Though the confirmed death toll is in the hundreds, many hundreds more are still listed as missing, presumed dead, after the Mexican earthquake last August that registered 7.0 on the Richter scale.

Among those missing is renowned geologist Dr Zigmund Silbermann, 38, who was leading a geological survey in the region when the quake struck. The field camp established by Dr Silbermann and his team was swept away during heavy rain in the aftermath of the quake. Dr Silbermann is presumed drowned.

Colleagues of Dr Silbermann's will recall his great zest for life. He was known by students and colleagues for his lively lecture style and, beyond his scientific work, for his love of music, poetry, and cycling. A memorial service is being planned in Dr Silbermann's home city, though he will be sadly missed around the globe, through fieldwork that took him to most of the world's continents.

67. FORTY-ONE YEARS AGO

Unaddressed letter, found at Silbermann field site, Mexico

[Illegible] August, 1973

My darling Rosa,

I write to you from the land. I lie here in the middle of my map, not yet made, in the midst of making. The land lies beneath me, stretches out around me, ready to be translated, though mine is just one translation of many possible. They will tell you, geologists will, that instruments measure the realities of the land, its now and its has-been, its present and past; that these are fixed points, true, factual, measurable. But mapping the land is – I know this – like translating from one language to another. There are many possible translations; here is the translation I choose, now, today. Here is my understanding. This – this translation, this understanding – this is where my art resides.

I have more words than my maps can hold. The words pour off the map, out of my notebook. My notebook cannot hold them. The words make poems instead. Each poem's shape maps the page, a cartography of words, as visual as the land, shape predetermined, integral.

I mutter my map as I annotate it, performing it to the canopy of this tent: *doubt, slip, no doubt*.

Every question mark on this map holds a [illegible] of meaning, signifies –

[The remainder of the letter is missing]

66. FORTY-ONE YEARS AGO

Letter from Mexico City

1st August, 1973

Dearest Rosa,

This, scribbled quickly: I have arrived in Mexico, and head into the field tomorrow. Our timing is terrible – the onset of the rainy season – but that cannot be helped. The local team is good. We will take 6 weeks for the survey, then I fly to you, and Iris, in Australia.

Until then, know that my heart is yours, beating rock-steady, my own love.

Zigi

65. FORTY-THREE YEARS AGO

From a geological report

Zigmund Silbermann, 'The Hope Fault: A Strike Slip Fault in New Zealand', *NZGS Bulletin*, Wellington, 1971 (MS completed 1969)

ACKNOWLEDGEMENTS

This study was carried out during a period of sabbatical leave in 1968, as a special project of the New Zealand Geological Survey. I am grateful to the NZGS Directorate for approving and arranging this research project. For valuable help in the field and with draughting and photography I thank Mr R. Hawkes, Mr A. McKenzie, Mr W.B. Christie and Mr A. Courtney. I am grateful to Rosa Golden for typing the manuscript, and helping in other ways.

64. FORTY-THREE YEARS AGO

From a geological report

CHAPTER 1. THE SHAPE OF THE HOPE FAULT

The Hope Fault is recognisable as a clear single trace, branching into a series of discontinuous fault traces. The most obvious of these runs along the foot of the seaward Kaikoura Range. This trace is intermittent, and does not reach the sea.

In detail, the most common shape of the fault trace is an arc concave to the north. The strike of the fault changes gradually along each arc, then swings back abruptly where the arcs join one another. Other reports have described the fault differently, for example as echelon segments, or consecutive arcs. The shape of the fault may be visualised in different ways, depending on the observer.

63. FORTY-THREE YEARS AGO

From a geological report

INTRODUCTION. A HISTORICAL NOTE

The earliest published reference to a strike slip fault can be found in the Bible:

> And his feet shall stand in that day upon the Mount of Olives, which is before Jerusalem on the east, and the Mount of Olives shall cleave in the midst thereof toward the east and toward the west, and there shall be a very great valley; and half of the mountain shall remove toward the north, and half of it toward the south.
>
> Zechariah 14:4

Apart from this biblical reference, the Hope Fault is, we believe, the first strike slip fault reported in the literature.

62. FORTY-THREE YEARS AGO

From a book of poems

Zigi, *The Hope Fault,* Hissing Swan Poetry Collective, London, 1971

THE HOPE FAULT

Fault leaves a clear trace.
It is intermittent and
does not reach the sea.

61. FORTY-THREE YEARS AGO

From a book of poems

THE CURVES OF HER BODY
For Rosa

I trace the curves of her body,
its terraces and
                    faults,
the lay of the land,
its beautiful
folds.

I measure the depth of her,
the width of her,
the height
of her; the steep
dips of her, the uplift of her.

I pace her out in yard-long steps.

60. FORTY-FOUR YEARS AGO

I have renamed the business, hung my own shingle over the shop. Golden Photographic Studio is no more. Fortune Photography it is.

Two years on and people still ask for Frank.

Is Mr Golden here? He did such a lovely job with my wedding/mother/baby.

Could I talk to your husband?

It's time to start fresh, though I call myself Golden still. I'm Mrs Rosa Golden, now that I am widowed, gaining back my first name at least, no longer Mrs Frank Golden as I was when Frank was alive. Dear old Frank. Solid as a rock.

Iris, next year, will start high school. She remains as quiet and solitary as ever. She is still sad for Frank, misses him greatly.

I have not yet shown her Zigi's letters. Maybe she already knows that he writes to me; but I think not. She never speaks of our time in New Zealand, those few months. It is as if they never happened. Perhaps it is all connected, in her mind, with Frank's death, and with the guilt of not being here when he died.

59. FORTY-SIX YEARS AGO

It is strange to be here, without Frank.

Though we both grieve, Iris grieves most for Frank, while I nurse a newer grief: the baby that had caught has slipped away. It's probably for the best; a menopause baby, so much can go wrong. This little thing had kept itself lodged through the trip across sea and land, all the way to here. A tiny thing, the size of a marble, or a pebble, maybe grown to a clenched fist or a stone you might pick up from the beach, to use as a paperweight, or keep in a bowl to remind you of place.

58. FORTY-SIX YEARS AGO

It ended as unpredictably as it had started, with the telegram from home, the sad fact of death. I booked us on the next boat back to Australia. We packed our things, caught the overnight train north to Auckland. I sent a telegram to Zigi at his field camp: FRANK DEAD. GOING HOME. SORRY LOVE. What else could I do?

From Auckland the boat crossed the Tasman Sea, berthing in Melbourne, then around and up to Adelaide, where Iris and I disembarked. We caught the bus across the desert to the west. Frank drew us back in death as he could not in life.

So it was. We returned home after the Meckering quake, following the fold in the landscape and the road that mapped it. I spent the whole trip west looking through windows, sideways. The tripped land made me think of Frank, dying alone.

I felt guilt, at fault.

57. FORTY-SIX YEARS AGO

From the notebooks of Zigmund Silbermann

UNCERTAIN / CERTAIN

No Fault? the map asks.
Elsewhere, No Fault's a statement,
on its side, sliding.

56. FORTY-SIX YEARS AGO

The voice on the radio stutters on the name of the place, Meckering, juddering at the unexpectedness of it. An earthquake! Over there in Australia!

The knock on the door comes the day after (juddering, unexpected; shifting everything). I sign for the telegram, read its non-sense.

REGRET TO ADVISE FRANK GOLDEN DIED TODAY. SUDDEN MASSIVE HEART ATTACK. ADVISE ARRANGEMENTS.

I equate the two events, imagine the earthquake shifting apart the plates of Frank's broken heart.

Iris's face, when I tell her, crumbles my resolve to stay.

Of course we'll go back, my love, is what I tell her.

And we will. We do.

55. FORTY-SIX YEARS AGO

From the notebooks of Zigmund Silbermann

THE ASYMMETRY OF DEPRESSIONS

They plunge gently
from the east to their deepest part,
west of their middles.

54. FORTY-SIX YEARS AGO

Letter from field camp

July, 1968

Dearest Rosa,

Another letter from me, from the field. Are you bored with them yet? I pour out my thoughts to you, as if I'm speaking to myself, love. I tell you my story in these letters. Each letter is just a fragment. You can piece them together, add in my poems – make me, like a puzzle.

You ask me, over and over, where I come from, where home is for me, and each time I give you a different answer. Here is my answer today. My imagination was formed first in Germany, then in my beloved Israel, my Dead Sea rift, and I see analogies and synergies with this landscape, a world away, an arc, half a circumference away. As far away as you can get, and still be on this earth. This ball of clay (and graphite), its carbon-based life forms; this ball of clay that seems so still, that hurtles through space – it is unfixed! In space! Held in its orbit by bits of nothing! By forces. By electricity, in essence. By tiny squillions of nothing, and also by the biggest bodies. The sun. The sun.

Sol, o Solomon,
o Sol. Bind me,
bind me, hold me – spinning
    – at arm's length. I'm
the third of your daughters, warm
in your distant embrace, cold
at shoulder's turn.

I wrote these words – this poem – today in my notebook. I

inscribed a hard-edged box around these words, marking them off from my work: an aside.

As a geologist, I can read the movements of the earth. For me, the earth is not stable, not still. The earth truly moves, for me. The earth is my text. I underline it with marker pegs. I run my hundred-foot tape along its lines, as an eye runs along the lines of a page. It is a language that makes sense to me, a language that I learned young. They say that learning a language young forms pathways in the brain that enable the learning of still other languages. My languages – my human languages – are German, and Hebrew, and English, and Latin. My earthly language is the language of the land, the solid, moving, transformative language. Doctor Freud wrote of the skips and slips in human language. I write my science in English, and so it has become for me also the language of my poetry, of the slippage of language that is what lets a poem become a poem. Language that is fixed cannot make a poem. That's why I write my poems in English: for the words that slip through, unfixed from their meaning, after I've written the science. For the science, I need to get the words right, fix their meaning. I can do that. But the meaning that slips through, that is left, that meaning makes up the poem.

The poem is the meaning underneath the words. It's the backdoor, the underbelly. It's the vivid colour that has not been paled by constant sun. A book, left on a bedspread – if it is left for long enough – will leave a book-shaped rectangle of pale, when it is removed. Or: in a pile of books, one book on top of a larger book – if the pile is there for long enough, the rectangle of the smaller book will remain, imprinted, once taken away. Its negative self.

When one day I bind my poems in a book, Rosa, I'll bind them for you; I'll write them for you; they'll bind me to you.

As my thoughts do, each day, with love,
Your Zigi

53. FORTY-SIX YEARS AGO

From the notebooks of Zigmund Silbermann

A SUGGESTED MODEL

A fault is straightened
by means of folds; a good match.
A narrow gap's left.

52. FORTY-SIX YEARS AGO

Note from field camp

May, 1968

Rosa, this brief note to let you know that though the quake was near here, and gave us a good jolt, I am fine, and all our small party hale and undamaged.

Two poor souls lost, the radio tells us. One in our party knew the helicopter pilot. A good bloke, he said (as all who are lost remain, forever, good blokes).

Rest easy, love. This shake puts us a little behind in our work, but I'll be with you again in two weeks, I hope.

Shaken, not stirred,

Your Zigi

51. FORTY-SIX YEARS AGO

From the notebooks of Zigmund Silbermann

TECTONIC COMPRESSION

Under compression
small gaps will not develop
but the blocks will tilt.

50. FORTY-SIX YEARS AGO

Letter from field camp

May, 1968

Dear Rosa,

As promised, I write to you from the field, to show you my days, the shape of them. Can I share with you the everydayness of it? The sharp edges of it, and the blunt quiddity of it?

I use *quadrillé* notebooks to record my field notes. I bought them at home – hard-bound, stacked and wrapped in brown paper and tied four-square with string – and shipped them ahead to my colleague in Wellington, in case I couldn't get them here.

Like all field geologists, I write in pencil, which writes in the rain and never smears, smudges, runs or fades, but which I can erase, if I need to. I sharpen my pencils using a knife – snick snick snick – the way my father sharpened his pencils. I like to snick a flat plane at the blunt end, the top end, to expose the raw wood – but not through to the lead – and use a pen to write my name. I like the feel of the pen biting into the soft wood.

In my notebooks, maps share the pages with columns of figures, with tables, with words on the page that might be poems, or might be observations. Or they might just be words on a page. I draw diagrams and figures, box them in with a border, doubled, crisscrossed with lines. I speak with my pencil, you could say, as I am alone much of the day. I make marks on the page, all manner of marks. There's no colour in the marks, though. They're all the silver-grey of my HB pencil, not too hard, not too soft, but just right. Like Baby Bear's bed.

When I have a question for myself, or an odd observation that doesn't flow with what else is on the page, I box it in, wherever on the page it sits. I draw a hard box around it, three sides out to the page edge's fourth. Questions sit next to, but separate from, the certainty of observations; measurements line up in parallel, away from the reach of my hundred-foot tape, my prismatic compass, my hand level, the tools of my rocky trade.

I work figures using a pencil sharpened to a fine point, hard enough for control, but soft enough to give depth and blackness. I favour HB in general, with B for the softer, blacker lines. H for Hard, B for Black. Soft black, lamp black; the more clay, the harder the pencil. Graphite softens, allows the pencil to slip across the page, as I draw the slips and faults. I letter words on the page, on maps: *Fault* and *No Fault*, questioned and unquestioning. I delimit the fault, sketch the land as it lies, and as it moves and has moved. Forever and ever amen. If another man should map this land, in fifty years' time, or a hundred, then shifting land will make it strange, will shift it from this shape I have mapped. That is the way of it.

Where one man might see solidity in a landscape, and never-changing, I see only change, movement, transformation. I see where the land has changed and moved, and I see where it will, one day, move and change; and move and change again. Its past and future are there to read in its present. I can read the land. I can move my eyes (my prismatic compass, my hand level, my hundred-foot tape) across the land and, each day, I read it, and I write it, marking its edges and ridges with my HB pencil in the *ivoire clair* pages of my *quadrillé* notebook. The ruling aligns my thoughts; and yet I can disregard the rules, make them a grid for my most abstract thoughts and ideas.

There I leave you for today, my love.

Yours forever,

Zigi

49. FORTY-SIX YEARS AGO

From the notebooks of Zigmund Silbermann

THE SHAPE OF THE FAULT

The most common shape
of the fault trace is an arc
concave to the north.

48. FORTY-SIX YEARS AGO

Letter from Wellington

May, 1968

Zigi love,

Here we are in Wellington, and you're there in the field. You know our life here, the shape of our days. Tell me about yours. Who are you?

I have taken on some work, a little typing for a local business, on the typewriter in the house here. That scrappy story I sent you last month, our shared shalefire song, typed in ghosts of letters, squeezing ink from the old ribbon like blood from a stone? Now that I've inked the ribbon, it's good as new – don't you think?

(I know you could read my pale and sorry shalefire story, though, as you sent it back to me as cunning verse!)

We can stay a little longer in the house. It's all arranged. I've cashed in our tickets home. It was easier than changing the date. And you will be with us again soon, in this little house that keeps getting colder as the light gets lower, the days shorter.

Hurry back to warm me.

Your love,

Rosa

47. FORTY-SIX YEARS AGO

Postcard from Wellington

May, 1968

Dear Frank,

We may stay a little longer, dear. The photography is going so well. Iris continues to enjoy her lessons. Can you spare us, Frank? You could get help for the studio if you need it. I've taken the house here for another two months.

    Your wife and daughter,
    Rosa and Iris

46. FORTY-SIX YEARS AGO

Letter from field camp, with poem enclosed

May, 1968

Dearest Rosa,

Your letter reached me! Thank Iris for her drawings. Tell her I have tucked them in my notebook, as I tucked my trousers into my socks when I cycled.

Ah, but you needn't have put away your red cellophane fish! You took my teasing too much to heart. Recall this: when I held it in my hand to ask it my fortune, it curled to the shape of *lucky in love* (according to the legend on its packet). I know it was only the warmth and humidity of my hand, my skin, that caused it to curl, yet I cannot fault its accuracy.

And your strange story of shalefire – what am I to make of that bawdy? It is so good to see you writing tales again! And this, from our talk of colour, and dyeing wool.

I continue our conversation: I have taken your words and versified them. I have tucked the paper in here, next to this short note. I could not help myself. It is just a doodle – I think this is a word to use? – repuzzling your words from prose into verse. Forgive me. I love your words as they are. This is play. This is me sounding your words back to you from here, an echo from the land, your words made strange.

Listen: that is love, echoing to you from

Your Zigi

SHALEFIRE SONG
After Rosa

It's time for celebration-o,
for singing, songing music-o!
For dancing drinking merry-o! When
shale bonfires are lighted.

Fires are lit at summersease,
(when summer's tailing, summersease)
and bracken's dry as ever be. Then
the shalefires shall be lighted.

Then the bracken is collected-o,
and shale is piled in bunkers-o,
then they all come together, and
the shale bonfires are lighted.

They burn 'til head of summer-o,
through dark'ning time of winter-o,
the shalewatch shall watch over-o,
while the shalefires smoulder.

Smoulder eyes of ember in 'em,
o you see 'em when they poke 'em,
o they burn with red eye gleaming, steaming
smoking smoulderfires.

In the summer time of wetting,
when the gleaming steaming's retting
there's the smell of woollen netting hanging
over all the town.

And the shalewatch's no more needed,
once the ash is raked and graded,
and the pots are where it's made up now, with
pants-off pints of brew.

And we all go pissing freely
in the buckets and the brewery,
and the smell of it is flowery if you
'magine well enough.

Mix the shale ash, mix the wettings,
mix them good and make them retting,
let it stew another season then
the paste is fit to dry.

45. FORTY-SIX YEARS AGO

Letter from Wellington

May, 1968

Oh, Zigi, love, now you've gone again and I can barely believe you were here.

To see you standing at the gate of this funny little cold little house was to see a ghost made solid. I remembered every inch of you, every moment of you, every smell of you, every sound of you. How could I not, with Iris your echo? I hold this in my heart: you, taking her hand in both of yours, shaking it softly, solemnly. The two of you, like a trick with a mirror.

The eggshells and stones remain on the windowsill, where you left them. They alternate there: the shells letting light through, the stones catching it, holding it. I see you now in my mind's eye, juggling those two stones (plucked from your pocket) with that egg (about to break for pancakes). 'The earth's like this egg,' you told Iris, 'just this thin mantle covering its molten centre.' Then you cracked it, for the pancakes, and she cried, for the broken earth! Perhaps you need to hone your teaching skills, my love.

You (rational scientist) laughed so much at my silly little cellophane fortune-telling fish that I (chastened) have tucked it away in the back of a drawer. Perhaps if you do not come back to us soon I will haul it out again, and ask it when I should expect you?

Remember while you were here, when we talked of photography, and of colour, of fixing brightness? You told me of the old process for making alum, that is used for fixing and brightening colour in wools, a process that takes piss and rock and time. It stuck in my mind, that story, and I have scribbled down this strange little version of a faery tale, a new faery tale. Maybe this is the beginning of a new book? Well, I send you this fair copy, typed evidence of your rocky mind finding its way into mine.

And Iris sends you this drawing. It's that nice man with the stones, she says, on his bicycle. Oh the sight of you, cycling down that hill! Freewheeling, yoo-hooing. I could see the little boy in you, your dark hair, your shoulders hunched over the handlebars, concentrating on speed.

How you will have slowed, now, to map your plodding, careful way across the land and its faults. Your bicycle awaits you here, as I do, love. Come back to us soon, as you promised you would.

Your Rosa

44. FORTY-SIX YEARS AGO

From the notebooks of Zigmund Silbermann

I AM A MAKER OF MARKS

Tiger-stripe terraced
fault lines stretch between questions,
marks order the land.

43. FORTY-SIX YEARS AGO

Letter from Wellington

April, 1968

My love,
We've made it to Wellington. When you are done with your measuring and marking the land, meet us here.

I wave across the water, towards you, just a ferry-ride away.

Your Rosa

42. FORTY-SIX YEARS AGO

Letter from Wellington

April, 1968

Dear Frank,

The trip has started with much excitement, as you may have heard in the news. We came into Wellington in time for a storm of such proportions I still barely believe it was real. A great ferry foundered on rocks in the harbour, and so many drowned. The storm was called Giselle, like Iris's doll named for the ballet. She clutches Giselle close to her, understandably perturbed when she hears people cursing her.

Iris sends you this drawing of the house we're staying in. I think I told you that we have it courtesy of one of the many girls who flitted through the flat in London I lived in all those years ago. What Iris's drawing doesn't show is the cold and dark, and the great up and down of the landscape of this place. I remember it from my visit here in '38 (thirty years ago!) viewed from the ship in the harbour, the houses tucked in gullies and on hilltops and hillsides, all in tumbledown glory up and down and everywhere, the streets winding narrow, wishboning (or do I mean herringboning?) from the hilltops to the harbour's edge. All the people here must have such strong legs and lungs. There's an old woman who lives in our street, and she walks the hill at such a speed, twice or thrice faster than I can manage.

Iris is doing her schoolwork as we planned. The travel will be good for her.

I have taken some snaps, although not quite the photographic essay I had planned, not yet. It is strange to revisit this place. You know how much I have always wanted to return, to revisit my time here in the '30s. It is much changed in some ways, though in others it remains remarkably unaltered. I'm not sure whether it's the change I wish to photograph, or its lack.

I hope you're enjoying your month or so of bachelor time without us. Thank you, again, dear, for your good-natured resignation in the face of your wife's itchy-footed whims. You're a good man, Frank Golden.

Yours,

Rosa and Iris

41. FORTY-SIX YEARS AGO

Letter from Perth

March, 1968

Oh, my dear Zigi,
I thought you were lost, but here you are, your pencil marks on paper, in my hand, bringing love and hope.

I have so much to say to you, but for the moment, just this: Yes.

I've booked passage for mid-April. I will write to you from Wellington, and see you there, soon.

Love,
Rosa

40. FORTY-SIX YEARS AGO

Poem enclosed with letter

TOGETHER, NOW

The steep tilt of it:
the valley of convergence
of this plain and that.

39. FORTY-SIX YEARS AGO

Letter, sent

1st January, 1968

Dear Rosa,

In the ten years since we met in London, first I found your name, then I found you. I have written you so many letters, though I have not, 'til now, sent one.

It's hard to know what makes this different. Perhaps it's something about the new year.

So today, on the first dark day of the cold new year, I'm writing this letter, a letter I am, finally, going to send.

Dear, in a month I fly to New Zealand. It is not your country, but you spoke – a decade ago, in London – of a visit you once made to this long line of land, thrusting out of the ocean. You spoke fondly of it, wistfully. You spoke of a wish to go there again.

I go there to map the land, a strike slip fault in the South Island. It was named long ago – not by me – the Hope Fault.

So: dare I? Hope?

Might you come to me, Rosa?

I will be out in the field, travelling as I work, but my base will be in the capital city, Wellington – I'll be there perhaps a few days each fortnight.

You cannot know this, for this is the first letter I have sent you: I have carried you with me in my heart these past ten years. Every breath I've breathed for you. Every step, walked with you. My stone-hard heart is hot and sharp with love for you.

It's a kind of madness, I fear. And it's madness – to a fault – to write this, to ask this, to hope.

And yet I do.
Madly, hopefully yours,
Zigi

38. FORTY-SIX YEARS AGO

Just like that, everything changes: with the arrival in the letterbox of an envelope I hardly dare open. But I do, and when I do, this is what I find: a letter, and a poem, and so much hope.

My world is rocked once more.

37. FORTY-SEVEN YEARS AGO

In the school holidays, I take Iris to town for the day. We catch the trolley-bus, get off on the Terrace and walk up Zimpel's Arcade to Murray Street. We stop halfway up the Arcade at Graham's, for iced coffee in a tall parfait glass (sweet and milky, a scoop of ice-cream) and buttery raisin toast. We sit in the dark room, on uncomfortable metal chairs, framed by the glass windows looking out onto the arcade, like mannequins in a shopfront, or in a tableau on stage. There's a slight incline of the arcade, up from the Terrace to Murray Street, so that if you let a marble go it would slide all the way down to the Terrace, out onto the busy, windblown street.

Most days in the holidays, though, Iris comes to the studio with me. Frank will have opened up early, been at work for hours, by the time we arrive. Iris sits in the back room, reading or drawing, colouring in, and painting. I clear a small shelf for her in the studio's little back room, and there she keeps the paint set we gave her for her ninth birthday, a metal tin with rickety hinges, twelve tiny pots, each a hard cake of colour, a space between the two rows of six colours for a brush. I give her water in a jar, and a white plate to test and mix colours. She paints flowers, and ballerinas, Giselle, the Swan Princess, in fanciful pinks and glaring orange.

Some days I give her offcuts or misprinted photographs, and she colours those, bends them to her own interest. She cleverly transforms brides to ballerinas, babies to dancing mice, Christmas family portraits to a scene from *The Nutcracker*. Poor Iris would love nothing more than to learn ballet. She's not the right shape, though, too solid, squat; she takes after her father in that.

36. FORTY-SEVEN YEARS AGO

Letter, unsent

November, 1967

Rosa, I have found you.

All these years, thinking of you in London – that cold night, your touch, the Englishness of it, the seasons northern, grey – and there you've been, on the other side of the world. You went home. I see you there, your name changed – a photographer now, the magazine tells me – but I know it's you.

I tore the page from the magazine. The photograph is in the box, with these letters – all of them unsent. I have contacted a colleague – the advantage of a busy academic career, I have colleagues everywhere my dear; I have become quite the professor in the ten years since we met – who has found your address. I have it here, on my desk. I am not yet ready to send you this. Not yet. If ever. But how can I not, now that I've found you?

Still at fault, your
Zigi

35. FORTY-EIGHT YEARS AGO

There is Iris, lying across the back seat of the car, her head resting on her arm, my leather coat over her. Frank is in the front passenger seat, his shoulder slumped against the window, his head back, his mouth wide open, his big throaty snores smelling of beer. I lean forward in the driver's seat, both hands steady on the wheel. I have to concentrate; that's what I said to Iris after I picked her up from where she'd fallen asleep, under the table, near the radio, a book in her hand, when I carried her out to the car and put her in the back seat, even though Iris is too big for this now, too big to be carried. I told her, shush now, I need to concentrate, you go back to sleep.

I turn the key, start the car. Before I back down the driveway I press the lighter in, wait for it to spring out. I hold the glowing metal to the end of the cigarette and huff and puff, until the cigarette glows, and cool menthol smoke fills me, wakes me, mixes with the gin.

On the road I lean forward, concentrate fully on driving. The cigarette is upright, jutting out from the steering wheel, standing like a flag between my index and middle fingers. The car fills with its smoke. I look back in the mirror at Iris, hunched under my coat, fidgeting. Her hands are moving near her mouth, her chin, as if in prayer. I wind the window down so there's a gap, just a little, the wintry night air mixing with the menthol, and Frank's stale beer.

I turn the radio on for company, but there's only static. I leave it on, turned down low. We glide through the night on static and gin and smoke and winter and tyres, and Frank's soft snores, and Iris's gentle back-seat fumbling.

Round a bend in the road it comes into view: a ship of coloured lights sailing on the river, the lights reflecting in the water below, the old brewery building behind it only just visible, a ghost, an after-image. We sail up and over the bridge, and I lose sight of it. I curve the car off the tail of the bridge and onto the riverside road that passes on the landward side of the brewery building. There's a wink of light at the edge of the building from the ship as we pass around behind it, and my nostrils fill with the yeast stink of fermentation.

In the driveway, I open the car door and lean in over Iris, while Frank lumbers inside and falls into bed. I bundle Iris up in my coat, the leather of it squeaking. She reaches her arms up and loops them around my neck, leans her cheek on the bare skin at my neckline. I carry her into her bedroom, lean down to drop her into her bed with her clothes still on. Her feet are bare, and smell of wet buffalo grass in the dark. I smooth the purple chenille up under her chin.

Clean my teeth, she says.

S'alright, one night won't hurt. Night love.

I push her hair back from her forehead, kiss her there, ghosting gin and smoke onto her skin.

34. FORTY-NINE YEARS AGO

In the May school holidays, I take Iris to be fitted for new shoes, before winter. And there is that sound, heard only twice a year, only at new-shoe time: the slick slip of the metal gauge as the fitter clamps it up the sliding scale and down to the mark where Iris's toes meet their measure. The slides and clamps of the measuring scale make me think of the metal calipers that the polio children wear. There is a girl down the street, Marguerite, such a pretty name, like the daisy. Her legs are not pretty, though; they are twisted, weak, and she clacks and clumps in her calipers as she walks. She has a crutch, too, a heavy wooden thing with a big black rubber stop on its foot. Marguerite's mother calls it her *stick*, though. Never *crutch*, which I imagine she deems rude, unseemly.

I have watched Iris watch Marguerite clump down the street with her crutch and her calipers, following her plain, prim mother. The look on Iris's face is not pity, but wide-eyed fear.

33. FIFTY-ONE YEARS AGO

There's a sad coda to our picnic this week. I saw it in the newspaper today. Those boys we saw: a raft upturned, its flailing captain topples and tips another. Two boys in the water, only one rescued, revived. They found the other boy the next day, bobbing in the murk at the edge of the lake, poor lost thing.

I develop the film from my camera. There is Iris, in the centre of the swans. She's crying, has her hands up in the air as if in surrender. The great black swans are all about her, encircle her, like a bad ballet, or synchronised swimming. In the next frame, there is Iris, in Frank's arms, encircled again, but safe.

And then there is Iris, with me this time. Frank had taken the camera, insisted; he had turned it on me, and Iris. I'm down at her level, squatting by the shore of the lake. My arm is around Iris's shoulders; her shoulders are hunched. She is not happy, but she is smiling for the camera. My face is in motion, a blur; I have moved, turned my head in the moment that the shutter opens, then closes.

Behind us, in the photograph, are the boys at the lake. They are background, out of focus, tiny figures blurred in the distance. I wonder which of them was saved, and which lost. Though I peer in close, I cannot distinguish their features.

32. FIFTY-ONE YEARS AGO

We walk to the lake, to feed the swans. Iris is slow, in the busy way that five-year-olds are slowed by chattering and finding and picking up and skipping backwards. She holds my hand when she walks by my side.

I carry my camera; Frank brings the Thermos, a rug, sandwiches. Iris carries the heel of a loaf of stale bread in a paper bag. Frank spreads the rug on the grass, close to the lake, and he and I sit down. I light a cigarette. Iris takes the bread from the bag, holds it in one hand, digs the other into the centre and pulls out a tuft of white bread. The swans turn towards us, start to bustle up the bank, their black necks snaking, beaks scooping, bodies waddling fat from the grubs and slugs of winter. They are huge, as tall as Iris. She runs behind me; stands there, her chin on my shoulder. I can smell the bread, warming in her hand.

Don't like them, she says quietly.

Give me the bread, then, I say.

Her hand snakes around from behind me, and the bread crust drops on the rug by my side as the swans reach us. I pluck bread from the crust, and throw it as far as I can down the bank. The birds turn away, follow the bread, move away from us; they scoop it, tussle over it.

I hand the rest of the bread to Iris.

Go on. You do it. I want to take some photos. Don't be a scaredy-cat.

She steps out from behind me and takes the bread, as I take up my camera and move off to one side. She breaks the bread, to throw it piece by piece to the swans, but instead she drops the whole damn lot at her feet. The swans move as a flock, crowd close to her, peck at the mound of bread on the ground, encircling her.

Frank lumbers up the slope from the lake, shoos the swans away. He lifts Iris up in his big arms, shushes her, pats her back. Her arms clasp around his neck, and she buries her face in his chest. I watch it all through the camera's lens.

There's a shout from the other side of the lake, where the bank rises up to the funny little dark old workers' cottages on the eastern shore. There are boys at the lake, big boys, almost men. They're messing about with rafts, or sheets of iron, standing on them, launching them into the water. They chiack, chivvy, muck about, curse in the air. They are spiky with poles that poke the mud, and press them out into the water. There's splashing and shouting. Two dogs stand on the shore, watching, barking, herding the boys.

A swan flies in across the lake, honking, large, majestic. Frank, Iris and I look up; the rowdy boys and their dogs look up. All of us look up into the air to watch the great fat bird pass overhead.

31. FIFTY-SIX YEARS AGO

Look at my little baby bird, her mouth open, greedy. I plug it with the teat of the bottle. I have weaned her off the breast. It's best, the doctor says. And ever since, she's fattened up; and she sleeps now, so I sleep too.

But even so, I remain tired. No, not tired: exhausted. I had not anticipated how terribly tired I'd be, how unable to do anything, in these first days and weeks, but feed the baby, feed myself. Frank doesn't need me in the studio, he says. But I find myself wishing he did.

So far, my camera has stayed in its bag. But sometimes, when she sleeps, I draw her, make soft pencil lines in a small notebook with square white pages. I draw the curve of her back, the clutch of her fist, the kick of her toes, the sweet soft fuzz of her big head.

I pick up the cigarette that burns in the ashtray by my side, draw on it carefully, so ash doesn't fall on the baby in my arms as she tug tug tugs at the bottle. I look at the clock on the wall. Another day stretches out ahead of us, endless.

30. FIFTY-SIX YEARS AGO

Letter, unsent

August, 1958

Rosa, my love.

I thought of you – as I think of you always – as I mapped the land. Mapping, marking with care, naming. And I named a place for you, dear. A fault – a breaking of the land – it marks my fault, my rending from you.

Though you are in London, now there is Rosa Fault, in the Rift Valley. The place where life began – perhaps? – I mark you on its map, mark you there always. You are there, in London, and you are here – in my Rift Valley, close to home – and I trace you, touch you, and know my own fault, my failure to connect, my slipping unseemly, unseamed, away from you.

Another strange note I will not send. I will kiss it to seal it, and place it in the box with the others. Why can I not forget you, Rosa love? You, lodged in my heart.

Yours, ever,

Zigi

29. FIFTY-SIX YEARS AGO

O! My daughter is born!

My daughter is born on the wave of this pill, this mask, this syringe, and I dive down into myself and hold her up to breathe.

There is Frank, with a flat box of fruit jellies, sugar crust, shaped mandarin and lemon and orange and cherry. I taste the sugar sweets, I mumble, and I stumble and, whoops, I am sick down my front. The nurse says, never mind, let's clean you up, I think it's time you popped off now, Mr Golden, Sister will show you the baby through the viewing window. Frank plants a kiss on my forehead, with beer on his breath to wet the baby's head, just about drowned the little fucker I'd say from the smell of it and oh, here it comes again, and oh that's mandarin, and sugar, and oh, they say she's a girl but I haven't seen her bits and pieces yet.

A doctor in the corridor says yes, an earthquake, in Alaska, the earth rent and rift (*Like me!* I think, *Like me!*). They say it might be an army. Soon-army, they say. Ah, imagine! A tidal wave, a giant flooding wave, like none ever known.

The nurse says: talk about giant waves, you should have seen her spew!

They'll bring her in the morning. My daughter. My daughter is born.

28. FIFTY-SIX YEARS AGO

It's a small ceremony, just me and Frank, with Mr Pritchett the dentist, and his receptionist, Marjory, as witnesses. I hold a posy of blowsy orange roses and crisp fishbone ferns, cut from Marjory's garden, the stems wrapped in a fat tamp of silver foil. A little water drips from the wad of damp cottonwool tucked within the foil. It's cool on my wrist.

I move into Frank's little brick house. He is gentle with me, quiet and kind, as always. He pats my hand, there, there, and brings me tea. We sit in his bed, upright, like a king and queen carved from stone. I reach for him, guide his bald head to rest on my breasts, as I used to, long ago, when he would come to Mr Pritchett for his teeth. He would smile up at me as I passed the instruments, handed water to rinse his mouth, and snapped the crocodile teeth of the metal clasp to fix the bib at his throat, and I would feel sorry for him, for his quiet kind shyness, and press him to me, brush against him gently, warmly.

Frank Golden is a good man. He will be a good father to this baby, when it comes. His big bulk will protect it, keep it safe.

Fortune's turned. I am Mrs Golden now.

27. FIFTY-SEVEN YEARS AGO

Letter, unsent

November, 1957

Dear, loved one, you whom I cannot forget.
Forty-five days have passed since I felt your touch. On every one
of those days, I have thought of you. Your hair. Your skin. Your
voice, telling tales, laughing. Your breath, mine. Our skin marked
and mapped with our urgency.

I cannot send this letter. I know your name – Rosa – and your
street. But you were not on the bridge, that night. Did you read my
note? I can only hope you did not. That you did not dismiss me. That
instead you simply missed me – no dis, just miss – or that we slipped
unseen past each other.

Oh, love, I miss you. You do not know it, but I miss you, and
remain, here – for now, from a distance – your

Zigi

26. FIFTY-SEVEN YEARS AGO

In London, in November, the sky is low to the ground, grey and fat with damp. The flat full of girls is riddled with cold, coughing, lipstick and crying. My hands on my belly, I dream, awake and asleep, for the first time in years of home: of the dry light, the faraway sky, the jellyfish stink of the river, the metal salt ocean, black swans hissing for water in shallowing lakes, the redbrick, flatland, heat-hazed, horizon-filling slab of it, calling me back.

I book passage on the *Arcadia*, send a telegram to Frank, and start to pack my things.

25. FIFTY-SEVEN YEARS AGO

Poem enclosed with letter, unsent

THE CURVES OF YOUR BODY
For Rosa

I have traced the curves of your body,
its terraces and faults,
the lay of the land,
its beautiful folds.

I have measured the depth of you,
the width of you,
the height of you, the steep
dips of you, the uplift of you.

I have paced you out in yard-long steps.

24. FIFTY-SEVEN YEARS AGO

Letter with poem enclosed, unsent

October, 1957

Rosa (oh dear Rosa),

I write to you as a maker of marks. I read the land, order its seams and faults, make sense of them, write them onto maps that men can read. The earth folds in on itself, heaves and cleaves and shifts and rises. And I read that, I map it. I measure it with a hundred-foot tape. I measure it, mark it, write it to paper.

The land has tells that people do not. Read the land, the faults are clear. They're a puzzle to be solved, and once solved, to be written. Slate and shale, graben and twist, schist and chert: incantations of the land.

But you, Rosa. You. O, I cannot forget you, the smell of you, your wild eyes. Your dark eyes. Your legs. Around my legs. Around me. Your schist, slate and shale. The slip of you. Your dark hair, the straight line of it, the no fault of it, cut straight across your forehead, the line of it above your eyes. Rose quartz your lips. The mudstone of your hair; the greenstone of your eyes.

Yes, I am a maker of marks. And the marks I made upon your body! Writing its curves and slips, its rises, its bulges, its slopes and terraces. I made invisible marks upon your body, inside and out, as you marked me. My paces stepped the length of you; I had the measure of you, I *was* the measure of you. As I might estimate distance on a map, so I estimated the distance between our bodies, between yours and mine. The closing of the gap – this diminishing value – can be achieved in one of two ways. I move towards you. Or you towards me. Or a third: we move together. We displaced

211

space between us, love, and filled it with ourselves. We measured the space between us with the volume of our bodies. The volume of this, the volume of that. The density of the space, now filled. The consequence of it.

Here is a poem for you, love.

I cannot shake you from me, and so I am

Your Zigi

23. FIFTY-SEVEN YEARS AGO

Note, slipped unread from a pocket through a hole, into the space between a coat's leather and its lining

Dear Rosa, beautiful Rosa,
I leave London tomorrow, for home, at the end of this geological congress. Can we meet again? God, I hope we can!

Forgive me this cliché; I'm still more than a little bit drunk, you're in the bathroom and writing this is all I can think of. Meet me in the middle of Waterloo Bridge, at 6pm tomorrow – no: today, Friday. I will wait for you there, but I must go straight to the airport, from the bridge.

You know me only as Zigi, but this is my name: I am Dr Zigmund Silbermann. You may write to me, if you will, at the Department of Geology, here at my university.

I wish only to see you again.

Dear, I wish it so much!

Zigi

22. FIFTY-SEVEN YEARS AGO

This is the night we meet.

Micky, wicked girl, has got them again, the purple hearts, and we pop them in the afternoon, and o o oh there we are in the bright and haze of them, the don't-know-where of them, the colours merge and wheel of them, the gorgeous buzz and hum. I leave my camera at home, but my eyes are my camera; I will never forget this, never not never not remember. Here is this pub, the two of us in this snug. This pint. The light of the fire of the stick of the match. Hold it still for just one moment, Micky, hold it, hold it, light another. Smoke sweet dusty full lungs blue smoke.

And look: look at you there, you, beautiful boy, there at the bar.

You're short, solid, an outline, coloured in, filled in. You wear wool trousers and suede shoes, movie star dark glasses. You stand apart from the others you're with, at the edge of the crowd of older men in their socks and gaiters and sturdy walking boots.

Micky leans in to me, her arm around my waist, whispers something, smoothes her hand down her skirt as she talks. Micky is looking your way. We are both looking your way. We are smiling. Look at you now, you've seen us see you. Yes. You smile back at us, show your neat teeth. Look at you take a slim book from your pocket, lean back against the bar, foot up on the stool. Yes, like that, and your cigarette burns, but let it; let the ash lengthen and teeter and drop, and you brush it from your sleeve. No, better still, you brush it from your thigh. Or better still: let me brush it from your thigh.

I'm at the bar now, Micky's with me. The music rocks, steady. We rock, we roll. I lower my eyes, lower my face; then I tilt up my eyes to you, raise my eyebrows, raise my drink. I'm by your side now, and I have my hand on your book. What's that, now; what is it you're reading? You flick the cover, show me this volume of poetry, this slim thing, and the pages splay, and you part the pages with your finger, at the page with the turned-down corner.

The poem's a dirty love song, rhythm skipping ugly on the page, rock steady, rock steady, words to part lips; something by one of the Beats, or translated from a language no one knows. And you read it, leaning in to me, your breath in my ear, your words, your rhythm. Your accent's unplaceable. You're there with your friends. My geological colleagues, you tell us, it's a rocky relationship, and you all laugh. Micky's there and she laughs loudest, with her hand on your arm, but you're watching me, and your pupils are large. You're drinking rum, the smell of it like cake, like spice, like perfume. The smell of you is all I can smell, not the beer or the smoke or the pickled eggs. Your hand touches mine as you hand me a glass. It fires my skin.

You're here for a geological congress, your first time in London, you should be with the others (over there now, sucking on pipes, scribbling maps on napkins). But you're in London. London! And you've escaped the scientists, the solid talk of rocks and maths, the petty hiss of academic rivals.

We sit in the snug, my hand on your chest, in your shirt, your hand on my leg, your blunt fingernails there. I move, so your hand slithers up the fabric.

Then there's a gap of not remembering.

And then I push you against the kitchen cupboard. You are my height, or shorter; my hair is short, so that your hair is almost as long as mine; I recognise something in you, like looking in a mirror, but the wrong way around, so that the reflection is other, is skewed but recognisable. I push you against the dresser, and plates rattle. You edge to the table, then to a chair, and ease yourself onto the chair and I climb you and take you in, and your face is hard then soft then hard again, and your hands, your blunt-fingered hands, find their way to my arse and push me and lift me, and your face disappears in my shirt, and you come up for air, smiling. And we heave and blow together; you rock me, back and forth, in the kitchen chair, your fulcrum, my weight. I put my hand across your mouth to catch your shout to God, and you bite me as you come, in the dark, in the kitchen that smells of sausages and tea leaves and laundry.

We huddle in the doorway, say goodbyes I can't remember. Drink and pills and lust still muddle my brain. You press my hand, and I crumple paper into the pocket of my coat. You slip away, into the grey light near morning.

21. FIFTY-SEVEN YEARS AGO

Here in London, I find that I'm playing art student, playing photographer, and not quite sure, day to day, which of these I prefer. I sport a severe look, my dark hair cropped short, high on the forehead, exposing my pale face, a slash of red on my lips; I dress often in black. There's a self-portrait I took, myself in motion, in and out of light and shadow. I'm in a pub. Smoke obscures me. I hold a cigarette in my hand, but as if I'm holding it for someone else, as if to hand it back.

There are endless parties, many of them in our flat. And there's an endless stream of people crashing in the flat, all of them Australians, friends from home, or friends of friends, or brothers of cousins of friends. They stay for a night, or for weeks or months. I come home late one night to find a man, naked other than his sleeping bag, camped on the floor, next to the kitchen table.

Gidday, he says. Barry, from Dardanup. Micky's cousin. The couch was taken.

I step around him to fill the kettle, put it on the gas burner to boil. He joins me, draped in his sleeping bag, and we sit at the table and drink tea, smoke cigarettes.

There are Australians everywhere, not just in our flat: at the school, in the pub, mounting shows in galleries. We congregate, whether we mean to or not. We hear each other's loud, flat voices across rooms. We drop the same social clangers, miss the same cues, and our Australianness earns us forgiveness. We're outsiders together, here, a little like puppies, or children, occasionally making a mess in the corner, but to be tolerated for our ability to entertain. We're *loveable rascals*. Although it's more than that; we have become, it seems, somewhat *en vogue*.

Micky has an invitation to an exhibition opening at Whitechapel Gallery for one such Australian painter currently courted by art connoisseurs. We go for the wine and the cheese, but stay for the paintings. They are flat, cartoonish, our mythic bushranger in his slit tin hat, lit with un-British sunlight. There are older myths, too: Leda, the swan curving up and over her, those great wings spread, so you can almost hear their beating. The swan is dark, like swans at home, the beak tipped red with threat, there against her thighs. I've watched swans here, in the parks. They're pretty and white, creatures from a faery tale. I draw them sometimes; I add a delicate crown in silver filigree, slanting jauntily over one serene eye. I draw them as *she*, always. But this swan, Nolan's wild dark bird! It menaces, the god come to earth as he-swan, neck snaking thick and hard with power against the soft caught curve of Leda. I shudder to look at it.

20. FIFTY-NINE YEARS AGO

Letter from London

May, 1955

Dear Frank,

I went to tea at my publisher's house; Babs (Mrs Swan to you!). She stays in a flat in London during the week, close to the office of Cygnet & Swan. She invited me to her cottage *in the country*, and I caught the train on Saturday. Oh, Frank, you should have seen it! A cottage older than any building in Australia – as old as Shakespeare! A thatched roof, low ceilings inside so I had to stoop the whole while (Babs is a tiny bird of a thing, so she flits about, upright, oblivious). There were faery tale flowers surrounding the cottage, and bluebells in the woods (the woods!) at the bottom of the garden. And inside, the rooms were stuffed with books and papers, with paintings and photographs, with old china and furniture.

She lives there with Cicely (whom she calls *Cygnet*) who is, I have discovered, her partner in publishing. It is Cicely who owns the house, I think, and lives there all week round, while Babs is in the city. Cicely, I think, is the money behind Cygnet & Swan. She is older than Babs and, I gather, content to leave Babs to run the business as her own.

We ate sandwiches and cakes, all made by Cicely, at a table in the garden. Cicely fed the scraps to the dogs, two of them, great beasts that lounged and lapped at her feet, followed her into the house, back out again, never let her out of their sight. I shot them, in black and white: Cicely with her hand feeding morsels to the dogs; Babs with her hand on Cicely's shoulder; both of them lighting cigarette after cigarette. Light and dark was playing on them, changing with the sun's movement across the sky.

Later, Cicely shooed us off while she cleaned up, and we walked, Babs and I, in the woods, after tea. Babs is eager for another book from me – but, do you know, Frank, I don't believe I have another in me. I avoided telling her as much, though. I held her off with talk of my studies, of this deadline and that.

My camera bag was slung over my shoulder as we walked, but I left the camera in its bag. I was mesmerised by the blue of the flowers, the bluebells in the woods, and couldn't bear not to capture it, but my camera was threaded with black and white film. I could have coloured the photographs, Frank, couldn't I? Added the blue in afterwards, like you taught me to. But I prefer, these days, to shoot in black and white, pure and simple, and let the shadows tell the stories (stories of dark and light, without colour).

My fondest regards,

Rosa

19. SIXTY YEARS AGO

The London flat is full of strange girls. It has been since the ship arrived, and the latest mob turned up. It was supposed to be one or two, a cousin of Ellen's, and maybe her friend; but four of them came, in the end. We'd met on the ship, and all got on so well, and here we are, so the flat is, yes, full of strange girls. The strangest of them all, in some ways, is me. My age hardly qualifies me as 'girl', though I never admit it. I'm too old to be a student, but most of the time I manage to get away with it. The others think I might be as old as thirty (imagine!) but could not conceive that I might be the age I am: forty!

I, like the rest of them, am red-lipped, bright-eyed, busy as a bee. They favour capri pants, ballet flats, tailored shirts in crisp white. But I play the art-school beatnik, hair *au gamin*, black skinny pants, black turtleneck or French sailor's top, a leather coat over it all. I carry my camera in a woollen bag stitched with big red blanket stitches, two leather toggles to close it with.

I thought I'd come away here to write more faery tales, to draw and paint them, but the camera seems to have taken me over. Having decided to stay a little longer, I've enrolled in classes at the Central School of Art, taking Photography and Composition, and I look to reality now, capturing what I see rather than inventing worlds. *Miss Fortune's Faery Tales* – now published – is almost forgotten. It seems another Rosa Fortune that wrote those tales. I have walked past bookshops and seen it there, and taken a while to realise: *Oh, that is mine. Rosa is me. I am Rosa.*

Being in this place is like being in a book, or walking through the image on a postcard. I know the streets and buildings so well, the buses, the taxi cabs; I know the very weather, the landscape, from reading it, from films, and from paintings (but from *photographs* of paintings; seeing the real paintings in galleries, walking up to them, seeing the light move on brushstrokes, seeing the size of a painting: these are remarkable things; remarkable). Photographing this place feels like photographing a fiction. Its commonplace is my unreality.

18. SIXTY YEARS AGO

Letter from London

March, 1954

Dear Frank,
This short note to let you know: I have arrived. I am Overseas, with a capital O!

Today I wore out boot leather tramping the streets (those streets and squares and railway stations so familiar from the playing board!), staring about me like the colonial yokel I am. Oh, the weather is dire, the streets are dirty, but even so, I find I love it already!

Tomorrow I meet with Mrs Swan, the publisher, for tea. Tea with my publisher!

Oh Frank, excuse my excitement, my rambling. If I don't tell you my news, there's no one I can tell.

I hope the new girl is working well in the studio.

With fond regards,
Rosa

17. SIXTY-ONE YEARS AGO

Letter from London

Cygnet & Swan, Publishers

November, 1953

Dear Miss Fortune,

I enclose a copy of the first review of *Miss Fortune's Faery Tales*. As you will see, it is extremely favourable. My dear, you should be very pleased with this reception of your debut publication – and in *The Times*!

I hope this will be the first of many such shining reviews for your delightful book.

Cordially,

Mrs Barbara Swan

Publisher

P.S. Have you thought further on a possible trip to Britain? All of us here at Cygnet & Swan would love nothing more than to show off our Antipodean author, here in London. We'd be fortunate, indeed, to be visited by Miss Fortune.

16. SIXTY-ONE YEARS AGO

Story from a book of tales

Rosa Fortune, *Miss Fortune's Faery Tales*, Cygnet & Swan, London, 1953

THE HISSING SWAN, *OR* HOW MISTER WILLOW CAME TO MISSUS MAKER

Once, long ago, in a land much greener than this, lived a good woman, old and wise, who had everything but love. Now this woman was an inventor, quite a talented one, and she fended very well for herself. She was surrounded by the products of her own clever mind and hands: from the mill that ground the flour for her bread to the chiming clock above her stove to the tiny mechanical mice that she made for fun, to scurry out from under the chair and worry the lazy cat.

She was the mother of her own inventions, and she could turn her creative mind and hands to anything, big or small, industrious or comical, for all the elements of her life. To even the rude mechanicals of lust she could deal, but true love can only come from another.

She felt this lack of love keenly, but managed, most days, to put it to the back of her busy mind. It was in the long nights that her thoughts would linger on it, mull the problem over. Finding no solution, she would most often manage to sigh with regret, then settle into dreaming wistful dreams of perfect love.

One night though, stricken with sadness and unable to slip into sleep, the old woman rose from her lonely bed. At a minute to midnight, wrapped warmly about with her quilt filled with finest down, she slipped out through the front door of her house. There she sat, on the river's cold bank, the tears on her cheeks quick like silver in the moonlight, dripping and mixing into the fast-flowing river at her feet, so the salt of her tears was made fresh.

As the clock above her stove chimed out through her open front door, striking midnight, a shadow passed in front of her and stopped just out of sight, in the middle of the river.

'What ails you, good wise woman?' asked the shade in a gentle hiss. The dark birdy voice drifted to her across the water's surface, undermuddled by the glisten sound of fat red feet paddling unseen. Peering into the darkness, she recognised the thick stiff curve of the black swan that lived on the river just above her mill.

The old woman sniffed a snotty sniff, wiped her nose on the quilt, and stemmed her tears for the moment it took to say 'O good wise swan, I really mustn't grumble. I can tend to all my needs, bar this: I need a lover. I have everything I need right here – forged by my own hands! – save this one thing.'

The swan paddled this way, and it paddled that way, then it stopped, hissed three times, and sang in its birdy voice:

O good wise woman, I too love lack.
Shall we scratch each other's back?
Do it yourself, as you always do,
Make plans, invent, use metal and glue.
Be here at midnight, at midwinter deep,
Bring a lover for you, and one for me.
Make them with love, and for love, and love will survive,
Lasting and true; a mate for life.

And he hissed thrice more and was gone before she could answer.

Midwinter deep was only a month away, so the good wise woman worked, as she knew she must, as if in a fever. She set pencil to paper that very night, making measurements, drawing plans, and by sunrise those plans were fixed. Then, over the days and nights of the month that followed, she made herself a lover, built him from the ground up, to her own careful specifications, so he was fit: fit for purpose.

She built his armature first, made him strong from willow wound loose enough to give, and tight enough to spring stiff. But she made him for love, not lust; made his skin from silk, white like marble, like sand, like milk. She framed his face with hair dark and thick as a bear's; she gave him eyes of cobalt blue, the colour of deep water hiding secret treasure; she spun him a mouth soft as faery tale kisses, from spidersilk purpled with beets.

Into his milky silk chest, last of all, she placed the heart she'd made him. It was this heart over which she'd laboured longest, sitting hunched at the high bench in her workshop, lit in the daytime by good low light from the sun through the window above it and, once the day's light had left, lit long into the night by clever lamps of her own design. Finally, after many days and nights of work, on the night of midwinter deep it was complete, and perfect: a heart of finest clockwork, quartz precision. She wound the heart with a wee silver key, inserted in a tear in the silk of his chest, til the mannikin's heart was ticking hot to trot, but still cold as only metal can be cold.

Over the tick tick ticking of her mannikin's heart, the clock above her stove struck eleven. She realised with horror that she had only an hour to make the swan's mate. Lacking time to make it with skill, she took extra care to make it with love. She fashioned the plump round body from her best sourdough, and covered it thick and warm with bright white feathers born through a slit in the quilt from her bed. She lifted the great hank of her own thick white hair and with silver scissors lopped it off at the neckline. She formed the hair into three thick strands and plaited them to make the swan's mate's neck, curved serpentine over a strip of yielding willow. She wove the ends of the plait through the loops of her scissors, so the scissor blades formed an open silver beak, and the loops formed dark staring eyes.

At five minutes to midnight at midwinter deep, she carried the heavy white swan outside and placed it by the river. As she arranged the white swan's head in place, she shivered in the cold, missing her hair's weight down her back; missing her warm down quilt over her shoulders. As she shivered, the scissor blade slipped and sliced her hand. Her blood stained the scissor blades a deep swan-beak red. Sucking the blood from her hand – staining her own beak – she hurried inside for her mate.

At a minute to midnight at midwinter deep, the good wise woman carried the cold little still little mannikin to the river, and seated him, naked, there with his milky silk feet toeing the water's edge. By the river he shone breathless in the midwinter moonlight, his cold heart tick tick ticking.

As the clock struck midnight at midwinter deep, she leaned in to kiss his cold beet-red lips, and left a stain of her own bright blood. Out of the dark midnight light, the black swan spread its wings and hissed at her from the middle of the river. The woman rose to her feet and stretched both arms wide, to the cold white swan by her left side, to the cold ticking mannikin by her right.

O good wise swan, I've done my part.
A mate for me with a perfect heart.
Scissors, and hair and blood and so
Make a mate for you, warm with love and dough.

The good wise woman trembled with cold, though she held herself steady and did not show it. She trembled too with fear, for she was not used to making magic contracts but knew, from tales heard tell, how easy it was to be tricked by word or deed into terrible consequences.

The black swan swam close in response. He reared up and seemed to grow to twice his size, snaking his sleek neck up to overlook the trio on the riverbank: the wise woman, the white swan and the tick tick ticking mannikin.

Good wise woman, you've done your part.

Now I'll do mine: make warm these hearts.

The black swan spread its wings and hissed. Quietly at first, then louder, the white swan's feathers bristled and rustled, and the willow of its neck creaked and stretched under the thick white braid. The red-tipped silver of its beak dipped down to the riverbank then raised up to meet the black swan's beak in a touch of recognition: like meeting almost-like, mirror-like.

The black swan spread its wings and hissed once more and the mannikin's stone-cold heart woke, hot and sharp with love, as nearly alive as invention and desire and spells could render.

As the little man's cobalt eyes flickered open, as a blush of life touched his milky silk face and body, as his willow stirred and strengthened, the woman showered him with kisses. Even in the face of such enchantment, such happiness, the good wise woman kept her wits (and her manners) about her. She looked up from her gentle waking man, raised her hand to the swan's dark breast.

'How ever can I thank you, good wise swan?' the woman asked.

The black swan hissed again, three times, in an answer she could not fathom, as the white swan stepped down from the riverbank and glided out onto the river's dark surface. The black swan and his shining mate swam to the centre of the river, their necks entwined. The good wise woman leaned in likewise to her little mannikin, and he to her. Four of them, two by two, paired now for life.

And so it was that the good wise woman lived happily with her warm-hearted mannikin year upon year ever after, in the house by the river. She called him Mister Willow; he called her Missus Maker. She never forgot what the wise black swan had done for them, and forever after made two batches of good sourdough each baking day. They never ever after went hungry for bread or love.

15. SIXTY-TWO YEARS AGO

Letter from London

Cygnet & Swan, Publishers

February, 1952

Dear Miss Fortune,

Thank you for submitting your manuscript (untitled) for our consideration. I apologise for the time it has taken to respond to your submission.

I found your manuscript, with its strange characters, colourful events, and its odd mixture of science and magic, delightful and surprising. These are *faery tales* (to use your quaint spelling) that disturb, in the way that the best old tales did and still do. I admit that some persuasion on my part was required to convince my partner that there is a place for your book on our list.

However, convince her I did, and so I am pleased to tell you that Cygnet & Swan would very much like to publish your book. We would like to give it a title which, as well as being informative, is a cheeky play on your name: What do you think of 'Miss Fortune's Faery Tales'?

We would hope to make a feature of your beautiful watercolours, and would print these as colour plates facing the title page for each story. Might it be possible for you to produce additional drawings or paintings for those few stories which lack them?

We anticipate this book having at least as much appeal to adult readers as it does to children, and this will prove a fascinating challenge to booksellers.

If you wish to proceed with a publishing contract for the book, please let me know by return mail, so that I may draw up a contract.

I look forward to working with you.
Yours sincerely,
Mrs Barbara Swan
Publisher

14. SIXTY-THREE YEARS AGO

Frank is good company, a pleasure to work for, and I continue to learn the photographic trade (I am even becoming adept behind the camera). I keep middling busy in the studio. Yet with every clatter of the postie's bike, my heart skips. Still nothing comes from Cygnet & Swan – not my own fat package back, rejected; nor a slim envelope offering solace, and publication. Month after month after month, nothing comes, until nothing is what I expect.

And so I focus on my work. Each day I sit at my desk in the studio with my brushes and gum and paints, and I tiptoe the brush to touch faces and gaps, bubbles of light. Specks of dust leave dots of light on photographs, specks of nothing, absence. I fill them in, make them good. I add colour, sometimes; that's the skill that Frank values, that's the showy side, but it's correcting the tiny imperfections that pleases me most.

As I make good the imperfections of others, I try to forget my own silly, imperfect faery tales, and the folly of my grand plan, to send them off to London to make their fortune, like Dick Whittington and his cat.

13. SIXTY-FOUR YEARS AGO

From manuscript sent to Cygnet & Swan, Publishers

THE UNCOVERY OF BLUE

Some of the best magic in stories is not magic at all, but simply nature, wisdom, and good chemistry combined; the magic rests in the uncovery, and the telling. This is one such tale. It has a woman and a forest, a journey and a fire; it holds a baby fast at its heart, and in the end, a great colour is revealed.

It may or may not surprise you to hear that the woman in this story is neither young nor beautiful; she's middling old, past bearing. The baby she holds is not her own, nor is it her grandchild. It is not of her blood but it is of her village and in her care, and she feels fiercely the need to protect it, to feed it, to love it as her own. Now, it happens that harsh times and bad luck have brought their once-fine village to despair and poverty. One by one, two by two, family by family, the people of the village have walked away from their houses to make a life in the city on the other side of the forest. In the near-silent village, when finally the baker, the grocer and the miller have all gone, the woman decides that she and the nameless baby must leave, too, and make their way to the city.

She packs her last half loaf of bread and her last dry rind of cheese, and they set out before dawn. They travel first on open road, then on well-trod way, until they find and take a faint path that she knows from long ago, that veers off under close-growing trees, through forest that lets in little sun. The woman carries the child close to her, strapped to her, shaped to her front. She stops only briefly, to eat bread and cheese. She puts her finger in the baby's mouth, and feels it tug at her. She spits bread she has chewed onto her finger, and the baby gums it, greedy, needy. Sometimes when she stops to eat, she stops a little longer. Then she feeds the baby goatsmilk and water, sweetened with honey and stored in a curdybladder that she carries on her back, tied to a cord slung over her shoulder.

She walks all day, until finally she comes to the forest's edge. She keeps to the thinning trees, not yet ready to break from their cover. She stops before it is night, and makes a small fire. While the food is warming, she lies the baby down on the forest floor, on a bed of leaves, in a pool of sunlight that comes to them through the thin cover of trees, breaking through their low canopy. The baby is in a little pool of light and warmth, lifting its arms and hands to the light, absorbing it. She cleans the baby as best she can, then wraps it in soft, fresh leaves, chosen carefully, picked from where they grow in the dappled light under the trees of the forest's edge. She bundles her fine woollen shawl around and over the baby, binding leaves close to skin, applying gentle calming swaddling pressure, until the baby's wrapped snug like a sausage, or a soft doughy pudding.

As she eats, and the baby sucks its goatsmilk and honeywater, and a little of her own chewed cud, she lets the fire die down. In the deep dark night she spreads the ashes to make a soft, warm bed, and together they lie down to sleep. Her sleep is deep and untroubled, and when she wakes with the first light of the day she is content, refreshed, and the baby too is smiling. The baby raises its hands to her, reaching, waving. She lifts the bundled baby and commences to brush the fine ash from the shawl. As the ash is removed, blue is revealed. Blue of the sky, picked out in ash patterns, in shapes and constellations, on the fine wool of the shawl. The baby's dampness, the soft leaves, the alkaline ashes – they have made colour, turned the wool sky-blue.

And that middling old woman, when they get to the greysky city, will pin the shawl to the ceiling of the room above their heads, so the sky is always with them. And the baby will grow up knowing colour, and – grown to adulthood, one day in the future – will become not just a great artist, but a watcher of leaves and trees and light and fire, noticing the science that is their magic.

12. SIXTY-FOUR YEARS AGO

In the daytime, when the light is good, in the gaps when we are not busy in the studio, I work on plates to illustrate my stories. From sketches I've made and coloured in my notebook, I make good copies onto acid-free card. I add mats and sleeves to protect them, using offcuts from the studio (or if they're not strictly offcuts, I'm sure Frank does not mind me taking them). At night, I offer to close the studio so that I can stay late. It's too dark to paint, so I use the typewriter in the office to type clean copy of my stories, double-spaced and with wide margins, onto good bond paper, bright white.

I fledge my manuscript (I have come to think of it as such now, as a *manuscript*, though perhaps *typescript* is more strictly correct), ready it for flight. I prepare to send it off into the world to make its way, to find its feet or spread its wings.

I do my homework. I look at the little symbols on the spines of books on Frank's shelves, and I go to the library and do the same, until I find what I am looking for. There is a publisher in London, Cygnet & Swan (est. 1921), that publishes very fine quality illustrated works, and some poetry. Their colophon attracts me: two swans, the larger with neck curved like a snake, bent down to the smaller, a fluffy bundle.

I write a letter in my head, ready to send to them when I have finished my plates. *I enclose my original illustrated manuscript for your consideration. My faery tales are, I feel, as much for adults as they are for children. I look forward to your response. Yours sincerely, Miss Rosa Fortune.* My hissing swan, my tiny dancer, my baby wrapped in blue, and all the others, all bundled in brown paper, flying away to London to find their own fortune.

11. SIXTY-EIGHT YEARS AGO

Oh, it is lovely, working in the photographic studio, after so many years in the dental clinic! Gone are the X-rays and ether, the probes and amalgam, the dusty smell of tooth enamel burning under the drill. I do not miss staring into mouths, rank breath, screaming children, the meaty tang of rotten gums. There is certainly less blood. Few people fear a trip to the photographer as they might fear the dentist's chair. I use different chemicals now, have swapped jars of sterilising liquid for developer, fixer and vinegary stop bath.

Mr Golden calls me Miss Fortune, his kind face never breaking into a smile until, a week into my employment, I invite him to call me Rosa. He teaches me the basics of photo colouring, in my first weeks working for him in the studio. Building on the watercolour skills I've taught myself over the years I learn fast.

I keep my desk at the studio just so, everything where I need it. It's a pleasing process, precise. I touch the tip of the paintbrush to my tongue, just lightly, then slip its tip between my lips and kiss it to form a point. There are the colours I've mixed, in shallow depressions in the white china palette on the desk in front of me. Just a little at a time. Mustn't be wasteful. I dip the tip of the brush into the pale pink wash that will form the undertone of the skin. The face in the centre of the photograph in front of me is tiny, a fine oval pale under the shelter of a great, broad hat looped with lace and topped with a pale silk flower. I touch the tip of the brush to the slim face, feel it slicken, see it bring colour to the face. I lift the brush. I purse my lips and blow on the photograph, blow on the face, just gently. The surface dries quickly; I watch it change from slick shine to dully dry.

I wash the brush, kiss it again to a fine tip, then dip its very tip into the deep rose colour. I touch it to the lips of the face in the photograph, brighten them, enliven them. I dab water lightly to the cheeks, using a damp cotton swab, moisten them just enough, then touch the tip of the rose-red brush to each shining circle. The colour wicks outwards from each of the tiny pink points, makes rosy apples of her cheeks.

I blow again to dry the surface, then work quickly and carefully to touch colour to the neck and shoulders, down to the soft line of lace at the dress's neckline. I touch pale pink to the hands that rest so, on the back of the chair, and so, on her husband's shoulder.

I do the same to paint the rose in a baby's apple cheeks, a rattle in its hand, or an alphabet block: add colour to bring the images to life.

10. SIXTY-EIGHT YEARS AGO

At one o'clock each working day, Mr Pritchett the dentist appears in the doorway of the treatment room, wipes his hands down the front of his white gown, says *You're in charge, Miss Fortune!* then turns and closes the door behind him, signalling the beginning of the lunch hour during which, according to his strict instructions, he is not to be disturbed. He eats his lunch in the examining room. I imagine him sitting in the leather dentist's chair, a bib around his neck to catch his sandwich crumbs (scraps of leftover chicken, or curried egg, or tomato gritty with pepper and salt) and wipe his mouth. I hear the tap run. Perhaps he rinses and spits when he is done.

Every working day, for the twelve years that I have worked here for Mr Pritchett, has been the same.

I am in charge, and left to my own devices, during that hour. Mr Pritchett expects me to mind the front room, to file records (to pin tiny X-ray films, their teeth gleaming white, to the top left corner of index cards, matching patient name to patient name), to type payment reminder notes, to fill the steriliser and straighten the small selection of magazines and newspapers on the table between the chairs in the waiting room. I'm to welcome the two o'clock patients, and bid them wait, if they're early (though people are rarely early for the dentist, I find). Most days, though, I spend my lunch hour alone, sitting behind the desk with my lunch and my notebook, writing or drawing whatever is in my mind, working on one or another of these odd stories, that come so freely now, and flow from my mind to my notebook. There are, perhaps, a few too many caves among my drawings. I put it down to all those mouths.

Today, the door opens early. A hat appears around the door, a face emerges below it. The face belongs to Mr Golden, from the photographic studio on the corner.

I wonder, might I? he says.

We're not — that is — we're closed until two. I wave my hand towards the clock on the wall.

Well, I don't have an appointment, but it's rather an emergency, he says. My tooth.

He opens his mouth, inserts a stubby finger.

Eeets thvery sthaw.

When he pulls the tip of his finger from his mouth, a thin line of saliva connects, thins, then breaks. Like gossamer, I think, in a faery tale.

I can't disturb Mr Pritchett until two. He may be able to fit you in then.

Very kind.

He takes off his hat.

Thank you. Uh — may I?

He waves his hat at the chair.

I suppose so.

He smiles, sits, clutches his hat on his substantial lap, then picks up one of the magazines I've not yet bothered to straighten. I return to my sandwich (cheese and gherkin), and my notebook, pick up my pencil, resume my drawing. I see him watching me.

Do you draw? he asks.

Oh, just for myself.

Might I?

He is risen before I can say no. He is behind me. He is a fat man, and tall. He leans over me, and I can smell the meaty smell of rotten tooth, like meat hung too long, or cheese left out in the sun.

That's very good.

He flicks through the pages, flicks backwards, so that I feel a little dizzy.

Yes, really very good. You have quite an eye. A sense of colour, too.

Well, I —

240

No, no, don't be modest, it's not everyone, you know. It's rare. I wonder – no, I'm sure.

Wonder what?

Well, I need a photo colourist. Someone to learn the business. I don't suppose you'd consider? No, I shouldn't –

I don't know –

And at that moment, Mr Pritchett opens the door, slapping his hands together, smacking his lips. Mr Golden leaps backwards, away from me. I hand him his hat, dropped by my notebook.

Who's our two o'clock, Miss Fortune?

Mrs Adams and her two bratty children are late, as always, for their two o'clock appointment.

Mr Golden, come this way.

As Mr Pritchett washes his hands noisily at the basin, Mr Golden makes his way to the big red leather chair. At the head of the chair, I fix the bib around his neck. I lift Mr Golden's head, curve the metal chain under at the nape of his neck, bring the alligator clip around at the side and fix it to the cotton bib at the front. I lean into him and shift his head, just slightly. He nestles against my chest.

9. SEVENTY YEARS AGO

I don't know why I've started writing these stories, after never writing anything more than a letter or a shopping list before in my life. They are dark faery tales, each one lightened with a flash of colour at its heart.

I'm not sure where the stories come from. Here and there and everywhere and nowhere. A fragment of song gives a nudge; words click together in my head. I sit on the bus, and a phrase occurs to me. I've taken to carrying a small notebook with me in my bag, with a small propelling pencil that fits through a loop. I capture the stories in the notebook, sketch figures and scenes to illustrate them. I have missed my bus stop more than once, found myself stranded at the trolley-bus terminus, instead of getting off outside the dental clinic.

At work, I slip the exercise book out when I can, at lunchtime, or when Mr Pritchett is busy, and jot down phrases, add to a drawing. The words for each story come first, but the illustrations to match those words seem always to follow close behind. Figures are elongated, often in shadow, drawn quickly. Closing my eyes, I can see the image as it needs to translate to paper. The image glows on the inside of my eyelids.

There are stories about children, abandoned or orphaned, by one or both parents; or children much-wanted, but unachievable. There is magic in the stories. It's not music-hall magic, not women run through with swords and knives but miraculously uncut; this is the older, earthy kind, the real magic of herbals and botanics, or pharmacopoeia; the magic of elements put together in the right way at the right time in the right proportions and sequence. They are more often recipes than magic, and more often than not they focus on colour. For the tales are often inspired by a colour. Not

Snow White and Rose Red, nor Little Red Riding Hood; not Rumpelstiltskin spinning straw into gold. There's a woman spinning green nettles into cloth to bewitch a stranger; there's a wet baby rolled for warmth in the gentle ash of a forest fire, releasing the colour from leaves. This is earthy magic; real magic. And god knows where it comes from, or why now – perhaps it's the War – but here it is, so I write it down.

8. SEVENTY-FIVE YEARS AGO

Back at my workaday job at the dental studio, it is as if I was never away from here. Now, three thousand miles and nearly a year away, I look to my notebook, and my feathered hat from Wellington, to remember my travels. How lucky I was to slip my New Zealand trip in before this war. But how long will I have to wait before I can get these itchy feet once more upon the road?

My New Zealand notebook is filled with words and little drawings. Its pages are fat and puffed, stuffed with mementoes and keepsakes I picked up on my travels. There are bus tickets and concert programmes, pretty picture postcards in colour and black and white, and a paper napkin stamped with the New Zealand Railways crest. Leaves, picked for their shape or colour, rest with flowers pressed between pages stained dark by their petals.

There is the photograph of me with Guide Ana, framed by the meeting-house gate. I wear my modish home-sewn coat, my Wellington hat with its fine feather. Her great feather cloak drapes down and out from her shoulders so that, at its base, it touches the hem of my coat. She looks like a queen. I look like a shopgirl.

My descriptions in the notebook are mostly those of a shopgirl, too, mundane, boring. *Today I caught the bus. Today I had tea and sandwiches. I shared my cabin with a lady from Adelaide, and her two married daughters.* Once in a while, behind my lacking, listing descriptions, I catch a glimpse of the adventure that I remember: the dark, rich smell of the forest, so unlike Australian bush; the unsettling rise of mountains, the deep wet green of hills, the ferocity of the weather, the sky so close, closer and smaller than home.

7. SEVENTY-SIX YEARS AGO

I continue my travels in New Zealand's North Island. Rotorua smells of sulphur and brimstone. All the earth's geology, its innards and workings, are there to see, exposed and raw and strange. It's as if the world is turned inside out, as you turn a ripe fig inside out to eat it.

I dress up to go to a fine show at the meeting house, to see the famous Guide Ana who has performed for Dukes and Duchesses. She sings in Maori and English, 'Pokarekare Ana' (is it about her, I wonder?), and 'Now is the Hour' in Maori, and other songs I do not know, but like none the less for that. She wears a skirt of native grass, not soft as I expected, but stiff, so it clatters and clicks as she moves. Her hands make waves in the air as she sings. Her voice is clean and clear and strong.

When the whole concert party takes the stage, the men and women are all in the same stiff skirts, all barefoot, the men bare-chested. Some of the women are draped with cloaks that are, I think, made of fur, or feathers, tufted, patterned. They have headbands, like Red Indians, and the women's hair is long, dark and thick. Their voices rise and hold together. The sound is not like a European choir, but has its own sound. There is a catch in their voices that sounds almost like sadness.

After the concert, I join the line of tourists eager to pose for a memento photograph with Guide Ana. She smiles at me as I take my turn. Side by side, under the high, carved gateway that leads to the meeting house, we face the photographer, and smile at his shout.

6. SEVENTY-SIX YEARS AGO

I used to dream about travel; now, here I am, after all those years of scrimping and saving.

New Zealand is green and beautiful. And cold, so I'm glad I took the time and expense to line my winter coat. And that coat has gained me a hat, for the fashions here are behind even ours at home, and I find myself modish, admired, a very strange state of affairs. In a shop in Wellington, the proprietress admires my coat so much that she asks if she might trace a pattern from it.

Leave it with me for an hour, she says. I promise I'll take good care of it.

I'll tell you what, she says in the face of my obvious uncertainty, you must choose a hat! Any hat! In return.

It's early afternoon, the sun high enough that I'm sure I can wander the long, curving main street coatless for the hour it will take her to trace my coat, to map its making. But the brisk wind soon sends me into a teashop for shelter, and I am forced to spend money I had not budgeted on half an egg sandwich and a pot of tea.

When I return to her shop, the proprietress meets me, grinning, at the door. I choose a pretty felt hat that I notice in the window, the same deep green as my coat, with a feather curving around from the brim. It is well worth the cost of the tea and sandwich, after all.

5. EIGHTY YEARS AGO

start a new job, working for Mr Pritchett the dentist.

The pay is better than it was in the office, so I can better afford to save my money to travel. Mr Pritchett says it doesn't matter that 've no experience as a dental assistant, he just needs a pretty face round the place. He pinches my cheek when he says it. He'll train me up, he says, and this way there aren't any bad habits to break.

Mr Pritchett doesn't look like a dentist. He has great big forearms covered in thick black hair, the forearms of a butcher, or a docker. When he washes his hands in the basin in the treatment room, the hair on his arms goes flat, dark, aligns like seagrass in the shallows on an incoming tide. He smells of disinfectant, carbolic soap, and the sweet, pink alcohol that the clean instruments are stored in.

4. EIGHTY-SIX YEARS AGO

Sister Bernard raps the ruler across my knuckles.

Stop dreaming, Rosa Fortune!

I jump, and blot my copybook.

There'll be no more looking out the window when you leave school, my girl, she says.

I am not her girl.

But I bow my head like the other girls, and I dip my pen and write.

I can't wait to leave the nuns behind, to go out into the world. stare at the map on the wall, its Commonwealth colours, its grea oceans, its land masses, its possibilities. I rest my chin on my hand and imagine myself anywhere but here.

3. NINETY-THREE YEARS AGO

Oh, but everything goes so quickly now! Here I am, at school with the nuns.

Sister Clotilde is kind and soft, and has a pretty face, but the other sisters frighten me. All in black, they smell of sweat and mince. I fear their hidden hair, their sharp ways.

Sister Mary Joseph has a wart on her chin, with a hair growing from it. Pongy Sally says Sister Mary Joseph's a witch. Betty Murray says that Pongy Sally would know all about witches, just look at her granny!

2. NINETY-NINE YEARS AGO

Pull me up on Mama, her breadsmell skirt. Bump on the floor, o o oh! Mama making pikelets, round like mouth, sticky jam. Want more!

I'm off! O o oh! Watch me crawl! Off I go, all the way back.

1. ONE HUNDRED YEARS AGO

Whack! Cry! O o oh, it is Rosa!

HOPE

'Now, Mistress Queen, what is my name?'

The Brothers Grimm,
'Rumpelstiltskin'

Sunday

THE YEAR'S DEEP MIDNIGHT

The baby wakes in the night. Only her mother hears her. Kristin rolls out of bed, stumbles to the baby's side. She has to hesitate a moment, half-remember where she is – this house, these rooms – but without coming to a full waking state. Actions come without connections to conscious thought – hold the baby, check her, feed her, pat her back, rub her tummy. Voice stays in that low register, that murmur. Words need not make sense. It's better if they don't. *Shush shush shush* sounds like the rain on the roof, like water flowing, like grass, like the ocean, the wind. And you rock back and forth, without thinking of it, just doing it. *Come, Baby. Sleep, darling. It's alright. It's alright. S'alright now. Sh-sh-sh-sh-shush.*

In this fugue state, random thoughts come. It's the longest night of the year, tonight. Midwinter. An image flashes through Kristin's mind: her mother's stories, growing up in Norway, Saint Lucia's Day, crowns lit with candles (the fear of them, and their beauty), lighting the year's deep midnight, its darkest moment. Saint Lucia brings light. The year lifts from here, the days lengthening, though imperceptibly at first.

The baby sleeps again now, her mouth petalling sweet breath. Kristin pads back to the room she shares with Paul, rolls back into bed, is asleep before her head hits the pillow.

LET HIM LET HER GO

He can't remember walking back to the house from the beach. He can feel the sticky wet of salt water in his clothes. Seawater feels somehow heavier than rainwater, sticks to your skin more. He feels the rain freshen the seawater, dilute it, lighten it. In his nose is the acid tang of sick.

Kurt stands on the lawn. He can see through the windows to the kitchen, but it's almost dark inside, just a faint glow that might be from the microwave, or the clock. The house is quiet, now. In the dark, in the quiet, he thinks about The Girl he saw and then failed to see again. He sees her head, her slender neck, the dark, straight, sleek hair floating, darkening the water around and about her. He sees her when he closes his eyes. That's what he sees. A girl. The Girl. The unseen, always-seen Girl, slipping away.

He thought he'd left The Girl behind, thought he'd eased her from his dreams. He thought he'd drawn her out in the comics. He thought the meds had let him let her go.

He opens his eyes. He stares down at his boots, their toe crust of grey river sand, their rime of salt. He swings one booted foot out in front of him. There's little resistance in the grass, the lawn. The sound of it – the swish of his boot, the parting of the blades of grass, the slick of the moisture on the grass – all magnifies itself, in his imagination, in his mind, mixes with the distant sound of waves. He's not sure what's close and what's far; what he feels and what he thinks; what's heard, what's seen, and what's imagined.

FALLING WITH THE WEIGHT

Driving back to the house from the hospital, Iris is careful, even though it's only a short drive. She sits forward in the seat, looking for animals on the road, or drivers coming out of nowhere. It's not yet light; it's that time of the morning when it's deep dark night, darkest before the dawn. Her car lights make a tunnel of brightness ahead of her, and she drives into it.

When she's only a few minutes from the house, the rain kicks in again, suddenly torrential, monumental. She flicks the windscreen wipers up to maximum speed, but they can't clear the view. She slows to a crawl. She can't see through the rain. It feels as if she's underwater, or driving at a building she can't see past. She indicates – though there's no other car around – and pulls the car over to the side of the road, feels the gravel pull the tyres onto the verge, feels the pull on the steering wheel. She turns the ignition off, leaves one hand on the key, one hand on the wheel. The rain thunders on the roof of the car, drumming as if to break through. How can water be so hard? The sound is powerful and gentle at once, like stones tumbled by the ocean.

Iris sits, in the dead-dark, waiting for the rain to ease. A phrase from the hospital sticks in her mind, morphs to this: *I have stones inside me.* She thinks of kittens drowning in a sack.

Just for an instant she feels herself falling with the weight of this, as if through time, or water, or a window into light.

The rain stops suddenly. Iris restarts the car, turns the demister up to full, wipes the inside of the windscreen with her sleeve to clear the condensation that's formed from her breath. As the view clears, she realises she's pulled off the road just metres from the rise of the bridge, just before their turn-off. She eases the car off the verge, back onto the road, up across the little bridge, then turns left into their driveway, and pulls in by the house to park.

As she gets out of the car, she feels herself sink into the ground. Dampness seeps up over the sides of her shoes. The house, from the outside, is quiet, dark. The cars that'd parked all around the house for the party have all gone now – there's just her car, and Paul's, and Marti's. She closes the car door quietly. The beep of the lock sounds bright in the still night.

The rain cloud is off to the south, and the sky above her is clear for the moment, star-ridden. Everything smells of rain, washed fresh.

She unlocks the front door, and steps inside the house.

The beep-beep chirrup of the car lock wakes Luce up, a little bit, but she doesn't wake up properly until Iris comes through the door, and nearly treads on her.

'What – Luce – what are you doing love?' Iris whispers. As if anyone would wake up.

'I – uh – couldn't sleep. I –'

Luce fumbles, puts her hands to the ground. She feels Iris's phone by her side, slips it into her pocket as she stands up.

'Oh, Lulu, I'm so sorry, I know I said I'd call, but I forgot my phone. Of course you were worried about me! I'm sorry, love.'

'No, I –'

Iris hugs her, and Luce is half asleep so she lets her. 'Oh, you're freezing! Come on, off to bed. You can sleep in tomorrow.' Iris shakes her head. 'Today. We can *all* sleep in today.'

Luce remembers why Iris was away. 'You okay? The hospital?'

'I'm fine. All sorted out. Nothing to worry about. A pebble garden in my gut.' She puts her hand on her belly as she says it. 'Gallstones. Not serious. Come on, off to bed.'

Luce is at the door of her room when Iris says to her, from where she's fumbling and moving books and bowls and papers on the hall table. 'Oh, I thought I'd left my phone here. Did you see it, Lu?'

Luce shakes her head. Her hand in her pocket feels for the phone's ringer, and flicks it to silent.

'Nuh.'

'Never mind. It'll turn up. Night love.'

'Night.'

Iris puts her bag on the kitchen table. She leaves the light off so she doesn't have to look at the party mess everywhere. She can smell the volatile dregs of wine and beer. There are no clean glasses or mugs on the shelves. She finds a plastic measuring jug in the pantry, stands at the sink, pours water into it, drinks. She feels woozy from being up all night, and from the low-level pain meds they gave her at the hospital. She stands, leaning at the sink, staring unfocused out the window.

Outside, something moves. On the ground. Is it –?

She leans in close to the window, fogs it with her breath; she leans away again. It's – something, on the ground, framed by the window. The shape lifts, an elegant arc of dark back rises up from the ground. Arms push up from the front and she sees a face – his face, her boy, her Kurt – pale in the scattered starlight as his shoulders heave and hurl, and he throws up in a dark torrent that disappears into the sodden ground underneath him.

THE FEEL OF HIM LEANING

They're in the kitchen, talking in quiet voices. Everyone else is still asleep. Kurt sits on a kitchen chair, a tartan travel rug around his shoulders. Iris has put a purple ice-cream container in front of him on the table, in case there is more vomit. There can, surely, be no more vomit. Iris is making tea. She has started washing mugs and glasses while the kettle boils. She puts teabags into clean mugs, tops them with water. She stands at the bench, jiggling teabags, watching Kurt. He has his head in one hand. The other hand clutches the rug closed at his throat. His eyes are closed, his mouth open. He stinks of bile. His wet clothes are in a pile on the bathroom floor. He's pulled on another identical pair of black jeans. She wants to reach out and touch him, but she knows not to. Outside, there's a glow of light in the sky. Kurt has been talking, but she can't understand what he's telling her. Something about the bay. Something he saw. She's so tired. She imagines lying down on the ground outside, where Kurt was, but off to the side to avoid the vomit. She imagines the cool of the damp ground against the side of her face, like the cool side of the pillow when you turn it over in the night. She looks at Kurt, who is looking at her now, as if he's expecting her to reply.

'Well – what were you doing at the bay, anyway? In the pouring bloody rain?'

'I don't really know. I was – I was just pissed. Like pass-out-in-my-own-vomit pissed.'

'Clearly.'

'Jesus. Alright. Sorry. Not something you've ever done.'

'Oh, love.' She reaches her hand out to his, covers it. His fingers are long, fine. His hands are cold. 'I was just worried. Seeing you out there, I thought –'

She doesn't know what she thought, and she can see the start of something – some kind of shutting down – in his eyes. 'Look, all that matters is you're okay. You can get rat-arsed if you want to, I don't care about that. Just don't do anything – stupid, when you're pissed. Anything could. You could. Look, I don't know. You could slip and go into the water. That's how people –'

He makes a noise in the back of his throat, annoyance or dismissal or frustration. A warning to shut up. But she can't.

'Love. I worry about you.'

He shrugs his shoulders. His head drops a little lower. She thinks of her teenage years, her own quiet, solitary drinking; she thinks of wine drained from the cask in the fridge into a pottery coffee mug (the suck of the fridge door opening, the tinkle of wine filling the mug), taking the edge off school nights. She remembers drinking at the oval before school socials, passing vodka bottles and beer cans, the glorious discovery of those first bedspins and boyfumbles. It wasn't often that she'd slip up and get completely pissed in front of her mother, but when she did, she remembers Rosa holding her hair back while she spewed sour wine into the toilet, bringing her a bucket, putting it by her bed, tucking a towel under her chin to protect the bedclothes; bringing her aspirin in the morning. She remembers feeling shame, bile-sour, gut-wrenched, head-aching shame. And she remembers it not stopping her. Not for years.

He is saying it again, telling her about something he saw. Someone at the bay, there and not there.

'What, you mean disappeared? In the water?'

'I dunno, Mum. I dunno.'

He so rarely calls her *Mum*. His head is in his hands, his hands mussing his hair; but this is how he sits, this is not unusual, this is a normal stance for him. Still: *Mum*.

'Well, if something happened, there would have been – someone would have got the police, or something. Wouldn't they?' She imagines it as a scene from a television drama, police sirens, TV cops in trench coats and perfect hair, crime scene officers zipping up a body bag. 'Wouldn't they? Kurt?'

He turns his head away from her and looks, his hair flopping over his eyes, towards the window. She wants to put her hand out and touch him; she wants to put her arms around him and hold him tightly to her. She wraps her arms around herself, instead, tucks her left hand into her right armpit, and her right hand into her left. She hunches over her arms, her neck curving, her head dropping, feeling her spine curving away from the back of the chair. She rocks, forward and back, but just a very little, so you'd hardly notice – she thinks – if you weren't looking for it. She is so tired. She unfolds her arms, lifts her head, uncurls her spine, and looks at Kurt, willing him to look at her, but knowing he won't.

'Well, was it – are you sure you actually saw something? If you were so pissed –'

He clenches his hand, digs his fingernails into the soft underbelly of his arm. His fingers lift; she sees white half moons, watches them flush to pink. Pull back, she tells herself. Go lighter.

'You know – sometimes we think we see things, but they turn out to be not what we thought we saw ...' She trails off, realising she's not making sense; she doesn't have anything to say. 'Oh, I dunno love.'

She swipes her hair back off her forehead, tucks it behind her left ear.

He gets up, shrugs the rug off his shoulders.

'Going for a walk. I feel like shit.'

'Oh don't, love. Stay here in the warm –'

'Fuck. I'm fine. Fuck! Don't fuss! I'm just going for a fucking walk! I'm not going to drown myself! Jesus fuck.'

He slams the door behind him. She stands, goes to the window, watches his shoulders slope, watches him walk away, out through the side gate that leads to the river path to the bay. She lets him walk away. There's nothing she can say to him. She doesn't know what to say any more. She's so tired.

She hears the sound of the baby cry, hears the bedroom door open, hears Kristin's voice, then the baby sounds soothe from cry to contented gurgle. She remembers when Kurt was small, she thought she'd never be able to protect him but, at the same time, she thought she always would. She was his protector. She and Paul were, both of them, but her most of all. She was his mother. Remember that feeling: when he was tiny, and she could hold all of him in her arms. All of him, held tight to her! And she could make it all better, always.

She remembers the feel of him leaning against her, when she was his safety, his world, his food and drink, his play, his sleep, his bath, his book, his story, his tongue, his word, his what's that, his why, his breakfast lunch and dinner, his apple cut into boats, his table fort draped with blankets, his clean clothes, his new shoes, his tickling, his counting, his archivist, his inconsistent scrapbook-maker, his don't do that, his garden buddy, his audience, his actor, his shouting mother, his bad role model, his inconsistent parent, his too tired to think, his doesn't make rules, his makes rules, his doesn't make rules, his walkover, his sheet-changer, his wake up at night and his singer to sleep, his doing all the voices, his back-patter, his worrier, his helper, his champion, his nurse, his cook, his scribe, his interpreter, his advance party, his problem, his solution, his excuse, his fan, his hairdresser, his stylist, his activities and entertainment officer, his disaster management expert, his trauma counsellor, his translator, his intermediary, his protector, his provider, his teacher, his student, his manager, his friend, his enemy, his understander, his not understander, his nervous observer, his never let go, his accommodation, his transportation, his photographer, his subject, his opponent, his team captain, his team member, his reader, his writer, his artist, his model, his researcher, his explainer, his question, his answer, his dictionary, his internet, his limit, his start, his where, his what, his why.

She puts her head on her arms on the table, and closes her eyes.

DEEP GRIEF, CROUCHING

When Luce wakes it's still early, hardly even light. She tries to go back to sleep, but she needs to wee. She rolls out of bed. On the way to the bathroom, she hears voices in the kitchen, and she listens, standing by the door like a sneak, standing in the dark of the hallway, behind the door that's open just a crack.

When Kurt storms off, she races back to her bedroom, pulls on her jeans and hoody. She picks Iris's phone up from the table by the bed. It's showing three missed calls. *Shit.* But – it's still early – the lady, when she'd phoned the first time, had said nine o'clock, right, *tell Iris to call any time after nine*, and it isn't even eight, it's still practically night-time – so technically, *technically* she doesn't need to tell Iris yet. She puts the phone in the front pocket of her hoody, and sneaks out the side door to follow Kurt.

She hangs right back, watches him walk out the gate to the river, and turn down the path to the beach, before she follows. As she reaches the gate, she feels the phone vibrate in her pocket. She pulls it out, checks the screen. Four missed calls. *Shit.* She presses the button on the top of the phone, and slides her finger across the screen to turn it off.

She follows Kurt down the path, but she's busting, can't concentrate. It takes her a while to choose a place, and her bladder knows she's getting close and it lets some out before she's ready. She squats down, just off the path, behind a bush. The air's freezing cold on her bum, and it's noisy when she goes, like a tap turned on full. When she's done, she wipes herself with her hand, and washes the wetness off by wiping her hand on the plants by her side, pigface and lupins, sopping with the night's rain. She wipes her clean, wet hand down the front of her jeans.

She slips back onto the path and follows it to the bay. She stops there, where the path comes out at the top of the beach, and watches

Kurt walk around the bay from the river mouth, and on out to the point.

Back at the bay, in the pale early morning light, it's as if the thing he saw (the thing he thought he saw) in the dark never happened. The river still flows, faster than even a few hours ago, into the bay. He stands at the point, where he saw – where he thought he saw – The Girl, The Man, them both, then their absence. He knows that if he took off his boots and his socks, and took off his jeans, and took off his shirt and t-shirt and put them in a pile on the platform rock, and if – then – he walked into the water, then out further, until the water rose to his ankles, then his shins, to his knees then his thighs, then further still – he knows that it would be cold; and that he could not do that, because all he would think about would be The Girl, the girl he'd seen, then failed to see again, that girl not gone, but always there, every night, in the dark at the edge of the frame of his dreams.

He doesn't know she's followed him (she *thinks* he doesn't know). He stands there now, all thin and tight in on himself. Luce watches him from where she sits on the big flat rock. Her knees are drawn up in front of her, her arms hugged in tight around them, making herself small. She rests her chin in the space between her knees, where it fits, filling the gap. Her jeans smell faintly of wee.

She curves her back so her face goes lower. She sniffs. It's not too bad. She can probably only smell it because she's this close. She thinks that a dog might press its nose at her, might breathe in deeply, move its wet nose about, taking it all in, pressing at her. There's no dog at the house, though, and that's good, because Luce doesn't like dogs much. She doesn't trust them. They can smell fear, people say. They can certainly smell wee. She prefers snakes. The idea of them, anyway. She's never touched one. Except the dead one, yesterday. She traces an S on the leg of her jeans. Snakes smell with their tongues, when they hiss. She pokes her tongue out, but it's cold, so she pokes it in again. She makes a quiet hissing noise, her tongue tucked to touch the back of her bottom front teeth. Then she stops, in case Kurt hears.

She looks out at him. He's standing so still, just staring at the water, at the waves. He hasn't picked up any stones to throw, or kicked branches to turn them over. He doesn't look as if he's going to go for a swim. It's too cold to swim, but he might go anyway. He used to swim when he was little – they both did, when they used to come here – and she wonders if he might now. Something in her wants to stand up, so she doesn't feel as if she's hiding. She could stand up and stretch and just sort of saunter down (she likes that – *saunter down*, that sounds good) and not say anything, just stand next to him and see what he does; see if he leans into her, puts his arm around her, or pushes her a little bit, like just for fun, like you'd do to your little sister or your best friend or something. She wants to talk to him about the comic, about which scenes he's going to work on next. She wants to ask him about the thing. The thing he saw. That she heard him say to Iris. She wants to tell him about the phone call. About the phone in her pocket. About Rosa.

But something about the way he's standing – the shape of his shoulders, perhaps the curve of them, the tightness – warns her away. He's alone, is what she thinks. He's alone.

He hasn't moved from the point. She gets up, slowly, straightens her legs and she's up, and she turns and she walks away as quietly as she can over the pebbly stones. She knows – somehow – that, even if he hears her over the sound of the waves, he won't turn to look at her, because he has other things *on his mind*. That stillness of his, it is a watching stillness. A waiting stillness. A stillness that does not watch, or wait, for her.

There Kurt stands, at the point, thinking of The Girl (whom he's tried to draw, before, but he just can't get her right). His shoulders shrug and twitch. His hand moves to his chin, to his forehead, worrying, then back to his pocket, for warmth; then to chin, to forehead, to pocket; and over again, anointing through the cold salt air. He can feel, somehow, the essence of what happened here – what he *thinks* happened here, what he *thinks* he saw – though he cannot be sure of its detail, or even its reality. It is an essence of grief, deep grief; maybe past grief. It does not move, the essence, the feeling. It just crouches in a ball, hugging itself to itself, making itself smaller, as small as it can without disappearing. It's almost as if it's afraid to move, or to stretch, or even almost to breathe. What is it afraid of? Kurt feels himself breathe in and hold the breath in, keep it there, feels it become stale – the breath – in his lungs. He feels a little faint. He lets the breath out – slowly – and it pushes out past his lips, a light whoosh, a whisper, a kiss. He breathes in, deep, then out, emptying his lungs. How very terrible it must feel to drown, to breathe water. How good it feels, the air, the oxygen. How good it feels to breathe.

STITCH KURT

There's black thread for Kurt. He's the letter K, leaning, as if into the wind (or into her). Soft stitches feather, fill the shape of the letter, leaving space: blankness, yet to be filled. In the only-just-light of early morning, Iris stitches a pencil, its tip touching the K, making marks, drawing itself.

TWELVE MISSED CALLS

Before she opens the door to the bedroom, Iris can hear Marti snoring, a deep rumbling, throaty and sour-smelling, fermented. As she steps into the room, Iris sees the mound of covers and rumpled bedlinen shift in the bed, hears it moan. Blonde hair tangles out from under the covers, a croaked voice manages *Rice*.

'S'alright Mart, it's early. Back to sleep.'

Iris hooks her toe in the belt loop of jeans that are on the floor by the bed, lifts them to her hand, steps into them, pulls them on. She lifts the armpit of the t-shirt she's been in since the start of the party yesterday, that she wore to the hospital; sniffs it. Rank. Jesus. She peels it off, gets a clean t-shirt from her bag.

She looks down at the bed. Marti hasn't stirred. Iris pulls the covers up over Marti's head, kisses her curls.

'Sleep tight. Pisspot.'

In the kitchen, there are empty bottles, or almost-empty bottles, on every benchtop. There are cigarette butts, rollies and roaches, by the back step, outside. The days of finding ciggie butts in beer bottles and stamped out in food bowls are over, thank god. There's a platter with dried hummus caked in a bowl in the middle, surrounded by a scattering of sagging sad carrot sticks, dry bread, grape stems. She spreads newspaper on the table, scrapes food onto it, bundles it into neat parcels and into plastic bags, bins it. She puts bowls and platters in the sink to soak in soapy water.

She remembers her phone. She checks her bag again, tips it up and empties it on the kitchen table – nothing. She goes to the hallway, checks the table there by the door, checks the floor behind it, underneath it. She's about to step out the front door to check the car – perhaps it fell down under the seat – when the rain starts again, dumping and bucketing. She's standing at the open door, framed in the doorway, trying to decide whether to make a run through the rain to the car, when Luce runs towards her, then past her, into the house. Iris steps back inside, closes the door. Luce stands there, pushes her hood back, off her hair.

'Luce! Where've you been?'

'Just – went for a walk. I woke up. Just now. Couldn't sleep.'

'Did you see Kurt?'

'No.'

'Shit. Did you go to the bay?'

'No. Just in the garden.'

'Oh. Look, why don't you go back to bed, Lu. Put some dry clothes on. Get warm. Everyone else's sleeping in.'

'Okay.'

'And Lu?'

'Yeah?'

'You didn't see my phone, did you? Last night? What I did with it? When I left, for the hospital?'

'Um, nuh.'

'God, I'm going mad. It must be somewhere.'

Luce stands with her hands in the pocket of her hoody, tumbling them under the fabric, as if she's doing the hokey-pokey.

'Off you go love. Do you want a warm drink? I could bring it to you.'

'Nah. I'm okay.'

Luce turns away, slips in through the door to her room, closes it behind her. Iris opens the front door again. The rain is dumping, torrential. She can't remember when she's seen rain like this. Kurt is out in it. She clutches her arms around herself, rubs the top of her arm with her hand, holds herself together.

The phone is not on the hall table, not behind it. She considers knocking on Paul and Kristin's door, waking them up; but it can wait. Iris takes her keys, slips her feet into shoes, dashes out the front door hunching her back at the weather. She lets herself into the car, closes the door on the rain. It hammers onto the roof of the car, drowning out other sound. She pulls the lever that lets the driver's seat back, feels around under it – coins, crumpled tissue, a used parking coupon – then reaches over and does the same to the passenger seat – supermarket discount vouchers for petrol, more tissues, bits of gravel. She puts her hand down the side of the seat, right, then left, reaches across the passenger seat and does the same at the far left, between the seat and the door. Nothing. She clambers over into the back seat, bends down, sweeps her hand under the front seats, into crevices. On the left side, one of Kurt's hoodies is on the floor. She picks it up, holds it to her, inhales, smells sweat, unwashed hair, and a stale chemical smell of deodorant or supermarket aftershave.

A shadow passes close to the car. Through the dripping condensation, she sees the dark Kurt shape walk slowly, as if in a procession, or in sunshine, to the door of the house. He disappears inside. She looks down, picks a long, dark hair from the fabric in her hands, rolls it between her fingers. His hair is thick, wiry, just like hers, but longer. She flicks her fingers and the hair drops to the floor of the car. She waits for a moment with her hand on the handle of the door before she opens it, and makes a run through the rain to the house.

Luce stands with her back to the bedroom door, pressed against it. She keeps one hand on the door handle. In the other, she holds the phone. She presses and holds the button to turn the phone on. *12 missed calls.* Fuck. A message flicks up. *Battery at less than 10%. Recharge now.* She pockets the phone, holds her hand over it in the front of her hoody. She chews the side of her thumb. One foot is crossed across the other, the feet aligned parallel, but on the wrong side. She shifts her weight across from her left to her right foot. She pulls the phone out, presses the button, holds it, swipes her finger to deaden it. Then she launches herself at the bed, lies across it and reaches under the mattress at the far side, by the window, to tuck the phone there, out of sight. She kicks her shoes off, and crawls under the quilt, pulls it up over her head to block out the light.

Iris has her hands in the kitchen sink, in the hot alkaline slick of soapy water, the squeak of clean glass against her fingers. She looks up at the clock on the wall. The shower has been running for twelve minutes. She listens to water hammering against tiles, the old pipes clunking in the walls. Outside, it's still raining. The sun's up now, but you wouldn't know it, the sky dark with cloud, the air thick with sheets of rain, everything grey, monochrome, colour stripped out, washed out, gone.

The shower stops running. The cupboard door opens, closes. The tap runs in the basin, stops, runs again for longer, stops. Iris lifts another glass from the soapy water, runs a cloth around the rim, smearing lipstick. She hears the bathroom door open. She worries the cloth at the red stain until it's gone, then places the glass mouth-down on the tea towel on the draining board. She feels Kurt behind her, close to her, but off to one side, just outside her peripheral vision. He smells of soap, shampoo. He puts one arm around her, leans his head down onto her shoulder. His wet hair hangs down her back, drips water. She wipes her hand on her t-shirt, lifts it to his hand on her arm, pats it, rubs it, squeezes it, pats it again. He removes his hand, and whispers something that sounds like *sorry*.

UNMAKING A HOME

Kurt, Paul and Iris sit at the kitchen table, finishing breakfast, drinking coffee in the warmth, putting off starting the day.

'Is Auntie Mart okay? Is she up yet?'

'I can't hear her snoring so she must be awake.'

'You're so rude about your sister!'

'She was so pissed. Christ. Will she ever grow out of it?'

'Marti?! Fat chance. And she wasn't the only one.'

'Yeah, yeah,' Kurt mutters into his coffee.

'Where'd you disappear to last night, Iris? Chas and Evie were looking for you when they left. We couldn't find you anywhere.'

'Oh, nowhere interesting. Now, if anyone wants anything from the kitchen, speak now or forever hold your peace. I'm going to start packing things into boxes, and I think most of this is headed for the Good Sammies. I've started a box for what I want to keep, and one for Rosa, things I want to show her. Books and things. Oh, and have either of you seen my phone? I had it last night.'

'Maybe someone took it? Last night, by mistake?'

'I'll ring it for you. Hey, Andy was funny, wasn't he? At the party. Pissed as a fart, as usual. Nup, sorry. Straight through to voicemail. Must be turned off.'

'Bugger. Thanks anyway.'

'Andy Wineries, or Andy Arsehole?'

'Wineries. See that woman he was with? The tall one? Poor Marie.'

'I can't believe you asked Andy Arsehole. And he came.'

'I didn't ask him. I thought you did.'

'You kidding? He's an arsehole. I should know, I worked with him for five years.'

'Taught him everything he knows?'

'Ha ha.'

'It was good though, the party. I'm glad we did it. Like the opposite of a roof raising.'

'A roof falling in.'

'A housebreaking.'

'Unmaking a home. Oh, god, that sounds so sad.'

Paul hugs Iris. She leans her head on his shoulder, her cheek against the scratchy wool of his jumper. 'Not sad, mate. It was good, this place. Good times.' He kisses the top of her head, unfolds his arms from around her, lets her go.

Kurt is sitting at the table, watching them. He shakes his head, almost smiles. Paul leans down to his son, surrounds him with his arms. 'Good times, eh?' He bunches his hand into a play fist, noogies Kurt's hair. Kurt shrugs away from him, shrugs out of his hug, but smiling.

'Sure. Let's go with that.'

'And here we are, the three of us! Our little old family. It's like we're getting the band back together for a final farewell gig.'

Kurt rolls his eyes. Iris shakes her head, but smiles. And then Marti's there, the whole great morning-after mess of her.

'Fu-u-u-uck. I need a coffee and a new brain.'

'Marti!'

'She lives!'

'Some might call it living. Is it morning?'

'It is. Kettle's boiled. I was going to make another plunger. Sit down, Mart, I'll get it. You look like you need looking after.'

'I have bruises. Drinking bruises. Look.'

'You were doing party tricks. Badly.'

'God.'

'There's your coffee.'

'Plunger coffee! Like the eighties all over again.'

'Mart, love, once you've had your coffee, could we get those boxes from your car?'

'Boxes?'

'Oh, Martina Diamond, don't you dare tell me –'

'Calm down, cabbage. I was pulling your rope. Car keys are in my bag. The boxes are in the back seat. I bathed in eau de cardboard box all the way down from the city. Oh, here she is! Morning, Lu! How's my little baby today?'

'Mum, get off. You stink like a pub.'

'Darling!'

'What? You do!'

The morning rolls on, and they're all in and out of the kitchen, the house's warm hub.

Paul says, 'I'll take a load of bottles into town, to the recycling.'

'Will the rain clear, do you think?'

'We should go for a drive. Do the recycling on the way. Make a day of it.'

'Oh god, listen to you! You're like a grandad. A Sunday drive. In your cardigan. With your slippers.'

'We could go to Sugarloaf Rock.'

'There's no point going in this rain.'

'Or the wineries.'

'Right. The baby's down for her sleep. Who's going where? Ah, Marti, I didn't expect to see you before lunchtime. How's the head?'

'Fucking awful.'

'Is there any coffee left?'

'In the plunger, Kris. We could go to that café. The new one. Out by the lighthouse.'

'I don't want to spoil the party, but someone needs to pack this house up. You go if you want. Take Luce and Kurt.'

'God, no –'

'Prefer to help me pack?'

'Actually, yes –'

'Excellent. Good on you, Luce. That makes one of you. Now, nobody's told me they want anything. I guess it's all going to charity, then.'

'Nothing for Faith and Hope?'

'Dad jokes. Sunday drives. It has come to this. Kristin, you're a lucky woman.'

'Aren't I?'

'How about we pack today, and wait and see what the rain does before any outings are planned. It's got to stop some time.'

'Rice is right, as always. Okay, well I'll get sorting in the shed, like a proper dad. Or grandad. Kurt, give me a hand?'

'Sure. I'll bring your cardigan and slippers.'

'Are they really doing this? Finally? Naming the sprog?'

The table's spread with plates, mugs, glasses, jugs, the contents of the cupboards all clean now, washed after the party. Marti's sitting drinking coffee. Every now and then she moves one of the glasses or plates in front of her, without actually packing anything. Iris sorts, wraps, and packs as they talk, slowly moving everything into boxes.

'Yeah. Kristin said they want to do it here, before we go. The plan is to do it tomorrow.'

'Why now? Why the rush?'

'Oh, I don't know. God, why am I bothering to pack this stuff? I should heave it all into a pile for the skip.'

'Have they decided? The name?'

'Don't think so. Said they would though. Obviously. By tomorrow.'

'God, they're hopeless.'

'Luce is all excited, so that's something. She's got some plan, I think. She's being secretive.'

'She's always secretive. She's fifteen. Fifteen's just another word for secretive.'

Iris wraps plates in newspaper that she's been stockpiling for weeks, that she's brought from the city down to the house for the purpose. Her hands are darkening with newsprint, words and images transferring themselves onto her skin.

'Remember when you chose Kurt's name?'

278

'God, I know. What were we thinking? I was mesmerised by that beautiful Cobain boy – a boy in a dress! That hair! That stripy t-shirt! – his music, his everything.'

'Did you ever think about changing your Kurt's name? When – you know –'

'Not really. Our Kurt was Kurt by then. You remember. He was only a year old, just walking, but we couldn't imagine him not being Kurt. Rosa got stuck into us, but –'

Rosa had hauled her over the coals, ripped strips off her, ripped her a new one.

'Change it! Just change it!'

'I can't, Mum. He's Kurt. He *is* Kurt. It's his name.'

Sometimes, though, a coldness passes over her, the thought that a name might determine fate. Her rational mind bats the idea away into the dark recesses of her consciousness.

'He got pissed last night. Kurt. Really pissed. He was passed out, out the back, this morning. In the rain. I saw him. He wasn't moving. He was just lying there.'

'Oh, love. But he's alright, obviously. A bit sorry for himself. He's a big boy.' Marti shrugs. 'You can't live his life.'

'I know. I just –'

'Yeah. Just worry about them, and want to look after them forever. I know.' Marti gets up, wraps Iris in a hug, smacks a kiss on her cheek. She smells of red wine and smokes and sweat. Her lips are lined red with winestain and old lipstick. 'You can look after me, lovey. I'm always in need of mothering.'

'You're hopeless. But speaking of. Looking after. I – um – went to the hospital last night.'

'What? Rice! What do you mean? Are you alright?'

'I'm fine. Fine. I just went to A&E, in town. I had a, sort of, attack, I suppose you'd call it? At the party. Kind of blacked out. No, more like whited out. But then I was fine. I drove to hospital to get it checked.'

'You drove? Jesus.'

'I was fine. It's just five minutes away. Everyone here was pissed, anyway. It was gallstones, turns out. So strange. I have stones in me.'

'Is it – what do they do? Do they operate?'

'Nah. They just keep an eye on them at this stage. I had an ultrasound. It was weird. Baby stones in my belly. Should've asked them if they could tell the sex.'

'You alright now?'

'Just exhausted. I was up all night. Then Kurt, passed out. The little shit.'

'Why don't you go to bed?'

'Nah. I'm just going to slowly work through the packing. The moving truck and the rubbish skip will be here on Tuesday, then the Good Sammies are coming on Wednesday to pick up whatever's left. There's so much to do before then. Hey, Mart?'

'Yeah?'

'I haven't told anyone. About the hospital. I'm fine. No one needs to know.'

'Oh-kay. Whatever you want.'

'Except Luce. Luce knows. I told her, before I went. In case anything …'

'Good. Good. That's sensible.' Marti brushes her hair back from her face, shakes her head. 'I shouldn't get so pissed. It's stupid.' She takes Iris's hands in hers, across the table. Marti's hands are cold, her fingers fine. 'I could've been looking after you. Not passed out like a sack of spuds.'

'Fermented spuds, like vodka. It's fine. I'm fine.'

'What's fine? Is something wrong?' Kristin walks in, goes to the tap, pours a glass of water.

'Everything's fine.' Iris lifts her index finger to her pursed lips, widens her eyes, mugging silence at Marti. She stands up, puts her hands on her hips. 'I wish I knew where my phone was, though.'

'It'll show up. Right, I'm all coffeed up now. Point me in the direction of some packing, Rice. I am yours to direct.'

'Brilliant. You finish the kitchen for me? I'm going to get started on the big room, books. Come and help me when you're done.'

STITCH STONES

In her room, between boxes, it takes Iris just a moment to stitch the stones. She mounds them in a cairn, marking the spot. She stitches six stones, one for each of them here, each one of the baby's mob: Kristin and Paul, Marti and Luce, Kurt and Iris. One on two on three, the stones form a triplet, a triangle, so that every way is up, and everything is stable.

THE NIGHT-TIME SMELL OF GROWN-UPS

It's cold in the big room, and Iris has added layers – a merino cardigan, a woolly hat, fingerless gloves – until she's warm enough to be comfortable as she packs books into boxes. There are picture books from when Kurt was little, novels with book exchange price stickers on the front cover, histories and magazines, books about the ocean, books about trees. She flicks through a history of their town, of Little Casse Bay and Point Geologue, and the mystery of Édouard Casse, a scientist who sailed on one of the early French ships in the area, who jumped ship and drowned, presumed mad, or drunk, or both. Kurt – aged about ten – was obsessed with the story of the missing geologist. The book falls open at a thick piece of paper. It is a drawing, signed at the bottom of the page, *Kurt Diamond*. It shows the geologist, Casse, at the bay – their bay – with a hammer in one hand, a sack of rocks in the other, in water up to his waist, holding the rocks up above the water. The geologist has wild eyes, outlined in red. The ship is off in the distance, and there's a figure on it in a captain's uniform, making a face at the drowning geologist, blowing a raspberry, *pfththt*. There's a ghost geologist, an outline with a gaseous tail in place of legs, floating up from the flesh-and-bones geologist in the water. And his ghost may be heard, that jolly geologist. It's a cartoon – the kind of cartoon that ten-year-olds draw, she knows that – but it disturbs her. She thinks of Kurt at the beach, in the night, slipping into the water. Like a sack of rocks, sinking like a stone. She puts her hand to her belly. *There are stones in me.* She slips the drawing back into the book, closes it, puts it in the box of things to keep.

Paul slips his head around the door, leans into the room with his arm pushing against the doorframe, counterbalanced.

'Ah, there you are. I'm going to make a run, do the recycling and rubbish. Got anything to go?'

'Just what's outside the kitchen door. Don't take any of the empty boxes. And leave all the newspaper; it's for packing.'

'Yes boss.'

She watches them move past the doorway like isolated frames in a film: Paul carries a box, clinking with glass; Kurt carries big garbage bags bulging with rubbish; more boxes, more rubbish, more clinking glass. The smell of wine wafts to her, just faintly.

She turns back to the bookshelf, removes another pile of books from the bottom shelf, tall books, pictorials, coffee-table books from the fifties, sixties and seventies; the production values getting worse the later the publication date. The earlier books are more like artworks. She remembers some of the early ones from their bookshelves at home. Later ones were Paul's purchases, celebrating the kitsch of them, then people started giving them to him as jokes – the cheesier the better. *The Majestic Swan*; *The West in Pictures*; *The Swan River*; *On the Banks of the Swan*; *On the Black Swan's Back*; *City to Sea*; *The Golden West*; *Gorgeous Girls of the Golden West*; *We've Golden Soil*.

There's one, *City of Light*. The cover shows the shot from space, when the astronaut was overhead and all the lights of the city were turned on. She turns the pages – lights in Hay Street Mall, bad modern lighting along the seafront, at the beach. The Boans storefront, all lit up on Peace Night, 1919. Then in a series of photos, there's the ship of lights.

Sailing along in the car, towards the ship of lights: she remembers it with such clarity. The old brewery building on the bank of the river – so close it seemed that it was built *in* the river – had ships patterned from coloured lights strung in place on the river side of the building. There were different ships, perhaps three or four different designs, so part of the wonder of seeing the ship was anticipation: which ship would it be, that night? The sailing ship? The ocean liner? Seen from the back seat of the car – in a state of sleepiness, late at night – as you crossed the bridge, the ships seemed enormous; they *were* enormous, the size of the building.

She remembers: lying on the back seat of the car, nursing the liberty of that night-time running about, of murder in the dark and fizzy drinks and chips, kids running wild while the grown-ups played cards and tinkled their glasses and smoked their stinky smokes. She remembers: the smell of buffalo grass in the dark, wet and cool from the sprinkler, crisp under their feet. In the car, there's the weight of her mother's coat over her like a heavy dog, calming, almost sedating her. There's her hand slipping into the pocket of her mother's coat, nesting there; then, when she pulls her hand out, sniffs the fingers, there's the smell on her of her mother's cigarettes.

Iris remembers: worrying her fingers around the hem of the coat, stepping her fingers along its stitches and seams, the feel of the stitches attaching the lining to the hem at the base. There it is: the feel of something sharp inside the lining, and the feel of working her fingers at the hole in the pocket, enlarging the gap that is there – slowly, quietly, working her fingers away at it – until she can reach in to the gap between the coat's leather and its lining. There's the piece of paper, the note, that she pulls out, pinching it between the tips of her fingers. She unfolds it, carefully, though it still tears along one fold. It says *Dear Rosa, Beautiful Rosa*. Something about London, and a bridge.

Iris remembers this: looking up, while she's reading the note, at her mother – *Dear Rosa, Beautiful Rosa* – driving, the darkness falling over her face as they drive into shadows, out under bright streetlights, back into shadows, into light again. And she remembers looking across at her father, Frank, his face all in shadow, only partly seen, his eyes – she thinks – closed.

She remembers refolding the note, very carefully, along its old fold lines, very quietly. She remembers thinking she could put the note back where she found it. Or she could keep it. Or she could hide it, poke it down the back of the seat, into that sandy gritty space where no one will ever find it; or post it through the gap where the window's wound down a little bit (to avoid the car fogging up), and it would float away on the cold wintry night air, into the Swan River, off with the jellyfish and prawns.

She remembers what she did, that night: she remembers tucking the note back into the lining of the coat, and pulling the coat up around her, sitting up on the car's back seat, looking ahead between her parents. And that's when she saw it. There's the ship of coloured lights, sailing on the river. Green and white lights billow its sails, red lights pick out cannons along its edge, all reflected in the river below. The building's invisible behind it. There's only the sailing ship, the ship of lights on the river, and Iris watching it, its lights reflecting colour – green, blue and red – onto her parents' faces, making them strange.

Then: her head's back down on the long back seat of the car once the ship's out of view, and she's rocked back to sleep by the car sailing, bumping, rough and smooth over bitumen, all the way home. She remembers waking up – that night, and other nights – to the slow glide, the turn with the flicker's tick tick tick into the driveway, her mother opening the car door and leaning in over her, the burnt, papery smell of cigarettes, and the smell of her mother's stiff going-out hair. There is Rosa bundling Iris up, carrying her inside. There is Iris, resting her cheek on the satiny bulge of her mother's bosom. There is Rosa carrying her into her bedroom, leaning down to drop her into her bed with her clothes still on. Iris smells it now, the smell of Rosa to send her to sleep: smoke and gin and perfume and sweat and hairspray, the night-time smell of grown-ups.

STITCH A SHIP

She uses green thread for the lights on the brewery, reflecting in the river's water, late in childhood nights. Two masts, sails billowing, pennants flying from the tips of the masts. Little tails of thread, left loose, mark telltales on the sails, to show the flow of wind. This ship sails into the wind, close-hauled, bow lifting up and on, ploughing through imagined waves. It's the brewery ship, and it's Casse's ship, too, poor man, jumping and diving and disappearing, sinking to the bottom (sinking like kittens in a stone-weighted sack), sleeping with the fishes. She threads brown-paper-coloured thread, and stitches a sack, flying off the back of the ship towards the unstitched water.

A SONG TO SING FOR THE BABY

Luce is on the bed, with her laptop open on her knees. She's humming at the screen, watching the audio levels bounce in the input monitor, humming just loud enough to register, not loud enough for anyone in the house to hear her (she thinks, anyway). Usually, the way she likes to work on songs is by building them, bit by bit, starting with a melody, then layering words onto that. She won't build layers of sound for this, though. This one needs to be simple. Just a song to sing for the baby.

'I'll write the song. There should be a song.'

That's what she'd said to Kristin and Iris yesterday. Iris was holding the baby, then, and its little hands were reaching out, and the idea just came to her, that that's what she wanted to do. Write a song. And now, with the phone thing, it feels even more important. If Rosa's – gone – then naming the baby will cheer everyone up. People talk about life going on, right? That'll be what naming the baby is like. And she can write a song – to celebrate – and sing the song, a gift to the baby. Like, *I believe that children are our future*. That song. But for the baby. Because the baby feels like *their* baby. All of their baby. Which is weird, and untrue. But that's what it feels like. And it can be for Rosa, too.

She wants the melody to be pretty, and simple. Like a nursery rhyme. Or maybe more like a hymn, or a folk song. Folk songs are like telling stories, like the faery tales in Rosa's book. There isn't a story for this song, though. The baby doesn't have a story yet. It's just got them. All of them, and all of their stories. She'd thought about laying down a melody using the keyboard function – sort of laborious, but it works if you're not doing anything too complex – then making words to go with it. But she's decided that the words and the music need to happen at the same time.

So, without thinking too much, she lets words come out of her mouth, and the music finds its way out, too. There's a magic of songs, that they can happen that way. She'll write the words as she sings. She selects *Record* on the screen, and the triangle goes green. She'll sing quietly, so the others can't hear her for now. She moves closer to the laptop so the mic will pick up her voice. The two green lines of the levels bump and bounce as she sings, softly, at the screen in front of her.

It starts as a nonsense of words, but some phrases stick – they feel sweet, and right, in her mouth – and the music forms around them. Then, at some point, the music takes over for a bit, bringing up words to match it. She sings the first line over again, shifts the end until it's right. She failed music at school, because the notes on the page don't make any sense to her; they're like an army of ants swarming up and over a farm fence. This is what she does, though: plays and makes it all by ear. This is how it all makes sense.

She'll listen back to the recordings, then write the words down later. It'll probably read like shit written down, but it sounds okay in a song, as if the music changes the meaning, lifts it up and away from the words.

'Do you have any paper?' Luce asks Iris. Iris is sitting on the floor in the big room, packing books into boxes. She's surrounded by stuff.

'For writing, you mean? Or drawing?'

'Anything. Writing. For the song. The baby's song.'

'In my bag. In the bedroom. There's a notebook. You can rip pages from the back of that.'

'Thanks.'

'Or ask Kurt. Or – hold on, I think there's –'

She moves over towards a shelf, takes a plastic basket from it; from the plastic basket, takes a pad of paper, A4, filled with thick coloured pages. There's a clown with a balloon on the front cover of the pad. From the side, the paper looks like layers in rock, or an ice-cream cake. The basket is filled with felt pens, bits of crayons, coloured pencils.

'Take it all, love,' Iris hands her the pad, and then the whole basket. Luce takes it, turns to go, and Iris says, in that tone, 'You're welcome.'

'Oh. Ah, thanks.'

'So, how's it going? The song?'

'Meh,' Luce shrugs, 'okay.'

She shrugs again – what's she supposed to say? What does Iris want to know? She'll hear it when it's ready – then turns, takes the basket and the pad back to her room, closes the door behind her.

Luce lies on the bed, headphones off, writing the words onto paper so she can walk around with them in her hand, learn them, maybe make them better. She's writing with a green felt pen onto orange paper. She's written a heading in purple, THE BABY'S SONG, at the top of the page. She hears footsteps in the hallway outside the bedroom, voices, her mother and Iris. Her hand curls over the page, without her thinking about it. Their voices get fainter, and she hears mugs clatter in the kitchen. Again.

She flicks through the rest of the pad, looking for more orange paper. Halfway through the pad, the drawings start. They are only on a few pages – she flicks through – maybe only on five or six sheets. Only one of them has a name on it: KURT, in the big, uneven letters of a little kid, pre-school age, just learning to write their name. The R is back to front, and the letters don't line up, they trail up the page, as if they're climbing it. They're not the classic little kid drawings that she remembers doing herself; these are buildings in miniature, and in section, like a building with the side removed – like a doll's house – so you can see inside. There are tiny figures in the rooms of the buildings, and stairs and slides and ramps and spirals, all with tiny people and vehicles. There are animal shapes, too, and guns and tanks, dinosaurs and birds flying overhead, all of them tiny. At the bottom of the page there's a wavy line to indicate water and, under it, fish shapes, and something bigger off to the side of the page – as if it's lurking there, offstage, out of sight – the head of a big fish or monster, just the face (do fish have faces?), with a grinning mouth and whiskers, the grinning mouth somehow threatening. As if it will eat everything else on the page. Some of the little tiny people are falling off the building, and into the water. It's almost as if the monster figure is licking its lips in anticipation.

She turns the page. Each of the four, five other drawings are variations on the same theme. She tries to imagine Kurt, when he was four, or five, which he must've been when he drew these. Before she was born.

She flicks through the rest of the pad, looking for more drawings. There, in the back of the pad – she turns it over – are her own drawings, the safe, expected drawings of the happy little five-year-old. There's the whole family, Mummy and Daddy and Lucy, all named in careful letters, each with a round balloon face, an egg for a body, sticks for arms and legs, circles for hands on the ends of the stick-arms, little spiky tufts for fingers. Mummy is biggest, a giant stretching the height of the page, her brush-stick toes touching the bottom of the page, her cloud of hair touching the top. The Daddy is tiny, with short legs and a black body – she remembers her dad always dressing in black, trying hard – and he's floating up in the upper right of the page, disconnected from the ground. *You got that right, five-year-old Luce.* Lucy is in the middle, and middle-sized. Her stick-arms reach out, lengthened to connect to her mother on one side, her father on the other. Her left arm is elongated and reaches up to grab the Daddy, who floats like a balloon, drifting out of reach.

Kurt lies on the bed, sketchbook closed in front of him. He has tried to draw The Girl, but the thought of her – the look of her, the gone of her – has drifted away, out of reach, as it does, always.

He hooks his sleeve up. The cat scratch has faded to a line of clean red scabs, like fine silk stitches.

He opens his sketchbook, and turns to the page with the swan.

291

– – –

Luce stands in the doorway. She has the sheet of orange paper in her hand, with the song lyrics. Kurt's on the bed, leaning against the wall. He has the sketchbook open on his lap. She rustles the paper in her hand. He looks up at her, and closes the sketchbook.

'Hey.'

'Hey.'

'I'm making a song. For the baby.'

'Oh yeah.'

Luce sighs.

'So. Can I. Can you. Tell me? What you think. Is that.'

'Sure. Go crazy.'

Luce sighs again. She can feel her eyes roll at him.

'Sorry. I feel like shit. Hangover. Stupid.' He closes his eyes, then, as if it's a huge effort, he opens them, sits forward on the bed. 'Go on. What've you got.'

She moves inside the door and has to push it with force, with the flat of her hand, to close it behind her. She takes a breath. Then, for the first time, she sings the song full voice.

Iris sits on the floor in the big room among boxes and books and paper and things. Marti is curled in the curve of the sofa, a rug pulled over her, nursing a mug of tea. They hear footsteps creak the floorboards, murmured voices. Doors open. Doors close. Then the sound of Luce's voice cuts clear, like a glorious bell, through the old walls, the closed doors, the gaps in the floorboards. Marti gasps; she puts her hand to her mouth, covers it. She is bright-eyed; they both are, and both smiling. Iris pushes herself up to standing, and moves to the sofa. Marti lifts the rug that covers her, and Iris slides next to her and they hold onto one another and listen together to their gorgeous girl.

'Kristin said I can sing it. She said we can all do something. Or say something. Whatever. Instead of presents. Because it's not like a christening or anything.'

'Yeah.'

'She said they're not going to tell the name until tomorrow, though. At the actual naming party.'

Luce sits on the floor. She's folded the orange paper to fit in her palm, tiny and fat like a miniature book, or a matchbox. She closes her hand around it, and the corners prick the folds of her fingers.

'So.'

She can't think of words to use to tell Kurt about the phone. About Rosa. He'd probably know what to do. But he's all shut down and weird. After the party. After the bay. Like he doesn't belong. Or doesn't care. Or like he's gone away, while he's still there.

She knows that once the words are out of her mouth – once she tells Kurt, or someone, about the phone – she can't take them back. She thinks of the screen, the last time she turned it on: *23 missed calls.* Then: *Battery critically low. Powering off.* Bricked, for the moment, it's back under her mattress, and – for the moment – only she knows it's there. Like a niggling pea; but that'd make her a princess, and she doesn't feel much like one.

'Well.'

She rolls over, stands up, puts her hand on the doorknob. Facing the door, she can't see Kurt.

'So, it's okay? The song?'

She hears him breathe in hard, like a sucked-in sigh.

'Yeah.'S'good, Lu.'

She turns her head a little bit, so she can see him, low over her shoulder, her hair hanging down in the way. His eyes are closed, his head leans back against the wall.

'It's good.'

A GOOD HOUSE

Paul slams back in through the front door. Iris hears his keys chime onto the hall table, the chirp of his phone, his footsteps creak down the hall. He moves into the frame of the doorway, moves past it.

'Paulie?'

He backs back into the doorway, leans in on the frame.

'Hey, boss. Recycling's done. Amazing what they've done down there. A whole recycling depot thing, everything sorted. I'll do another run tomorrow. When the rain stops. If the rain ever stops.'

'Yeah. Ta. Hey, is Kurt okay, do you think? You know, the drinking, last night. Passing out. The bay thing.'

'What bay thing?'

'He went to the bay. Last night, in the pouring rain and the dark, so pissed he couldn't stand up. It's so stupid. Dangerous.'

Paul blows air out through pursed lips, a kind of sigh, opens his hands in a whaddya-gonna-do gesture.

'He's a grown-up, love. You can't tell him. Not any more. You've got to let him be stupid if he wants to be stupid.'

'But,' Iris shakes her head. 'I just —'

'I know.'

Paul walks over to her. He reaches his hands out. Iris reaches hers out to take them. He pulls her up to standing, pulls her in to him.

'He's okay.' Paul rubs his hands on her back. 'He's okay, you know?'

'I know. It's just. Seeing him like that. Passed out. I just. And — the house. It feels so strange to be. I don't know. I'm — just tired. Last night. I didn't. Not much sleep.'

They break apart. Iris sits on the sofa. Paul stands in the middle of the room. He stretches his arms out wide.

'Iris. This was a good house.' He drops his hands by his side. He looks her in the eyes. His mouth is sad for a moment, then not. He nods at the truth of it. 'The three of us. A good house.'

'It was.' She nods, too. 'A good house.'

The rain squalls in at the windows. The baby cries in another room. Paul leans down and kisses the top of her head as he goes to the baby.

WINGS IN THE NIGHT

They're all around the table, now, all of them full as googs but still picking at bread and chocolates and the sweetest little mandarins, muscat grapes dried on the stem, almonds. Candles light the table, are dotted about the room, on the windowsill above the sink, on top of the fridge. It feels celebratory, like Christmas, or a wedding.

'That was amazing.'

'I can't stop eating.'

'Move the chocolates to the other end of the table before I eat them all.'

'I'll put her down in a tick.'

'Her last night nameless.'

'Here's to Baby.'

'To Baby!'

'Babycake.'

'Baby!'

Empty mandarin skins curl on the table, glow orange. The tang of them scents the air, mixes with candlewax and chicken skin, garlic and wine.

'Has anyone checked the forecast?'

'I've never known it to rain so hard, for so long.'

'It was supposed to stop today.'

'Is the café even open tomorrow? On a Monday?'

'Holiday Monday. Course it is.'

'We should go for a drive to the recycling depot. It's bloody amazing. They should do tours. I'd pay good money for that.'

'A fool and his money.'

'Café at the tip. Not sure there's a market for that.'

'Les Deux Maggots. Ba-doom-tish.'

'I don't even know what –'

'Dad joke.'

'Existentialist Dad joke. The worst kind.'

'Why did the existentialist cross the road?'

'To be.'

'To be nothing.'

'You're so weird.'

'You're so right.'

'You're so welcome.'

'Come on. Back on topic. Where'll we go tomorrow?'

'We don't have to decide.'

'Let's see what the rain does.'

'I think I'll stay here. Keep packing.'

'We can take two cars.'

'Do you know where the café is?'

'Head to the lighthouse. Can't miss it.'

'I don't want to go if it's raining.'

'Shall I open another –'

'No!'

'Jesus.'

'Marti!'

'You're remarkable.'

'And then when I get back to the city, I've got so much to do.'

'God, me too. I've got to finish sorting out what we're doing for Mum's one hundredth. It's only a week away.'

'She'll go on forever, old Rosa.'

'I hope not, poor love.'

'Come on, your mum's unstoppable. Good old Mrs Golden-Fortune.'

'Are there –'

'What, love?'

'Are there, like, lots of people invited?'

'No, it'll just be family. Just us. And Kurt, for his twenty-first. It'll be quiet.'

'Do you really get a telegram from the Queen?'

'What if –'

'I think you have to send off and request it.'

'I did.'

'Iris!'

'Just for a laugh.'

'But, say if you don't make it –'

'Rosa'll have a laugh at that.'

'What about if you're *almost* a hundred, but you don't –'

'I think you have to actually tick over. Like turning over the speedo.'

'Time to replace the cam belt.'

'What year are you even living in? Cam belt.'

'What's a cam belt?'

'What about opening another –'

'Oh, Mart, you reckon *Rosa's* unstoppable!'

They're all inside the house, now, all of them spread out, each in their room. Iris stands at the kitchen sink, looking out through the window into the dark blue night, and listens. The house breathes. You can tell it's full of people; it does not sound like an empty house. And it's not as simple as the sound of people breathing; it's not snoring or footsteps, not even hearts beating. It's a fullness, somehow; it's their presence, filling the house again.

She walks to the back door and opens it. It creaks in the middle of its arc, as it always has. She stands in the doorway, not quite outside. The rain has stopped, for the moment, but the air – everything – is sodden, saturated. The night sky hums with the sound of wind in trees, the distant whisper of the river, the waves. There are wings in the night that might be birds or moths or bats or bugs, but are night sounds, never heard – not like that – in daylight. The wind gears up. She hears it before she feels it on her face. It bites through her clothes, straight through to her skin.

She shivers, hugs her arms around her, hunches in. She breathes in, then breathes out, emptying herself. Tomorrow's the last day with all of them in the house.

STITCH ROSA

Iris stitches a rose for Rosa, makes it rose-red, open, blowsy. Around the rose, cupping it, holding it, she stitches C for one hundred. She forms the C with care, with one hundred tiny stitches, one for each of Rosa's years. She stitches it in fine gold thread, for Rosa's Golden married name. Gold serves to mark her maiden name, too; Fortune's golden, after all. The stitches make Frank Golden, too (dear Frank, long gone; there's only Iris, in this house, to remember him).

Monday

HERE COMES THE SUNSHINE TO DRY
UP ALL THE RAIN

It's the absence that wakes her. The missing of it. The quiet, where noise was before.

The rain. It's stopped.

Luce sits up in bed, reaches out, lifts the edge of the blind. The sun's not quite up, but the sky is bright. The clouds – the big black clouds that've hung over Cassetown for days – are gone.

Everything around her drips and drains and sops from the days of rain, but no more falls from the sky. She can hear it, softly now, still draining from the spouting and pipes. The waterspout. *Down came the rain and washed the spider out.*

Here comes the sunshine, *to dry up all the rain.*

Luce pulls her hoody on, and tiptoes to the loo on cold, bare feet. In the bathroom she can see her breath. She looks in the mirror and blows out, watching herself, her mouth like an O, breathing smoke.

In the kitchen it's so quiet. The house. Everyone. She opens the tin on the table, takes a shortbread biscuit and puts it in her mouth, then takes two more and puts the lid back on the tin. She opens the back door, walks out on the cold cement to the edge of the back verandah, then past it, out from under the roofline, onto the back lawn.

The sun's higher, now. The sky is so clear, crisp blue, diamond-blue, diamond-sharp, edged with gold, and cold as ice. Under her feet the grass, too, is crisp, but under that, the earth feels full, like a sponge, or a soft mattress.

She flicks her hood up over her head, and wraps her arms around herself. She hops from foot to foot, eating biscuits, until the cold sends her back inside, back to bed.

STITCH THE RAIN

Now that it's stopped, Iris stitches the rain. She sits up in bed, surrounded by thread, lit by the light on the wall by her head. First she stitches a ground of gold, and onto that, an outline of the house in pencil-coloured silk, quick tacking stitches (first to hold, then to unpick). Then over this she makes the rain, in long stitches of dark satin grey and deep dark black, angling down, elemental and solid, to flood the world with water.

ALL TOGETHER NOW

All of them are in the big room, they're in and out of it, and in and out of all the rooms of the house, as if the sun's got them moving, like ants in summer. They're all together now, working together to get it all done. Sun is streaming in through the windows, through the glass doors that line one side of the room. They open the doors to let the sunshine in, but the cold drives them to close them again. Still, the sun makes it feel warm, and they warm, too, with the lifting and carrying and packing and bending and hefting.

'I think this box is too heavy.'

'Split it between two. Use the small boxes for books.'

'No more boxes.'

'Are you keeping this? Iris?'

'Kettle's boiled.'

'Mnh, I don't think so. Have it if you want it.'

'Yeah, there are. In the other room. I'll get them.'

'I'm going to scream if someone's packed all the mugs. Tell me they're not packed.'

'Is there any more newspaper?'

'They're not packed.'

'They're packed, aren't they. Crap.'

'I can do a coffee run. Now that the rain's stopped.'

'Pastries!'

'Extremely large skinny flat white, extra shot.'

'Make that two.'

'If you're going to the shops, see if they've got any weekend papers left. Grab a couple, we need more for packing.'

'Hot chocolate.'

'Long black.'

'Make that three.'

'Right, I'm off. Last orders! I've got a long black, three extra large skinny flats, pastries galore, papers ditto.'

'And whatever else you need for the cake, Mart. We've got flour and sugar. And there's a cake tin.'

'Cornflour? Caster sugar?'

'Yep, all good, all in the pantry. And icing sugar.'

'Okay, I'll get eggs. And cream.'

'I'll come too. Help you carry.'

'Um? Hot chocolate?'

'Sorry love, got that. A hot choc for Lu. Rice?'

'Oh alright, a skinny flat white, then.'

'– never listen to me –'

'Right, we're off.'

'The roads'll be oily, after the rain. Drive carefully.'

'Yes, boss.'

STITCH THE HOUSE

Now that the rain has stopped, Iris sits outside and stitches the house. She stitches its face like the child's drawing it resembles: a box for the house, a door in the centre, a window on each side of the door; a triangle roof overhead, and a chimney up from the triangle, with a cloud of smoke billowing up to the sky. She stitches the door in bright red thread, its knob a French knot in black. She outlines the windows in red, as well, crosses them, quarters them, makes panes. Long teal-blue weatherboards finish the front of the house. Steel grey lines on the triangle of roof map its corrugated iron, patterned with rust brown patches, satin stitch. She stitches the smoke, tinges it with grey.

INSIDE, OUTSIDE, AT THE SAME TIME

'It's the only thing I bake but, by crikey, I do it well.'

Marti made her first sponge at ten years old, guided by her mother, Alba. Alba soon acknowledged that Marti had the knack, and handed over the family sponge duties to her daughter. Since then, it's the rare Diamond family occasion that goes by without a Marti Sponge (like a Victoria Sponge, only bigger and ruder and noisier) in the middle of the table.

Marti knows the ratios off by heart. Five eggs is her standard recipe, but she can scale it to four eggs, or six or ten, as the occasion demands. She can make it in her sleep. Just flour, eggs and sugar. Magic. Perfect. But the thing is, if it's not quite perfect when it comes out of the oven – uneven, or broken, a little under- or over-cooked – you can't really go wrong with those good, basic ingredients. And there's no imperfection that can't be masked by cream and jam; or booze, custard and fruit. And more booze.

Iris (Marti had told her: *Be my kitchen bitch, Rice*) has found and unpacked the old rotary beater, the wooden spoon, the whisk. She's unpacked mixing bowls and the conical metal baking measure. Inside the cake tin's base she's fitted a circle of brown paper, cut from the bakery bag the pastries came in.

Marti measures sugar, whisks flour in a bowl to sift it. She separates eggs, slides the whites into a big mixing bowl. Each yolk she leaves cupped in its own half shell, all six of them resting on the table, each rocking gently until it find its balance.

'One for each of us.' Iris nudges the eggshell closest to her, and it wobbles then rights itself, stable again.

'Hmm?'

'The eggs. You, me. Kurt and Lu. Paulie and Kris.'

Marti screws her mouth up. 'What about the baby?'

'The whole cake's for her.'

Marti beats the egg whites with the rotary beater, working up a sweat. She tips in sugar – beats – then a little more; then more. She rests the beater against the side of the bowl, looks up at Iris, grins, wipes her forehead.

'Jesus, quite the workout.' She grabs the flesh of her upper arm, judders it. 'Got the bingo wings going.'

'Fadoobadahs.'

'They're like slabs of pork. All ready to roast. Slice me and coat me with olive oil, rub salt into my wounds.'

'Marti, you're not roast pork, you're ham.'

Iris reaches out, rubs her right hand on Marti's arm, at the top.

'And I love your arms. They're like an old sofa –'

'Iris!'

'No, no, I mean they're lovely. Soft. Velvety.'

She stands up and hugs Marti, then releases her and stands next to her, one arm around Marti's shoulders. Iris is shorter than Marti – not much, just enough to have to reach up to reach across her shoulder. She leans her head on Marti's shoulder, smells cigarettes light on her skin and clothes – not stale, not unpleasant, just the smell of Marti.

'We're a couple of old sofas, Marti love. Soft and pink.'

'We're comfortable.'

'We're luscious.'

'We're sink-into-able.'

'We are.'

'Oh, Rice. I don't want to be a sofa.' Marti's mock-sad, joking, but she sounds as if she means it, at least a little.

'You're a lovely sofa. Quality. Mid-century modern. We shouldn't be stick insects at our age, anyway.'

'Kristin's a stick insect.'

'Kristin's half our bloody age, and lives on seeds and nuts. Of course she's a stick insect.'

They hear Kristin's voice from the other room. Marti mugs, wide-eyed, to Iris – *shhh!* – a floury finger to her lips. They giggle like girls. Marti tips a gold yolk from its shell into the bowl, mixes, adds the next, and the next, until all six yolks are combined. She folds the flour in, turning it lightly and gently with the wooden spoon to bring the mixture together. Then she tips it into the tin, pale yellow flowing to cover the brown paper.

Marti picks up the cake tin in both hands, and holds it in front of her at chest height. Then she moves her hands apart and lets the tin drop to the table: getting the air out, settling the mixture. Iris opens the oven door, Marti picks up the cake and slides it inside, and Iris closes the door on it.

Everyone's ready to go for a drive. All of them, except Iris, are going, glad to get out of the house, into the sun. But Marti makes them wait until she's taken the cake from the oven. She doesn't trust Iris to judge it.

'Gas ovens are tricky. The moisture. The heat. You've got to get it just right. Leave it to the expert.'

They all stand and watch. Marti takes the cake from the oven, assesses it, touches her finger gently to the cake's surface. She nods, kicks the oven door up with her foot to close it. She slips a plate over the cake tin, inverts them, turns the cake out onto the plate. Perfect. She places a rack over the bottom of the cake, inverts the lot – plate, cake, rack – and lifts the plate off, puts the cake on its rack in the middle of the table. She opens her arms, jazz hands, shimmies.

'Ta-daah!'

They all applaud. Paul jingles his keys.

'The famous Marti Sponge! Nice one, sis. Right, we good to go now?'

Iris herds them out the front door, the five of them and the baby. She leans in the doorway watching them, her hand held over her eyes to shade them from the sun. Car doors bang. Luce sits in the back of Paul and Kristin's car, next to the baby. Kurt's with Marti. Motors start. Gravel crunches under tyres. As the car pulls away,

Luce lifts her hand, presses fingers to the window. Her fingertips are white pads on the glass, like the underside of a chameleon, or a salamander, or a frog. Iris lifts her hand, waves her fingers to the backs of the cars, to Luce's pale face in the dark frame of the window.

When they're gone, she stands in the doorway, and soaks up the sun and the quiet.

Iris cleans up after the cake, after Marti. She washes and dries and repacks the beater, the whisk, the bowls and the wooden spoon, the cake tin. She sweeps the six empty half eggshells from the table into a bowl, then wipes the table. The cake, on its rack, sits in the centre, fragrant with eggs and sweetness, still cooling.

Standing at the sink, she carefully cleans the eggshells. She runs water over them, slides her fingers on their satin silky insides to remove membrane. The feel of them: the chalk-rough of their outside, the glide of their inside, so strong and so fragile all at once. The look of them: the smooth of the curve of the egg, the sharp of the broken edge; inside and outside at the same time.

When they're all clean, she wipes the halfshells dry and puts them in a line on the windowsill, where the sun – when its angle is right – will catch them, and light will shine through them. She lets the shells settle and find their balance: all on the same ground, each facing in a different direction.

TO THE LIGHTHOUSE

The car shoots down a road edged by trees that are tall and straight, like light poles, but for giants. The trunks are bright orange-red, as if painted for safety. The trees make a wall you can't see past. At their tops (the *canopy*, they learned that in Ecology) they reach across the road and almost touch, high above them. Luce puts her head back, looks out the back window at the world the wrong way up. The sun's out, but everything's still soaking, the road steaming, trees dripping. Luce presses the button and the window glass moves down, widens the gap, lets in damp fresh air.

Kristin's driving, the seat pushed back so far that Luce, behind her in the back seat, has to angle her legs and wedge them in place. In the back seat of the car, behind Paul and next to Luce, the baby's asleep in its backwards-facing pod, its hand clutched tight around Luce's finger.

She can't see Kristin in front of her, on the other side of the huge leather seat. She can just see the side of Paul – the side of his face as he turns to Kristin, his hands as they fiddle with his phone. She can't hear them properly, but they're talking to each other, anyway, not to her, as if they've forgotten she's there. Kristin says something about Iris, and boxes. Paul says *Mrs Ramsay*, something something; and he says something about the lighthouse, and Kristin laughs.

Luce wants to go to the lighthouse, but she's been outvoted.

'Nah, we'll find that new winery. With the art gallery. Barry's stepdaughter's the manager. He told me how to get there the back way.'

Paul has his phone in his hand. He holds the screen out towards Kristin, and Luce can see it between the big leather seats, the blue flashing dot that's them moving closer to the upside-down teardrop on the map.

'I dropped a pin to mark it. Barry said you take this back road.'

He pinches and swipes to zoom and pan, all proud of himself.

'I sent the pin thingy from the map to Kurt, so he's got it on his phone. We can just meet them there. They're amazing, these things, aren't they. Don't know what we'd do without them, eh Luce.'

He leans around and looks back at her for a moment, grinning, winking a big comedy uncle wink as he swipes and clicks the bright tiny screen.

'Should be a road off to the right, but it's a way ahead. Just go straight for now.'

He settles back in his seat, and she can't see the phone in his hand any more.

She remembers the lighthouse. They went there only once, that she can remember. She was little – so was Kurt, but he always seemed like a big boy to her – and her dad had to carry her part of the way, up the path and the steps to the lighthouse. She remembers a sunny day, hot cars, stopping for an ice-cream from the shop. She remembers all of them – Iris and Paul and Kurt, and her and her mum and her dad – and the two cars, like today. The two of them, she and Kurt, always wanted to ride together, so they'd go out in one car, and come back in the other. She remembers sticky ice-cream hands, and her mum not having anything to wipe them with so she put Luce's hands in her mouth – one at a time; one whole hand, then the other – and gobbled them clean. It was their silly game, the python swallows its prey, her mother's mouth tight and slick and warm around her hands, sucking gently.

Luce sticks the tip of her finger in her mouth now, sucks hard. She remembers standing at the base of the lighthouse, that day, and craning her head back to look up, but she couldn't see the top. Her dad lifted her up on his shoulders, said now she was as tall as a lighthouse. Then he lifted her down and swung them around, turning circles til they were dizzy.

There are two photos of them from that day. In both, Luce is on her dad's shoulders, right at the foot of the lighthouse. In the first, she's leaning down, holding both of her little hands over his eyes, peek-a-boo. Her face is leaning down at the side of his, so she can see him, not seeing. In the other photo, he has his hands up in her armpits, tickling her, and her head is thrown back with laughter, pure joy. Off at the side of the photo, not quite complete, her mother's face watches them.

His Auntie Marti is waving her arms as she talks, as she always does. She mostly keeps one hand on the steering wheel. She keeps turning towards Kurt, in the passenger seat next to her, to make eye contact as she speaks. She can't help herself. He turns his head and looks back through the rear window, and he can see the front of Paul and Kristin's car, tiny in the distance behind them, coming in and out of shadow as it moves through the trees. Kurt turns back to face front. He stares out through the windscreen, keeps his eyes on the road dead ahead, as if he can steer the car, keep it on track for her.

His phone beeps quietly, vibrates in his hand. He swipes and taps. A message from his dad.

Map point for café and gallery attached. Meet you there, chief. Over and out.

Kurt taps, saves, taps again to bring up the map screen. There they are, a blue dot moving, pulsing. He taps again, hits send.

Got it. See you there.

Marti laughs like a drain at something he hasn't heard her say. He stares out at the road ahead, keeping them safe.

'Yep, they've got it. They'll see us there. See, that's the beauty of it. All this technology. It allows you to be so flexible. Spontaneous.'

Kristin reaches out with her left hand and pats Paul's knee. That's all Luce can see in the gap between the leather seats: the slim hand with a gold ring, pat pat pat then resting on dark denim.

Then Kristin looks back over her shoulder at the baby – checking her; Luce has seen her do this a hundred times each day – and her eyes catch Luce, and her mouth makes an O of surprise. Kristin turns back to face front, but she fixes her eyes on Luce in the rearview mirror.

'Luce! For a moment I forgot you were there.'

Paul's phone beeps. A message flashes.

'Oh crap. No signal.'

Kurt's phone beeps, and he takes his eyes from the road. A message flashes up on the screen.

No signal.

He flicks to the map screen. No pulsing dot. The teardrop pin is fixed on the centre of the screen, but the map – the lines of the map, the meaning of it – has gone blank. They're on their own.

'Ah, shit, the map's –'

His phone beeps again. The message disappears. The five vertical bars at the top of the screen go solid, one after another, from the shortest to the tallest, like climbing a hill. The blue dot that is them flashes again, pulses, moves along the lines on the screen that map the road ahead of them.

'What, love?'

'Never mind. We're good.'

The road turns a corner, then straightens out before the crossroad ahead. He looks back through the rear window. He thinks he can just see Paul and Kristin's car, a tiny flash in the sun on the road behind them.

He looks down at the pulsing blue dot, the thick line joining them to the teardrop pin. He looks up at the road, checks that it matches.

'Go left at the crossroad, then veer right at the fork straight after that.'

Marti takes the right-hand fork in the road.

Kristin takes the left-hand fork in the road. She indicates to turn, even though there are no other cars.

Paul had remembered the first turn, left at the crossroad, but at the fork, he'd gone blank. Kristin pulled over and idled on the side

315

of the road while Paul climbed out and walked around, waving his phone in the air, trying to get some signal. He'd climbed back into the car seat, huffing and sighing.

'They could've waited.'

'Well, just try to remember the map. Close your eyes, think of it.'

Paul had finally lifted his hands in the air and waved them both in parallel towards the left-hand fork, like the cabin crew on a plane indicating the exits.

'We go left. I'm certain. And we're bound to get signal again as we drive, anyway. Probably once we're out of the trees.'

So they'd taken the left-hand fork in the road; and here they are, driving on through the trees.

The road is sealed at first, then it starts to narrow, and the big trees give way – quite suddenly – to low scrub, to tea-tree and banksia, then they're bumping along a sandy track, the grey-green low-growing trees scraping against the side of the car. Paul holds his phone up the whole time, waves it about, trying to recapture the map.

'This isn't right, Paul. We should turn back.'

'Nah, this has got to be it. Barry said the track's a bit ratty.'

Kristin just sighs, and keeps driving.

The baby squawks, next to Luce, waves her hands about as if conducting an orchestra. Luce puts her finger out, wiggles it in front of the baby. The baby grabs onto her, and pulls Luce's finger to her mouth. She sucks, warm and wet, and Luce feels the little pull of it like a string to her heart.

They continue down the road, even when it becomes nothing more than a sandy track until, finally, they drive up over a dune and emerge out of scrub, almost at the sea.

Marti pulls the car into the carpark between the winery building and the gallery. Kurt checks his phone is on, and they've got coverage – they have – and pockets it as they walk across the gravel, following the blackboard signs advertising TASTINGS, to the cellar door.

The track ends in a sandy clearing, roughly circular, surrounded by low scrubby trees. Kristin stops the car, lets the engine idle a little before she pulls on the handbrake and turns the motor off. They sit in the car, at the end of the track, and stare out the windows. Light patches dot the perimeter of the clearing, where tracks lead off up and over to the beach, or to snugs in the dunes. Luce winds down the window. She can hear the booming waves on the other side of the dunes, and smell their salt.

It's a picnic area, or a drinking spot, used for camping or fishing, or all of the above. The remains of a campfire mark the centre of the clearing. Stones – burnt over and over again – edge the firepit, contain a slush of ashes and bottles, charred coals and empty cans. They spill outwards on one side where the stones have been dislodged, breaking the circle.

Luce leans on the sill of the car window, watches Paul walk up to the firepit. He kicks a can, then kicks a bottle, and Luce hears them roll. He kicks again, and releases the smell of campfires and burning, of charcoal heavy after the rain.

The baby whimpers, then sucks in her breath, then releases a wail that fills the car and threatens to break it apart. Luce opens the car door and scrambles out onto the sand. Her bare feet break through a light crust, then a thin sponge of damp on top of fine, dry powder, with the sticky feel of salt.

'Shush shush, Baby.'

Kristin unclicks herself from the driver's seat, walks around the car to the back and opens the door, leans in and unclips the baby. She lifts the baby out, unzipping her jacket as she does it, lifting her t-shirt, all at once, as if she's got four hands. Kristin walks to Luce's side of the car, the baby already nudging against her. Luce sees a flash of white skin, the roundness of Kristin – a thread of something, is it spit? – as the baby lifts away for a moment. Then the baby nestles back into her, and Kristin backs into the back seat of the car, where Luce had sat. Kristin waves at Luce. Luce looks away. She puts her head down, and walks to the other side of the clearing, past Paul, still kicking cans and waving his phone in the air.

Kurt watches his aunt tap carefully at her phone. She holds up the screen when she's done.

Don't know where you've got to!
K and I at winery.
Meet u back at house.
We'll bring wine / bubbles / champers.

He nods at her, shrugs, all in one movement. She taps to send.

Kurt nurses his second coffee. Marti waves and clicks her fingers in the air to summon more wine.

Luce watches her uncle walk from the clearing. He takes a track that might lead to the beach. He holds his phone in the air, and out to the side, then peers at it, then pockets it, then takes it out again. Luce looks over at Kristin in the car, with the baby. She should be used to it – the baby feeding – but she isn't, and it makes her feel a sort of shame.

She chooses a track that leads off in a different direction from the one Paul took. The track is narrow, sandy underfoot, with the same thin crust of darker, sodden sand over dry white sand that was in the clearing. The scrub gets sparser as the track starts to climb the side of the sand dune, then before she knows it she's up above the scrub and the stubby trees, out on a great lift of bright white dune dotted with beach plants here and there: pigface and lupins, cattails, marram grass.

She climbs, up and up, then down into a valley in the dunes and she rests there for a while in the quiet, alone, just standing there, as if the world has gone away. She listens to the waves. They boom in, crashing, bigger than the waves in their bay. This is a wild bit of coast, big surf that comes in from the south with the full force of the ocean behind it. She shivers, though the sun's on her.

She climbs out of the dip and up the angle of the next dune, higher than the first, and her feet dig into the sand as she climbs, and the dry sand underfoot squeaks and sends another shiver through her.

And she comes to the top of the dune, and there, off in the distance, on the point at the end of the far, far curve of the great long bay, is the lighthouse. She can't see its detail – it's too far off for that – but she remembers it: the limestone blocks of its base; the great red and white lift of it; the feel of thick paint (like candle wax, molten then hardened, liquid then not) under her little hand as her dad lifted her up to touch the first red stripe.

She reaches her arm out towards the lighthouse, pincers thumb and forefinger together and squints her eye along her arm, to take its measure, to pinch it. She looks down in the other direction along the bay, and sees the tiny dot that is Paul, walking on the beach. She measures him too: a tiny man on a beach, but as big as a lighthouse, from where she stands.

On the top of the sand dune, Luce plants her feet so she's as stable as a lighthouse, and draws herself up as tall, and she sings, quietly at first, because she doesn't want them to hear her. But Paul's far away, and she knows Kristin and the baby can't hear her – they're in the car – so she sings louder and louder, sings the baby's song.

And she gets louder, and louder still, until she's shouting out to sea. As she sings, she turns slowly on the sand dune, arms out, like Julie Andrews on a hilltop wearing a curtain, or like a lighthouse beaconing into the night.

When Paul and Luce arrive back at the clearing – both of them popping out of the scrub track and into the open ground at the same time, as if they've responded to an offstage cue, or a siren's call – the baby is fast asleep in its car seat, and Kristin is busy. She's picking up the burnt-out cans and bottles from the firepit's charcoal and ashes, and from all around the clearing. She's already filled two shopping bags (taken from her stash in the boot of the car), and has started on a third. Luce stands at the edge of the clearing and watches Paul take the bag from Kristin. She watches him snake his arms around her, and kiss her on the top of her head, and she watches them both stand still like that, together, in the middle of the clearing.

Kurt drives Marti's car back to the house. Marti snoozes in the passenger seat, her mouth open, her glasses crooked on her nose. The bottles of wine in the box on the back seat chime against one another, all the way home.

BURST THROUGH THE DOOR

They all arrive back at the house together, though the two cars come from different directions.

Kurt and Marti are first. Iris hears the car pull in on the gravel, and goes to open the front door for them. She sees Kurt step out of the driver's seat, duck around and open the door for his aunt. He carries in a box of wine, plants a kiss on his mother's cheek as he passes her in the doorway of the house. Marti breezes past Iris and blows her a kiss (blackcurrant, tobacco, a hint of vanilla, oak and plum notes) on her way to make coffee.

Next Paul pulls their big car in and parks on the gravel. He goes to the boot and lifts out shopping bags filled – as far as Iris can see – with rubbish, while Kristin unclips the baby in her seat, and lifts her out and swings her up and around, the baby pouring gorgeous liquid giggles.

Then Luce is up and under her. She bursts through the door like a flash of light. There's high colour in her face (is she sunstruck, just a little, or is it the cold?). She stands in front of Iris, her eyes wide and shining, her arms held out from her body, in an upside down V.

'We went to the lighthouse!'

She whispers it, then her arms are up and she hugs Iris, hard, her face beaming, her cheek cold against Iris's warmth.

Then just as quickly her arms drop, and her face goes back behind its mask, hiding itself, and she steps away, and skips to her room, where Iris hears her humming.

STITCH LUCE

Take up silver thread, and gold, for Luce. Stitch her as Saint Lucia, a
crown of candles on her head, marking the year's midnight, lighting
the year to come. Stitch her with a smile, and with song. Make her
with stitches small and true, well placed. Stitch a lighthouse behind
her, tiny to indicate distance, but float it in the air, ungrounded, like
a medieval painting. Stitch its rays, beaming, bringing light.

TO THE BAY

Luce walks away from the house, through the gate, and follows the river towards the sound of the ocean, to the bay. When she gets to the sand, she takes off her shoes, ties the laces together, loops them around her neck so that the shoes both hang in front of her, banging her chest. The sand is sun-dried now, fine powder underfoot, sticky still with the feel of salt. She lowers herself to sit on the sand, pulls her knees in under her chin, hugs them tight. She cups sand in her hands and drifts it down onto her feet, feels the tickle of it, then the weight. She covers her feet with sand, up to the ankles. She draws her finger through the sand to trace a line down the top of her right foot. The sand falls back, fills the space her finger leaves behind, covering her trace.

She looks out at the ocean, stares dead ahead. There isn't anything you can see, if you look straight out from here. Not land. Just sea and sky that go blue, all the way to Antarctica. Or maybe Africa. With nothing in between. Somewhere out there, but further than Luce can see, is her dad. Somewhere out there, and one day she'll see him again, and she'll know it's him, and he'll know it's her. He'll walk up to her – slowly – and he'll put his arms around her (tightly, slowly, but not creepy), and he'll hold her so tight she'll think she can't breathe. But she will. She'll breathe in the smell of him. And it'll mix with the smell of her, and be perfect.

Kurt walks around from the far side of the bay, and as he rounds the point, he sees Luce sitting there on the beach, small and quiet, her back rounded, rocklike, solid, grounded.

He lifts his hand to hail her and, catching the movement, she lifts her face to him, and it is full of light.

He walks towards her, his almost-sister, moved by the tractorbeam pull of blood and love.

— — —

'Are you going back? Paul said could you go back. The party. To help set up.'

She has to shade her eyes from the sun. It's shining behind him, so he's in shadow, lit from behind so she can't see his face, or anything but his outline. It's like talking to a special effect. He's a tall black shape, a curve, a line, and the sun behind him makes him shimmer, like a mirage in an old desert movie, or a genie from a bottle.

'Yeah, alright. I'll head back.'

He stands there, still for a moment, then his arm moves to his glasses, nudges them in the way he always nudges them, always has, ever since she can remember. His arm drops back down by his side, then reaches out from his body, his hand towards her, sitting there on the sand, reaching towards her hand.

'Come on.'

She puts her hand out and rests it in his. They're the same shape, with the same long fingers, and they fit together like twins.

'In a bit. I want to —'

'What?'

'Nothing. You go. I'll see you back there.'

''Kay.'

Kurt's hand moves away from hers, slots into his pocket. Then he moves, and the sun is no longer behind him, and she can see him — the detail of him, but from behind, so she's missing the look on his face — as he walks away towards the path that leads along the river and back towards the house.

When Kurt reaches the track at the top of the beach, where it meets the river to follow it home, he turns and looks down the slope of the sand, past the great stones that both interrupt and anchor it, to the sea.

He pushes his glasses, puts his hand back in his pocket, then lifts it again — push, pocket. The shape of Luce appears up out of the curve of the bay, unfurls like a great round stone coming to life, until she's standing, straight and long and true and fine, facing out to the sea and the sun.

Then he hears it, faint at first: three notes in descant, rising to the sky.

Luce stands and sings – for the last time alone – the baby's song that she has made, singing out to the ocean, pouring crystal notes out into the blueness of it all. She sings for the baby, and she sings for Rosa, and she sings for herself and for Kurt and them all. And when she's finished, she sings it again.

He stands, watches, listens. And maybe it's Luce singing; or maybe it's just the sun, as it dries up all the rain; but everything clears, and he knows that it (whatever it is – the feeling, the darkness) will come back, but it's lifted, for the moment. Into his mind comes the image of his mother stitching, running stitch that is visible on the fabric face, making shapes and words, but invisible where it runs underneath.

Iris is on her way to the bay, to find them both, Kurt and Luce, when she hears it. She stands with her hand on the latch of the gate, and listens, for a moment, before she walks towards the song.

Along the path by the side of the river she walks, and she comes to Kurt, standing there at the top of the bay, listening to Luce, and she stands with him too, and they lean into one another, and he hums under his breath, matching Luce; and Iris holds her own, holds *her* breath, and listens to the sound of their voices, together.

STITCH MUSIC

Take up blue thread for the bay, and black for notes, and stitch
music, voices merging. Stitch the stave, and stitch each note fat —
egg-shaped, stone — upon its line. And stitch the ocean at the bay.
Turn the stave into horizon, striations of sea and sky and stone.
Stitch the bass clef a drape of seaweed; stitch the treble clef broad at
base, neck-fine above, tail trailing below like the feet of a fat black
swan, paddling under the water's surface.

MARK IT WITH B

While Marti cuts the cake horizontally through its middle, Iris draws a B onto brown paper, in the centre of a pencil circle she's drawn, marking the size of the cake. She sketches the slope of the back of the B, then its full breast, and its fuller belly below. She fattens the lines, thickens them, makes them curve. She adds curlicue serifs breezing out from the B's back — but not too fine, so they're thick enough to cut.

Marti's knife slices through to the other edge of the cake, and she flips the two halves apart, the insides egg-pale, flour-soft, circled round with gold.

Iris holds the paper up, shows it across the table.

'B for Baby.'

'B for beautiful.'

Now Iris cuts — blunting tiny silver scissors meant for thread — around the B, releasing the shape from the paper, while Marti whips cream, and they both laugh again at her paddling arms, her bingo wings. Marti spreads jam, blood-red, rose-red, to top one half of cake. Iris snip snip snips to cut the centre from the belly of the B. Marti scoops cream, satin-stiff on a broad metal knife, and spreads it thick on top of the jam. She licks the knife, her eyes closed, licks her lips. Iris snip snip snips to cut the centre from the breast of the B. Marti lifts the bare half of the cake and flips it, then centres it above the laden base, and she places it, carefully, to crown the baby's cake.

Now Iris holds up the paper B, suspends it above the cake. As she holds it, the paper starts to curl at the base, moisture lifting it up, tugging with life. And she thinks of a long-forgotten fortune-telling fish, a novelty tucked in a wax paper sleeve, in the back of a drawer of the dresser in the house where she and Rosa stayed for a time, long ago, far away. She thinks of its red cellophane curling in the palm of her outstretched hand, and of matching its curve to the words on the wax sleeve in which the fish hid: *lucky in love*; *warm of heart*; *full of grace*; *fair of face*; *sharp of eye*; *quick of mind*; *fleet of foot*; *just and fair*.

And she places the B in the centre of the top of the cake; she rests it lightly, then shifts it slightly, into its perfect position. She presses down its lifted curve. And Marti rains icing sugar over it all, the cake and the B and the plate and the table, and Iris's hands by the plate, and they laugh at it, at the too-much of it, and at the scrape of the spoon against the metal mesh of the sieve. And they sing, or at least they think of singing:

Pat it and prick it and mark it with B
And put it in the oven for Baby and me.

And when everything's covered in white, Marti lifts the paper B with both hands, as careful as Iris has ever seen her; and there's the golden B left on the top of the snow-white cake. They both hold their breath, and Iris holds her hands cupped under the lifting B, to catch anything that falls.

STITCH THEM ALL TOGETHER

Almost done, now.

Stitch lines onto the quilt. Like contours on a map marking height of the ground (the level of the ground, where things are the same), lines join them. All together now, on the blanket for the baby.

Fix the backing to the blanket, now, fine wool to sit soft against skin, and to mask the stitches' backs. Fold its edges over, and stitch it around, neat and strong. Stitch a tiny bee – slip slip slip, bee for B for Baby in a few quick stitches – in one corner of the blanket's back; and stitch a trail of running stitch behind it and before it, looping and crossing itself, escaping off the edge, taking flight.

How will she stitch herself? She's already there, in the stones, in all the stitches. On the blanket's backing, she stitches an eye – eye for I for Iris, Eye-Rice – in the bottom right-hand corner, like signing a painting. Eye for an I; for I will watch over you, little one. The sister of my son. The daughter of my son's father.

Then she leaves the backing fabric unstitched, unfixed along one edge, so she can reach up inside and finish it, once she knows the baby's name, and can stitch it, front and centre; then she'll stitch them all together, happily, forever.

'Will you get the cake –'

'Not yet!'

'Glasses then. Plates.'

They have opened the heavy wood and glass doors along the side of the big room, the music room, so the room only has three walls, now. Luce has cut coloured paper into fat strips, looped them to form paper chains, hung them across the top of the doors, so they frame the outside. Across the room, the table is covered with an old batik sarong, pale in patches from sunlight. There's a jug in the centre of the table, thick acid-green, filled with branches from the garden, soft cattails from the beach, early freesias that Luce found around the edge of the garden. A big glass bowl, thick blue glass from the 1950s, is filled with ice (bought in a bag from the petrol station), a bottle resting there, waiting to pop. Rosa's book is on the table, propped open at the back, on a stand.

Luce unpacks plates from a box, wipes them with a tea towel and stacks them on the table.

Marti arranges forks for the cake, glasses for toasting.

Kristin holds the baby, who is sleeping through it all.

Next to the piano, Kurt and Paul prepare to sing. Iris stands in the doorway, leaning on its frame, and watches them. She leans in, leans towards them. They both stand, Paul and Kurt – father and son – close to one another, closer than she has seen them for a long time. They stand by the piano. Kurt hums a note. Paul hums it. Paul reaches out to the piano and hits a key. They both drop their hums to match the piano. They look at each other. Kurt counts in, *one, two, three*, then a fourth beat with his finger, then he starts – Kurt does – at the high end of his range, on a wobbly note that strengthens and holds, then Paul comes in under him, supporting the sound but not taking over.

Kurt closes his eyes as he sings, as if he's forgotten anyone else is there. When he'd started, he was standing awkwardly: one hand on his chest, the other hanging by his side; almost Napoleonic or as if recovering from a stroke. The hand is still on his chest now, but it's activated – feeling his breath, working it. The other – the hand by his side – is now tapping the rhythm of the song, tapping in counterpoint.

Marti's voice joins them – in this old song, that the Diamonds always sing – then she walks across the room, to stand with them. Marti and Paul bookend Kurt, their arms around him, smiles big as the day, or the year. Marti's free hand is moving, marking time, her fingers picking notes from the air, pinching them, then letting them go.

Their three voices match in the way that only blood can make voices match. They loop together, the notes in the air; they fit. If you looked at the waves their voices made – the recorded sounds, displayed as signals on a screen – they would share signatures of waver and quaver and lick and tone that would match them, as surely as DNA profiles, as father and son, and as sister and brother, twinned.

But all Iris can hear is her boy's voice. His beautiful voice; her beautiful boy.

While they sing, Luce slips the phone – the dead-battery phone – out of the pocket of her hoody. She composes a look of surprise on her face, then she nudges Iris, holds out the phone to her, whispers.

'I found it under a bed. Battery's dead. I checked.'

'Oh, love! You're wonderful!'

Iris takes the phone, pockets it, puts her arm around Luce and kisses her on her cheek. There are tears on Iris's face, and they touch Luce and make cool wetness. They stand together and listen to the song, and Iris does not let her go.

— ⋕ —

'Bravo! The von Diamond Family Singers.'
   'Look, I've found my phone!'
   'How do you solve a problem like Martina?'
   '– under one of the beds. I thought I'd checked them all –'
   'Mittens on kittens, my favourite things.'
   'Speaking of which –'
   'Settle down, Marti. Wait for the name.'
   '– completely dead. I'll charge it later, in case the movers need to contact me.'

'I know you said no gifts –'
   'Oh, Iris –'
   'But I wanted to make her something.'
Iris hands the folded blanket to Kristin, and leans in to kiss the baby's head. She kisses Kristin – awkwardly, catching her ear – and then Paul has them all in his big wild arms and they're all together for a moment before they break. Kristin unfurls the blanket – a flick of her wrist, like a magician's sleight of hand – and Paul takes the other top corner and they hold it between them: a banner, a sail, a map, a scroll.
   'There's space for her name. In the centre. If you –'

'I made this for her.'
Kurt brings a book, square, small. He has stitched the pages together through the spine, inside a cover of cloth glued to stiff card. He flicks through the pages, and lines and colours move into action, like a zoetrope, or something glimpsed from the corner of your eye.
   'I drew one of Rosa's faery tales. The swan one.'
He nods with his head towards the table, where earlier he had placed Rosa's book, *Miss Fortune's Faery Tales*.
He places the book that he has made in Kristin's hand, and leans in to kiss the baby's head, then kisses Kristin on the cheek. 'There's

space for her name in the front. This book belongs to –'

He stands by his mother's side, and leans into her.

'Well, I made her a cake, the first of many.'

Marti carries the cake up and out in front of her, holds it up on high like a gift of gold, and they all whoop and cheer, as she places it on the table. She waves a knife in the air as she speaks.

'No space for her name, so we marked it with B. Time for cake and bubbly, now –'

'I made something too.'

Luce moves to the centre of the room, and she stands like Kurt had stood: one hand flat on her heart, the other by her side. She closes her eyes and starts to sing.

In the house
Where we all are

She gives full voice to the words. She's written them for the baby, for all of them.

At the bay, in the rain

She opens her eyes, and sees her mother watching her, nodding in time to her voice.

Unmake this house around you

Words from the house, from the bay; from that poetry book that has made its way to the table, too.

Map the world, mark it
Name it fresh, illuminate

She sings for Rosa, her long life.

All that it may become

She sings for the baby. She looks at Kristin, holding the baby, smiling at her. The baby is half-awake. Kristin rocks, sways out of time with her voice.

Light the house
Bring it home

She's left space for the baby's name, in the breath round the words at the end of the song.

While we name you, here in the rain

Those were the words when she wrote it. But the sun's here now.

While we name you, here in the sun

The baby's arm lifts, and its fist pumps the air in a rock'n'roll salute.

Iris – with all of them – waits to hear the baby's name. She might be Rosa. She won't be Hope. She will be herself, her own name. And Iris will mark it, map it in the centre of the blanket, stitch it to fix it, to finish.

ALL OUTSIDE THE HOUSE, NOW

There's a certain point, about now, once the words have been spoken and they have all cheered and sung and wept, and wet the baby's head, when they realise it's warmer outside the house than inside. Marti lifts what's left of the cake in one hand, grabs the half-empty bottle in the other, and so the procession starts: the party moves outside. They bring chairs, one by one. Paul and Iris lift the table, and carry it between them, place it in the sun. Luce brings Kurt's book, reading it as she walks. Kurt brings the baby's blanket, reads its stitches like a book. Luce goes back for the paper chains, loops them from chair to chair. Iris brings Rosa's book, the Hope poems, and a pot of tea. And Kristin brings the baby, with her fresh, new name.

ACKNOWLEDGEMENTS

This novel was completed with the assistance of a Creative New Zealand Arts Grant. I'm grateful for that grant, and for three short residencies: R.A.K. Mason Fellowship at New Zealand Pacific Studio (thanks Chris and Derek Daniell); Varuna Second Book Fellowship; Mildura Writers Festival Residency.

Thanks to those who, whether they knew it or not, helped me write this book: Tracy White, Anna Borrie, Lydia Karpenko, Vlad Papish, Denise Batchelor, Madeleine Slavick, Mary Chan, Janis Freegard, Jessie Cole, Eliza Henry-Jones, Peter Bishop, Sheila Atkinson, Danielle Hanifin, Donata Carrazza, Helen Healy, Sheridan Stewart, Stefano de Pieri, Pam Shugg. Dylan Horrocks and Sarah Laing led me (back) to comics. India Flint's writing on mark-making, landscape and textiles provided early inspiration. Mardi May lent enthusiasm, and a Meckering line. Junichiro Iwase's art resonates through this novel. I borrowed (again), though lightly, from my grandmothers.

I was inspired by the unexpected beauty I found in the writing of Dr Raphael (Rafi) Freund (1933–1984), geologist. Thanks to Simon Nathan, Keith Lewis and Maggie Dyer for geological and publication information; any geological errors are mine (or retained with poetic licence).

Thanks and respect to all at Fremantle Press (especially Georgia Richter) and Aardvark Bureau.

Love and thanks to Craig and Spencer, as always, for everything.

The author gratefully acknowledges:

Permission from GNS Science to reference Raphael Freund, 'The Hope Fault: A Strike Slip Fault in New Zealand', *New Zealand Geological Survey Bulletin 86* (1971).

Epigraph: *Hicksville* by Dylan Horrocks, Victoria University Press, Wellington, 2010, used with kind permission from Dylan Horrocks.

'RAIN' epigraph: excerpt from *Tree and Leaf*, HarperCollins, London, 2009. Reprinted by permission of HarperCollins Publishers Ltd © J.R.R. Tolkien 1964.

'ROSA' epigraph: 'Counting Backwards' (music and lyrics Kristin Hersh), used with kind permission from Kristin Hersh.

'At the bay' first published in *Good Dog! New Zealand Writers on Dogs*, Stephanie Johnson (ed.), Vintage, Auckland, 2016.

For further notes on source material, visit **tracyfarrauthor.com**